# All The Way Under

# All The Way
# Under

INTERNATIONAL BESTSELLING AUTHOR
## RACHEL ROBINSON

LN
♡P

**All The Way Under**
Paperback Edition
Copyright © 2025 by Rachel Robinson

Love N. Books Press
An Imprint of Wolfpack Publishing
1707 E. Diana Street
Tampa, FL 33610

www.lovenbookspress.com

Internal graphics design by Rachel Chaya Design
Edited by My Brother's Editor

Paperback ISBN 979-8-89567-169-6
Ebook ISBN 979-8-89567-168-9
LCCN 2025942750

*For the dreamers of big dreams.*
*You can make it happen.*

# All The Way Under

# *saylor*

"BUT DARLING, IT'S COLUMBIA." She drags out the center of the last word. "You don't just turn down a master's degree from Columbia because you want to putter around on a dinghy getting sunburnt. It sounds positively evil," Mom says, a martini balancing perfectly in one hand and her latest romance novel in the other. "Just get the degree and then, if you're still inclined, go for the little boat ride. The master's is good for your career." Puckering her lips, she sips the tiniest of sips.

"My career has been just fine without the master's, and it's a yacht, Mom. It's not a dinghy. You and Dad bought it for me, remember? Because I've loved sailing my whole life. Dad taught me everything I know! I've been working on my boat all year, getting it ready for this. That was before I applied for my master's program. That can wait. I can defer a year. I'm twenty-eight. I'm not getting any younger, and sailing takes a lot out of you." I play the one card I know she'll respond to. "Don't you want grandchildren this decade? I must do this sail first." If I make it sound imperative, she may bite.

She rolls her eyes, sitting down in an oversized chair facing the window. "Daddy only taught you that as a childhood hobby because he loved it. You are a lady of wealth and standing. You can't be bruising yourself in boats anymore. Grow up, Saylor."

The irony that my dad named me after his passion is lost on her. A lot is lost on her, but this is all she's ever known. She went from her daddy's money to her husband's. This is the path she wants for me.

Another puckered lip sip makes my fingers curl into a fist. "Archie is at Columbia getting a law degree because he's finished his master's. You should be there with him, so he doesn't find another suitable woman to marry. Out of sight, out of mind, darling. You need to keep that one. He deals with your incorrigible behavior without too much fuss. That's not easy to find."

The way she talks about me like I'm an object makes my skin crawl, but I remind myself this is who she is, and it's fine that I don't want this life.

I thought I did, while I was in undergrad. Who wants to be poor? Who wants to struggle to make ends meet? Who wants to worry about money at all? I think most humans would choose the path my mother wants for me because it's a sure bet. I've heard the saying that money can't buy happiness, but I'm here to tell you that when money isn't a worry at all, you have more time for the things that *bring* you happiness.

That's what the phrase should say. Money can't bring you happiness. You have to find it, make it, do whatever it takes to be happy.

I could marry Archie, who would cheat on me regularly but provide a life so lavish I'd be expected to look the other way and ignore his indiscretions. I'd never worry about money, and every material possession my heart could dream up would be mine. This is just the way things work in the small elite circle I'm a part of. I don't have to quit my career, but it's expected of me when kids come along.

Sailing is what gave me a new perspective. Daddy would take me to places all over the world, and I'd see the way other people live. As a child, their lives seemed to be so full of love, emotion, and family. Their customs and foods were better, and the way they treated each other seemed more genuine than anything I'd witnessed. Sailing gave me a way out.

I humored my parents with the Columbia undergraduate degree because, even though I'm meant to be a high-priced breeder, the piece of paper proves I'm *of class*. The master's degree is just plain insanity for the sake of living close to my boyfriend. Ex-boyfriend. One engineering degree is enough. I'm smart, and I know it. How long will I have to do what she wants? I don't want a lifetime of being a puppet.

Back to the banal conversation at hand. "Archie broke up with me," I say, rubbing the bridge of my nose.

Her head nearly twists off her neck as she looks at me.

"What was that? Why? Get him back, darling. Whatever it takes. Do whatever it takes. We can't have you on the market at this age. It makes us all look bad. This boating nonsense is just a hobby, like your father does. It is not something to fill your time with. Look what you've done."

What I've done is cast her in a negative light by being a twenty-eight-year-old spinster who enjoys yachting.

Unknown to most, this is still a thing with the upper class. Everything is about how an action makes a family look. I groan.

"Archie said we weren't a match." I lift my arms and

let them fall by my sides. "He cheated on me all the time. It's hard for me to overlook it when everyone around us talks about the infidelity. Don't you care about how that makes our family look? Saylor Wyndham lets people walk all over her," I say, mocking her tone. "Isn't that just as bad as being single and following my actual passion?"

"Darling, all men cheat and lie. You might as well be rich while they do it."

I put my hands on my hips. "Dad doesn't cheat. Or lie."

She lifts a shoulder. "Yes, but I'm special. Most aren't."

I don't think she means to be offensive, honestly. It comes naturally. It's a defense mechanism after years of being surrounded by false personalities and empty promises.

"Dad doesn't cheat because he has high morals."

He also went to military school and served our country, even though his trust fund had nine zeros after it. After his military career, he joined the family business, Wyndham Technologies, and still works harder than anyone I know.

"He is a worker, Mom. He loves you despite everything."

I refuse to stoop to her level, but I do often wonder what my dad saw in her all those years ago.

"I am like Dad, Mom. I like adventure and seeing new places all over the world. The challenge of sailing is something I need."

"It's going to get you killed, Saylor Jean. You mark my words right this second. Your father stopped going out so much because the world is a dangerous place for people like us."

"You mean rich? Rich people?"

She scoffs and sips her martini.

"I hate that word. It's gauche. *Wealthy* people, Saylor. Wealthy people have targets on their backs. You're not just any old Joe off the street. You are a Wyndham."

"I know all there is to know about sailing, and I know the safe routes. Dad is worried, but he will let me go if you give your approval. Please just let me do this one thing, and I'll come back and be the perfect Wyndham specimen." It kills me to give her this open-ended promise, because I know she'll make it hurt.

Her gaze lights on my face. "Dad said he'd let you go?"

I nod, eager. It's not a direct no. She loves that man.

"Yes. He's been helping me prep the boat. He taught me everything I know, and you know how much this used to mean to him. It will be the voyage of a lifetime. It has all the high-tech gear—some I helped design myself—and it's safe."

"And when you return, you'll get your master's and find a husband?" Another sip, then she holds up her finger. "A respectable husband. Perhaps even one of *my* choosing."

My stomach flips. I knew it would be this, though. Mom and her hammer of control.

"Oh, you really are going to take it there? Can't I fall in love the same way you and Dad did? Remember Aviva's arranged marriage? He was gay! She had to pretend for years that they were happily married until the clubhouse manager saw him going at it with the towel boy in the locker room! Arranged doesn't work when both parties aren't all for it." I clear my throat. "All that shame Aviva brought on her family's name, and she didn't do anything except what was asked of her."

My mother's face looks ashen as she recalls the scandal. "It is absolutely horrifying how little Jude cared about his family's name." She groans. "Poor Avivia and her family. I heard they're working on a new suitor for her. A really nice man from Europe. He doesn't know how to act in social settings, but he has standing and power. You can overlook some things for the right individual. I tell you that all the time."

Except she doesn't have to overlook a single thing with Dad. Not one thing.

I stare at her blankly. "You're serious, aren't you? You let me go on my world record sailing trip, and I'll go get my master's. Bronwyn didn't even get her master's before she got married."

My older sister got out of this house as quickly as possible after high school. I envy her every day. Going back to college is the lesser of the two evils, for sure. I cannot have Bianca Wyndham select my husband. It will end worse than it did for Aviva and Jude. I shudder at the thought.

My mother finishes her drink and twirls the metal toothpick holding her garlic-stuffed olives.

"You always were going to give me gray hair, weren't you? Bronwyn was too easy. I should have known this would be a battle. I'll agree to let you go if you let me talk to Archie, and you get your master's from Columbia when you return."

She closes her teeth over the olives and pulls them off the pick.

"Lastly, you will be finished with your crazy adventures after that."

She tosses the metal pick into her glass. It clanks loudly.

"Do we have an understanding?"

She requires me to give, give, give.

"Archie moved on the second I hung up the call. I'm

sure of it. Mom, he moved on *before* he broke up with me. I agree to everything else."

Giving up sailing sends a lump of lead to my stomach because I know she'll strong-arm me to obey her wishes in some form or another, but this voyage is what's important to me. I'll do anything to make it happen.

My dad saves me. Like he always does. He slides into the room, scraps of metal in his hand. The man is constantly working on taking something apart or putting something back together in his free time. He says it quiets his mind. I wish I had something other than sailing that did that for me.

"How are my girls doing?" he asks, a smile beaming. Bronwyn got our dad's olive-toned skin and toothy grin. I'm Mom's twin with Dad's mind. It's like being trapped in a beautiful cage with all the wrong tools to escape.

"Mom said I could do the record sail," I say, tone high and voice quick. "The big one we've been preparing for."

Dad grins, so I bluster on. "She gave me some qualifiers, because nothing is free with Bianca's bidding, but she said I could do it." Hopping up and down in tiny little steps, I finish, "I'm so excited. You'll help me finish off the checklist, right?"

His eyes light up like they do anytime he looks at me and my sister.

"You can count on me, Sweet Pea. We'll get her safe and secure in no time," he replies. "You were nearly there the last time we checked her out."

Mom lets out a tortured moan. "The way we're even talking about this right now is ghastly. We should be planning an engagement party or a spring mixer, not a dinghy ride, Roger." She calls it a dinghy this time to offend us both, her narrowed blue gaze bouncing between us.

Dad leans over and puts a hand on Mom's shoulder.

"It's not just a boat ride, honey. You know how much sailing means to me. Well, it means even more to her. It's scary to think of her out there by herself, but this could be her life's great adventure. We can't stand in her way."

That's the catch. Alone. Without a crew. That's the record that hasn't been broken before. It's easy to do something like this when five people are taking turns. Everyone is well-rested and highly skilled. To do something like this alone is unheard of.

"Plan the spring mixer. There's no reason we can't do both, Bianca." Dad waves his arm out to one side, fingers splayed toward the grand window. "Picture it. A seaside soirée, clinking champagne flutes, floppy hats, and crisp linen. Saylor's boat will be anchored on our beach, right over there, and everyone can take a tour of the craft before she sets sail and smashes the world record. You can decorate it."

I must hand it to him. He's animated, convincing, and giving Mom exactly what she desires to make our lives easier.

"All our friends will be captivated by Saylor's quest. It's going to be fantastic. The party of the year. Nothing less than perfection. They'll be chatting about for months."

"When you put it that way, I think this could be a wonderful thing, darling," Mom says, eyes twinkling with wild, albeit expensive, plans.

Dad winks at me, then smiles when he sees how happy Mom is. "It's going to be fantastic. Sweet Pea, tell me all about your plan. What's left of the checklist?" he says, holding out his arm to the hallway that leads to the kitchen.

We can't talk about sailing in front of her, or all the

tech projects we've installed, either. Tech bores her because it also confuses her.

We leave Bianca to her own devices, scribbling down ideas on a half-wet cocktail napkin she pulled out from under her novel. The piece of junk Dad is fixing clunks on the kitchen counter. Black dust leaves a film on the stark white marble. It doesn't belong there. I don't belong here. Dad doesn't either, but he's adapted like a chameleon.

"You're going to have to take all the precautions that you can, Saylor. We've been talking about this trip for a long time, but now that it's real, there are real conversations we need to have. There are protocols, and bail out spots, and not to mention the hostile waters you'll have to travel through if you're taking the agreed-upon route." He clears his throat. "The world record-setting path," Dad amends.

I've planned it all. There are plans and contingency plans. There are ports marked on my charts, and the highest quality of navigation gear is purchased and installed.

"I know. I'll show you everything. I have it all laid out and written down in the passage plan. I'll email it to you."

He narrows his eyes as he slides a finger across the black dust to make a "t."

"I overheard the conversation before I walked in," he says, eyes flicking away from mine. "Archie wasn't ever going to be your forever, Sweet Pea. I'm sorry you went through that with him."

"It's fine, Dad. I was just trying to do what Mom expects of me. Archie was a mere figurehead—a guy I knew she'd approve of. Figured if I could keep her happy in one area, she'd let up in the other areas, where I'm not reaching my potential." I air quote the last word. "I delayed the master's with work for longer than I thought possible."

He cups my cheeks.

"You reached your potential the second you came into this world, Saylor Wyndham. The way you look at life is something I've always admired. You will be the one to follow your dreams and create a life so fantastical it will be beyond your wildest dreams. Archie wasn't a man who deserved to be on that ride with you. You'll know when you meet the right person. He'll challenge you, but he will never break your trust, or your heart."

I nod. "That's it. She challenges you. That's why you love her," I say, drawing a circle in the black dust next to his mark. "Doesn't it feel like a...a pain in the ass?"

Dad chuckles, eyes crinkling in the corner.

"She's *my* pain in the ass," he replies, holding my wrist to stop me from spreading his mess. "I wouldn't have it any other way. She brings my life full circle." He laughs softly, his face wrinkling in a comforting way.

I think about what my mom said on my twentieth birthday. *You'll only regret the wrinkles you didn't tap with Botox, darling. Nothing else that's regrettable can't be fixed.* Here, Dad is in all his perfect, natural, wrinkle-filled glory, and no one loves Dad more than her.

Shaking my head, I move out of the way as our home chef bustles over to clean the counter where we've made a mess.

"Sorry, Angie. I didn't realize this was that dirty."

He picks up the piece of metal, and Angie wipes the marble, a smile playing on her lips.

"We'll get out of your way."

He grabs an apple from the fruit dish, and I follow him out to the garage.

"I've been working on this one all week," he exclaims.

I see that it's part of an engine he's working on. A ride-on lawn mower. We might be wealthy, and Dad grew up wealthy, but this man still does everything he can on his own without hiring help. Sitting on a little stool, watching him fix things, is my earliest memory.

"A week? Not time to throw in the towel and buy a new one? It must be *really* broken." I emphasize the really by raising my eyebrows.

Dad is a mechanical engineer, so this hobby makes sense. As a software engineer, it doesn't bore me, but it doesn't make me as excited as he is. I prefer code and virtual systems.

"Your mom only lets me mow the side lawn by the garden these days. The gardener does the rest. I have some time before it needs mowing, but I don't give up on things when they're hard," Dad says, picking up another piece outside of the engine. He makes eye contact with me over his shoulder. "Never have, never will."

I grin. "That explains so much more."

He chuckles. "Hand me the torque spanner."

I rifle through the top drawer of his red toolbox and find it. "What millimeter?"

He tells me, and I hand it to him.

"If you don't want to do your master's degree, you don't have to. You know that, right? Sometimes Mom is set in her ways of thinking things need to be done a certain way. She's sharp how she goes about it. If you're anything like me," he says, looking at me with raised brows. "Then more school is the last thing that's going to make you happy. You're rising through the ranks at Wyndham Technology without my help because you're a brilliant engineer. It comes naturally without sitting in lectures."

He moves back to the exposed engine.

"Go sail. I'll take care of your mother. She'll come around. Don't let her qualifiers scare you. You're an adult now, Saylor. Do what makes your heart happy." He pauses. "Your job will be here when you get back. No one can spitball big-brain ideas like you. Martin said you constantly wow him."

Dad's great-great-grandpa started Wyndham Technology, and luckily for him, we've all been math-brained and love the family work. Martin is my boss, but I do find him asking me things I'd expect him to know.

"We love you no matter what and no matter how," Dad adds.

He always says they'll love me no matter what. Angie pops her head in and asks, "Salmon and quinoa?"

"That sounds great," Dad replies. "With a Sauvvy B for Bianca?"

I cackle at the use of Mom's nickname for Sauvignon Blanc. "I love your salmon, Angie. Yes, please. Sounds great," I say.

"I would never serve salmon without Bianca's favorite Sauvvy B," she replies, lowering her voice, a smirk on her lips.

It's like we're in the normal club at the Wyndham Manor, and Mom can't know it exists. Bronwyn used to be part of the club before she moved out. It's getting smaller and smaller. Poor Dad will only have Angie soon.

Our chef heads back inside, and I'm left watching Dad tinker. I take my seat on the stool and watch him in between going over my sail plan and schedule. It's just like old times, except there's promise on the horizon—something exhilarating brewing.

I email the sail plan documents I've been working on for weeks to my dad when I'm sure they're perfect.

"For the first time in my life, I'm doing something I

want to do. No one can tell me to act a certain way or dress a certain way. No one is watching my mannerisms to make sure I'm behaving in a way dictated for me since birth. I can just be myself. *Saylor's Delight* is going to set records. I just know it."

Dad stands, hands on his hips. "There's nothing that makes me happier than seeing you and your sister following your dreams."

Bronwyn followed her escape plan, not her dreams, but did happen to fall in love while doing it. Lucky rat.

There is a touchscreen panel on the wall that helps communicate with almost every room in the house. It's as if my mom hears my excitement about something she has no part in and must interrupt. She beeps in. "Darling, when you're finished, join me on the deck before dinner. I have big plans for our party, and I need to share them with you."

"Of course. Give me ten," he replies to her before she clicks off. He ruffles my hair, gentler than he used to do when I was a kid. I tell him I emailed him the plan, and he promises to go over it tonight. "This is the beginning of something fantastic, Sweet Pea. Your grand adventure"

After I kiss him on his scratchy cheek, I skip out of the garage and into the foyer. My cell phone rings in my back pocket. It's Bronwyn's ringtone.

"You already heard the good news," I chirp, heading toward the kitchen stairwell.

We don't get cell service in the elevator. Despite all the code and tech in this house, it's insane we haven't been able to fix it. I concluded it was built this way for a reason. It's a dead zone.

Bronwyn jostles the phone, then says, "No, I didn't hear anything yet. I want my cashmere sweater back. I just bought a long silk skirt, and it will match perfectly.

Edmund is taking me to the Savoy Cellar this weekend, and I want to wear it."

I round the first set of stairs and begin the second. Our house is large by our neighborhood's standards. By the average American standard, it's monstrous. I'll be out of breath soon.

"I'll have to make sure I have it at home. There is still a closet full of clothes at my apartment in the city," I say. "Not that the Savoy Cellar isn't exciting, but they agreed to let me do the sail, Bronwyn. I'm going to leave next month when the tides are perfect."

"Are you kidding me? Not that I'm not excited," she says, her voice lacking all enthusiasm. "But didn't you say the prep would take years?"

"Yes, the prep takes years. I have been working on this for so long and know I can be ready quickly."

She stays silent but for breathing, then finally says, "I have a bad feeling about this, Saylor, but I know nothing will stop you from trying. Mom agreeing to this is insane. I can't even imagine what she made you give up." Bronwyn knows, because she's experienced it as well. "I don't know what you have to prove. You've already won sailing competitions. Everyone knows you're an excellent sailor. The whole thing seems unsafe and unnecessary. I don't want to sound like Mom, but you are my only sister."

Even Bronwyn, my biggest fan and cheerleader, is concerned, though it would be suspect if no one cared at all, I suppose. I'll prove them all wrong. I must. It's going to change my life completely. It will fulfill me in a way that nothing else can. And if it doesn't, I can at least say I tried before I throw in the towel and become Bianca 2.0.

# brody

"I SUPPOSE I should say hello, but I'm not sure it's worth the effort," I chide when my twin brother scoots into the booth in front of me. "You're late," I add, raising one brow.

Nolan smiles.

"By two minutes, Brody. Late by two minutes. I was wrapping up at a job site and was training a new kid." He shakes his head. "You're in true curmudgeon fashion today. Is it normal cynical, ill-tempered disdain, or did something happen at work that you want to tell me about?"

Typical Nolan. Kind and good-natured in the face of evil. We've always been opposites.

"I mean, it's my usual pessimistic sarcasm, though I wash it with a little love because you're my brother. Why are you training the new guys?" I ask.

He's an electrician, and business is booming. Straight out of high school, he went to trade school for it, and I thought he was crazy. I marked him as less than for pursuing a trade instead of college, like me. Now, he owns his own company and makes more money than anyone we know who went to college. I feel like no one talks about that enough.

Nolan runs a hand through his longish, rogue, wavy hair. Hair I can't have in the Navy. It's not to standard. Mine is clipped close with a few motley inches on top.

"I'm the boss, Brody. I want to make sure they're doing things the correct way. My name is on the line. Literally." He sighs, then flags the waitress when she passes by.

We order drinks and the same lunch we always order: two burgers, medium rare, extra cheese, with a side of BBQ sauce for our fries. She taps her pen on the receipt and nods before she leaves for the kitchen.

"We're opening the fourth location this year. It's more important now than ever before that our quality is the same across the board. I have to have my touch on everything, including the new guys."

I nod. "That makes sense." I sip the water the waitress just dropped off. "I'm on alert right now," I say, exhaling, changing the subject to my work.

"That means you could deploy at any given moment, right? You have to be within a certain mile limit from the base?" Nolan asks, even though he knows he's right.

He's a good listener. Way better than I am. I'd say it's something I've been working on, but I just don't care, nor does anyone in my life dictate I have to.

"Yep. I had dinner with Mom and Dad yesterday, and we said our goodbyes. They never get used to me leaving," I say. "It's been seven years, and they still act like it's the first time I deploy every time."

I mentally cringe thinking about how sad they get. It's awkward and makes me nervous and uneasy. I have no clue how to handle that from people who have loved me my entire life.

"Just because it's not the first deployment doesn't mean the outcome will always be the same. That's why it makes them nervous. Hell, it's why it makes me scared, and I've been dealing with your daredevil personality my whole life. You coming home safe all the times before doesn't guarantee you will come home safe this time."

Nolan looks away, but I know what he's feeling. I've always known what he's feeling. We have an extra sense when it comes to our connection. It's almost as if it's a type of telepathy. We leaned into that when we were kids and tried to distance ourselves from it when we were teenagers. Somehow, now that we're adults, we've circled back to appreciating the twin connection.

"Nolan." I say his name to get his attention. "I'm going to come back, okay. I'm too fucking mean and nasty to die. You know this. It's always the good men who don't come back, the ones who people only have wonderful things to say about them. What's that saying? Only the good die young? The bastards live forever." I smile, happy with my analogy.

I'm a bastard. That's the way the scales tipped the second we were born. Nolan was good, and I was not. I cried more. I needed to be tended to first. My ballad of discontent was the loudest.

Nolan doesn't crack a grin. "You play a bastard as armor. You aren't a bad guy. You're not fooling anyone. Well, maybe you are fooling some people, but you don't fool me. You are one of the good ones. We will always worry, brother. We love you."

My chest tightens.

"Yeah, yeah, I've heard it all before. It's fine. I'm going to be fine."

Nolan cuts me off with a headshake as our food arrives.

"Repeat after me. I love you and will miss you too," he says, tone slow and monotone, like he's trying to get a baby to pronounce the words correctly.

Rolling my eyes, I dig into my meal.

"Right back at you," I whisper around a bite.

I hate emotions. It doesn't make sense because my brother and I were raised in a loving home by the same compassionate, nurturing parents. He obviously soaked it in, and I'm made of nonporous lead. Nothing enters. Nothing exits.

"Anyway..." I hiss, the end of the word. "How was the weekend at the lake?"

He exhales noisily, annoyed by my irreverence. "It was fun. You should have gone with us. Liddy brought his jet skis, and Sam towed in his boat, so we wakeboarded and buzzed around the lake. I don't know why you've only gone once. I bought the house so we can enjoy it together."

All our friends from high school seem like a distant memory. I have a hard time connecting with my past life. After becoming a Navy SEAL, a detachment formed from most of the things I used to care about. I guess that happens when you understand real problems exist outside of yourself. That, and living in life-and-death situations on a regular basis, forces a perspective not many people can understand. I'd have to fake too much with them, and I suck at faking anything.

Swallowing, I speak. "You know I don't have anything in common with them. I didn't before, and I certainly don't now. Nothing against Liddy and Sam. I know they're great friends, but it's just...it feels like...work social-izing with them."

I take a mouthful and chew with puffed-out cheeks.

"I'll go with just you if that opportunity ever arises," I add.

Nolan chews, eyeing me thoughtfully.

"You act like wakeboarding requires so much socializing. You know you're going to have to wear a figurative mask and try to be normal if you're going to have friends outside of the SEAL Teams...or get a girlfriend. You aren't getting any younger, McBrode," he says, eating his burger gingerly.

I scowl. "A girlfriend? Toss me to the kraken and call me dead. The last thing I need is someone telling me what to do or how to live my life. I like my routine and my work. The friends I have are just fine."

He flashes a half grin, but it falls quickly.

"Your biceps aren't keeping you warm at night, and the friends you have are just like you, so it doesn't feel like work. Doesn't that get boring? We're turning thirty next year. Isn't there something outside of work you want to accomplish? Don't you want your life to be well-rounded?"

"Well, your multimeter isn't keeping you warm at night, either," I clap back, cramming more into my mouth. "You need to practice what you preach."

He looks down, then away. A tell. He's lying or keeping something from me.

"Wait a damned minute. Do you have a girlfriend you haven't told me about?"

Nolan takes another bite instead of replying. Then another, his gaze on his plate. He drinks a sip of water, and by the time he finishes, my heart is pounding, and I don't know why.

"Nolan," I chide. "Tell me."

"This was supposed to be your goodbye lunch. I don't

want to talk about myself. I wanted to try to crack your shell again, so you know you're loved and cared about, even if you'd rather live in a one-room shack up in the mountains and never talk to anyone ever again."

I ignore his emotional sentiment.

"About your new girlfriend?"

"She was at the lake house this weekend, Brody. You don't do life normally these days, so I saw no sense in mentioning her until I'm sure if it's going to work out." He pauses and stares into my soul. "You don't give a shit about minor details these days."

My heart pounds a bit more.

"Of course I care about you. Tell me about her."

He's right about details, though. Most of them aren't a value add, so I let them bounce off me.

It was always only a matter of time before Nolan McCoy found the right woman. I'm shocked he hasn't already, honestly. He focused on building his empire. This would be the next logical step, even if it scares the shit out of me. I don't tell him, of course, because I can't, but I'm afraid to lose him to whoever he marries. She's going to hate me. She won't want me around. I'll be too brash and dangerous to be around his kids. It's a legitimate fear of mine, and these days I don't have many of those. I may not want a lot of things, but I want my brother in my life.

He clenches his jaw, working it back and forth.

"She's a nice woman. She's an RN at a pediatrician's office in Sag Harbor, right by the main McCoy's Power Pro office. Her name is Catherine. She has her shit together and doesn't have any baggage that she's shown yet." He exhales after taking another sip. "She has no kids, and she's never been married. It's been six months, so even if I'm not one hundred percent yet, I'm confident she'll be around for a while."

Six months. My stomach sinks. He's kept this from me for half a year because he didn't think I'd care.

"I can't believe I haven't met her yet," I say, homing in on something normal instead of the disconnected heartbreak I feel.

Has he seemed different these past months? Am I a bad brother? It's one of the things I thought I was okay at. I haven't had a girlfriend for a long time, when I was innocent and didn't have to pretend.

"I want to meet her."

He raises his brows. "You do?"

I cock my head in question. "Why wouldn't I? It's been six months. That's serious. I want to meet her."

He shakes his head. "I never know with you, Brody. I don't. It's hard to tell what you'll care about and what you won't."

He is the only thing I care about outside of my teammates and work. *Just say that,* I think. Tell him you love him.

"Well, now I guess I must meet her when I get home in three months. You think she's going to be around then?"

"She will," he says, finishing his burger. "She wanted to meet you," he adds quietly.

"Oh?" I counter.

"I told her you weren't really the type to meet until things got more serious," he explains. "Which started a whole argument. The last thing I wanted was to burden you with a social interaction that may cause discomfort."

Now he's being a prick, and I guess I can't blame him. It's not like he's saying anything untruthful.

When we were kids, I took the blame for everything because I could just stare at the wall and take the heat. My parents were stern, but loving, and even still, Nolan didn't deal with stern well. I can turn it all off when it's anger or disappointment. When we're talking jokes or trying to find something in common with someone, that's where Nolan picked up my slack. Together, we equal one damn awesome human. Apart, we are a little fractured. Me more than him.

I grumble under my breath. "She's already got a bad impression of me. Great."

"You care what she thinks about you?" Nolan's eyes widen.

Clearing my throat, I say, "If you're staying with her, then my seeming like a lumbering, dumb troll who can't meet people isn't great. If she matters to you, she matters to me."

"I didn't call you dumb. I said you were away a lot because you were a Navy SEAL, Brody. That was the main excuse I gave. You know I think highly of you."

"Whatever," I say, looking away. "Tell her I look forward to meeting her after this deployment, I guess."

He laughs once, loudly. "Your sarcasm will win over any heart that your pure charm can't. Remember that."

Scowling, I finish my water, shaking my head.

"I won't remember that, but I will remember Catherine and will want to meet her when I get home. And I will be home, so don't worry about that part, like I know you tend to. It's supposed to be a quick deployment," I say, trying to get down to brass tacks now that our time together is winding down.

"I'll be safe." I air quote the last word and pull an ugly face.

"I won't come back any more fucked up than I already am."

I pull another ugly face.

"I will email you when I get a chance, and you can

pass on the info to Mom and Dad. Everything is going to be okay. I know what everyone thinks, but not everyone gets PTSD from deployments and death. It is possible to look at my job as just a job and the things that go with it, just go with it, same as any job. Think about the doctors who work in emergency rooms or paramedics who scrape motorists off the highway. More people need to know it's not all doom and gloom because bad things happen. I'm unscathed. Many SEALs exit this career path unscathed. I promise you, Nolan. I hate the stigma that we must be fucked up because of what we see and do. *It's not true.* I am really good at putting things into boxes. It can happen, and I can put it in a box. I don't have to think about it when it is done. It can stay in its box."

He stares, waiting for me to go on, but I just gave him more than I usually do.

"I'll call you when I leave my house so you can go pick up Grimace." My dog is the only annoyance I willingly allow in my life, and he's a big one for a man with a career like mine.

"I trust you, and I know that you've always been this cranky, so I'll try not to worry, but I am concerned about balance in your life. I'm sure it will come, eventually. I was wondering when you would mention your prized possession. Yes, I will pick up Grimace and care for him like the prince he is. Are you still taking him to the groomer on Sixth and Paramount every four weeks?"

"Yes, and please don't try any new groomers like last time. He's used to the woman at the Sudz Bucket. She doesn't even have to muzzle him anymore. He gets a wash and trim."

Nolan chuckles. "It still baffles me how you ended up with a dog as mean as you."

That's the crux of why I have him. I walked past a

farmers' market on my day off, and the local animal shelter was there trying to adopt out a bunch of dogs. Grimace was in a cage in the back by himself. Hair matted, and teeth jutting out from the bottom in the grossest underbite I've ever seen. He has a permanent grimace on his face. They said he tried to bite someone before I walked by. They mentioned him not being adoptable, and when someone tells me I can't do something, I'm almost always going to do it. I took him home, and that dog cherishes the ground I walk on. Vice versa, if I'm honest with myself. He's four pounds of stringy hair and one hundred percent heart.

"That's why we get along," I say, grinning. "Thank you for caring for him. I'll have his go bag packed. Remember, don't touch him on the paws. That's what he hates. Tell everyone not to touch his paws. Catherine needs to know."

Hah, I worked her in again, so he knows I'm serious about getting to know her.

"If she gets bit, that's another unfavorable mark against me."

Nolan cracks his knuckles on the table and picks up the check the waitress dropped off. We always take turns, and it's his turn today.

"I know Grimace well. He loves me because I look and sound like you. He does get sad for a few days, but he gets used to my amiable personality quite quickly. I bring him to the office, and the receptionist keeps him in a heated bed under her desk. He lives the life. I'll make sure no one touches his paws."

I smile, thinking about Grimace in a heated bed in Nolan's office.

"I'm glad I don't have to worry about him while I'm gone. You're the only person I trust, you know that?"

"That's the first real smile since you sat down," Nolan points out. "And it wasn't because I told you I love you, and I'll miss you. It was because of Grimace. What needs to happen to give you a different life perspective? So you'll see what's important in life?"

He's always a little philosophical. Nolan looks at life differently than I do. There's no arguing he has it right, and I should conform, but I *can't*. I don't know how. Not yet. It is coming time that I'm going to have to face my past head-on and forgive myself, though. Time is passing, and I do understand that.

"Eventually, I'll come around. You said it yourself. Probably need more time to figure it all out," I say, standing after our check is taken care of.

We make our way to our trucks. Mine is black and tinted, and his is white, and the windows are still standard.

Stretching when Nolan faces me, I wrap him in a hug. He holds me for a long time, and I hold on just as tight. I don't care what people think or what it appears as. I do love my brother. I will miss my brother. *Just say it*, my subconscious whispers, but nothing comes out. I just close my eyes and will him to know. When he pulls back and looks me in my eyes, the same blue eyes I own, I know he knows my heart. Without saying a word.

He ruffles my hair. "I'll see ya, McBrode," Nolan says, eyes glassing over.

I push the emotion down, as far as it will go, but I still feel it leaking from my eyes.

"Yeah, I'll see you, McLan." I ruffle his hair back, and then I get into my truck.

I wait for him to pull away first, making sure he's safe on the busy road before I head for home.

Grimace is sitting on the back of the couch, staring

out the window when I pull into my driveway. I smile at him, and he hops down to greet me at the door. I scoop him up and lock my door. We're going to head to base, and he comes with me when he can.

I transferred to the SEAL base in Southampton a few years ago to be close to my family, and so far, they haven't asked me to transfer yet. I'll admit if they do, I will be upset. This is the most settled I've felt in a long time. I like my little cottage house and the fact that Nolan and my parents are close. I like that it feels like home when I'm not deployed or on a training trip.

"All right, Grimace, we need to make sure I have everything I need, and you need to guard the high bay while I do it," I explain, petting his head at a red light.

He sits in my lap, his tiny paws on one thigh and his butt on the other.

"You can't be mean to Catherine, Grim. You hear me? You're going to meet a nice lady, and you need to be sweet to her. Sweet like you've never known how to be. If she doesn't like us, we're in trouble, okay?"

He looks at me, and I swear he has an understanding.

"We need to blend in, Grim. We need to be good. Nolan deserves it." I say the last sentence quieter. "He deserves it," I repeat. "I'm going to miss you so much. I am going to miss him so much. I love you."

I whisper the words to my dog that I couldn't bring myself to say to my brother.

## CHAPTER THREE

*saylor*

"THE HYDROFOILS ARE FAILING," I say to myself as I check the gauge for the tenth time.

Hydrofoils are underwater wings that lift the hull out of the water and lessen the drag, allowing me to sail quicker.

"Sea Tracker is also failing," I whisper in absolute horror.

That's the newest mod Dad and I installed before I set sail. Sea Tracker is an AI GPS that sails autonomously, so I can sleep with more regularity. Sea Tracker makes real-time adjustments for weather conditions and the wind. Without it, I'm completely self-reliant. It's still doable, but it's much harder. This is something I didn't anticipate doing without a crew. *I can do hard things*, I remind myself.

I'm crouched down in front of the control panel, sweat pouring down my face as I stare at the worst-case scenario unfolding. I'll be facing the toughest, most powerful current in the world, the Agulhas current, without the equipment I'll need for safety. Even though I can see land, it's not friendly territory. I pulled up the charts of my friendly ports, and I'm still a few days away from being close to a port that I'd be comfortable docking at.

There was a storm last night, and while I didn't think it was anything concerning at the time, I now realize it did more damage than I thought. My VHF radio is working, though there seems to be a jam in the lines. Channel sixteen, which is only used for emergency situations, would work, but this wouldn't qualify as life-threatening. Not yet, at least.

*Come on, Saylor. Pull your shit together. You can do this. You've trained for this.*

The Mozambique Channel is wildly dangerous, filled with pirates, and it requires a lot of technical sailing, but it's the closest route to get out of open water to try to repair my GPS. It's the patch of water in between Africa and Madagascar. Wiping the sweat from my forehead on the hem of my shirt, I head back up to the deck for fresh air.

At the helm, I catch my breath as my heart hammers. This journey has been mildly challenging up until now. I had all the luxury items money could buy to make my job easier. I squint in the distance to recognize land shapes and the entrance to the channel. I give myself a mental pep talk. I can fix this when I get to the next port. This doesn't have to set me off track.

Yeah, but can I get to the next *safe* port before another storm hits, without sleeping, and sailing at a lower knot without my hydrofoils? At night?

"Damn it," I hiss, slamming my fist down.

My mom always says if you're feeling angry, eat. If you're feeling sorry for yourself, take a shower. If you're feeling confused, sleep. What if I'm all these things at once?

The winds are shifting, and I won't have time to do any of those things soon. I decide to pause before the next storm comes in. I do need to eat and shower. Sleep probably won't be something I'll have time for, though. Grabbing the boom, I adjust the main sail before setting my anchor. I shovel a meal down and then hit the button to turn on my hot water to shower. This is when I need to think and weigh my options.

Showering in this small tube is one of the only true comforts of sailing for this amount of time. I do pick up fresh fruit when in port, but that runs out quickly, so the freeze-dried meals and shelf-stable canned stuff are what I live off of in between. My nose is continuously sunburnt, no matter how much H Mart sunblock I use, and my body hurts from sleeping in the berth. My bed isn't as comfortable as the one at home, and the constant rocking from the variable sea states makes for a lot of rolling around instead of deep sleep.

I turn off the water as I lather my hair and body with my shampoo and soap from home. I mean, a girl has her standards, and if this were to be my only guilty pleasure, I figured it wouldn't hurt to bring the good stuff. I turn on the hot water to rinse, then off again to shave and wash my face.

I could reach Mozambique before nightfall, I think, doing the math in my head. The wind will be in my favor. Even if it's not a friendly port I marked on my plan, it doesn't mean they wouldn't welcome me. It just means it has a higher risk factor for a single woman sailing an expensive boat.

When I'm clean, I slather on sunblock and dress in a light pink long-sleeved SPF shirt and a black stretchy skort. I put on my socks and sneakers and pull my satellite phone off the charger to call my dad. He answers on the first ring because he's on alert, given my situation.

"Sweet Pea, is everything okay?"

I try to call him when things are good and when I have a small issue, so he doesn't have a heart attack every time he sees my number.

I turn it on speaker phone as I braid my hair into two long pigtails in the small mirror in the saloon.

"Everything is going well, but I do need to make some repairs, Dad. I'm going to have to stop in Maputo or Beira." I say it all so he can soak it in. "The AI GPS and the hydrofoils are down," I add so he knows I'm not being outrageous for no reason.

I hear his breathing rate increase.

"It'll be daylight when I make it there. Which port do you think is the better option?"

"How many nautical miles is it to the Mozambique Channel, hon? I don't have my computer in front of me, so I'm not sure where you're at exactly."

My phone has a tracking device so he can keep tabs on me, but he's only able to get a precise location on his computer because of the software that's required for pinpoint accuracy.

I exhale when he doesn't question anything. It tells me I'm making the right decision.

"At six knots, which is doable without the hydrofoils, about five hours. Plenty of daylight left if I start when I get off the phone with you. Which port?"

Dad blows out a long breath. "Neither if you had another option, but it's unpredictable on the Madagascar side, so I wouldn't recommend porting there. Maputo is a big city and will have more sailors and foreign folks who could help you, but it's dangerous, Saylor. The pirates cruise those waters no matter the time of day. Do you have the .22?"

"I always have it on me, don't worry. So...Maputo over Beria. Got it."

"Your boat is worth more than some of the locals make in a lifetime. I hate giving you this advice, but I don't think it's safe until you have everything back online. You're between a rock and a hard place, for sure. Any idea how the GPS went down? Was the storm that bad last night? Was cloud coverage severe?"

He tracks everything from home, and I love him for it.

I shake my head, back in front of the control panel.

"It wasn't. It seems like a hardware malfunction. Maybe a geomagnetic disturbance? Sea Tracker relies on the satellites, and my phone is working, so that doesn't track either."

I don't say it, but it could be caused by jamming or spoofing, which is terrifying because that means there's a ship or a boat somewhere doing this to me intentionally. Many military ships jam to block interference from enemies. To a military ship, my equipment may seem too high-tech to be a civilian sailing. This is something I spent time worrying about.

"When you port and troubleshoot, let me know how long it will take to fix. I'll reserve our jet and put our pilot on alert so I can get to you if there's enough time, Sweet Pea. Please be careful."

"Promise. I'm going to make it all the way around, Dad. Just you wait!" I offer a little optimism because his worry is evident from the tremor in his voice. I hate to hear it. "Don't tell Mom until you have to. I love you!"

He explains what to expect at the port and where I should go for help. He tells me a few phrases to use in Portuguese, a language I can understand and speak a little, and tells me the indigenous language is Xichangana in case I encounter it and need to translate on my phone. Then he bids me farewell.

"I love you. Fair winds, Sweet Pea," he says, then clicks off the call.

The large phone trembles in my hand. It's my only link to civilization when I'm out here. The only love I feel. My world lives inside this heavy, ancient-seeming technology. Extending my arm, I connect it back to its Velcro home and plug it into the charging cable. One of the improvements I made before I set sail was the addition of solar power. I always have electricity in plentiful amounts because of the conversion system we installed.

Now it's time to get to work. I strap the .22 into the leg harness and pull it up high so my skirt covers it, raise the anchor, and change course to head toward the Mozambique Channel. Words that would have seemed impossible to even think about before I left.

Mom would be throwing a fit if she knew I was going off course, but I doubt she'd understand the risks involved with it. She's always just thrown money at a problem to make it go away. She's never done anything like this before, but I'm comforted knowing that if the worst happens and some random ass pirates succeed in kidnapping my ornery ass, they'll have to deal with Bianca Wyndham for the ransom money. She'll drive the hardest bargain they've ever encountered. They'll rue the day they chose me. She'll ask if they have wealthy sons and what their real estate portfolio looks like. Bianca will make them regret they were born. The morbid, yet enthralling thought keeps me occupied as I sail.

As the port comes into view, the AI GPS flickers on and off once or twice, my heart swelling each time, but it's dark again, without any signs of coming back online.

The seas were choppier as the onshore winds began affecting my sails, so it took longer than I expected. The lights on shore beckon, but the fact that it's dusk gives me pause. I could anchor here for the night, tucked into the corner of the channel, sheltered from the swells of the current further behind me. Or I could push on for Maputo and take my chances. Because I need to sleep and the fear of not having my GPS is strong, I decide to dock and sail as quickly as I can to get help.

After the flicker of life with Sea Tracker, I know I'm being jammed. If it were a hardware failure, it would be flatlined without any bounce back.

I fixate on the shore as I adjust my rigging and make sure the cleat is holding the ropes properly. The fenders are inflatable bumpers used when docking to protect the boat from landing against other boats or hard surfaces. They're in place, as well. After my checks are done, I take my place back in the helm and watch my backup GPS just as it begins to rain. Tiny, hard rain that ricochets off the water in sharp little circles.

It went from dusk to black in what feels like seconds, but I know that's not true.

"Fabulous," I mutter as I throw on my rain jacket and tighten the hood.

I've barely made headway in the channel when I hear the roar of a speedboat engine. I see their flashing lights bouncing off the sails and landing on random places on my boat. Then a spotlight lands on me and holds. They found what they were looking for.

As they grow closer, I recognize Portuguese words over the pelting rain that's blasting like spiky sand against my face. The words I can understand aren't pleasant or helpful. They're talking about money and my boat.

As quickly as I can, I get to the stern, turn on a large

spotlight, and tilt it until their speedboat is illuminated completely. Let's be honest, it's blinding, it's ostentatious in size, and their momentary stun gives me time to grab my gun and aim it directly at them before screaming in Portuguese, "Stay away from me or I'll shoot."

There are five men on the vessel. I know how to fire this gun, but I don't know if I'm a good enough shot to take all five of them out, and that can be the only viable option when I begin shooting. The one steering the boat will be first, the second will be the one next to him, then the three in the back. That's the plan.

The men rub their eyes against the bright light, then draw guns far larger than mine. One of the three in the back shoots into the air twice, in rapid succession. They could sink my boat with rounds that big, and I realize this is bleak. I hate that I made a joke about Bianca when I thought this wasn't a likely scenario, and I realize I'll be lucky to get out of this with my life.

"Everyone on board, stand in front of the light and put your hands up. We are boarding."

They pull up closer to the boat, holding onto my fenders as two men try to board my boat. Bounding toward the helm, I tune to channel sixteen and send in my mayday, but I don't have time to talk as I hear them sliding up the stern. I head down to the berth, grab the satellite phone, and dial my dad. I know he's picked up, and I know calling him is more valuable than calling anyone else.

I tell him in a low voice what's happening, and I describe the men and their craft as detailed as possible. Then I tell him I'm going to leave the phone on for as long as I can so he can track me. He stays quiet, and I can hear him cursing and praying over and over. We aren't religious, and his reaction heightens my fear.

I can hear the men on the deck, so I grab all the ammo I have and put it in my pockets with the phone tucked in an interior jacket pocket. I rush the deck, gun aimed in front of me.

I shoot one man who is heading down the stairs. I move out of the way and shoot him in the back one more time to be sure, then continue, targeting another man starboard. I fire the gun once more, hitting him in the chest. The momentum causes him to fall over the side.

Unfortunately, that's where my luck ends. I'm grabbed around the waist, and the gun is taken from my hand.

"Little bird, little bird, here all by yourself in this fancy boat? How dumb can you be?" he says in his native tongue.

"Let me go!" I scream, trying to wiggle out of his grasp without luck. I'm zip-tied, hands and feet, and being lowered into the speedboat before I can even process what happens next. My phone, I think.

"Where are you taking me?" I wail in broken Portuguese. "Where?"

He seems surprised I'm speaking his native tongue. "Somewhere safe," he growls.

It's the man who was captaining the boat who has me. The other two men are aboard my boat, rifling through it. I can see them now that they've turned off the spotlight.

I'm never going to see this boat again. It seems a foolish concern considering I may die, but as the craft crashes against the water heading in the opposite direction, I don't take my eyes off my boat until it's vanished completely. After that, I consider dumping myself into the water to drown, because nothing off this coast is going to be safe.

He lessens the force on the throttle and says, "You killed my men, and you will pay."

I shiver against the memory—something I can't process now. I'm shaking with shock.

"You stole my fucking boat, and you're going to strip it for parts. You will pay. When you realize what you've done, you're going to be sorry. So, so very sorry," I say, in English this time to drive my point home. "They will find you. They will hunt you down. They will cut you open one by one and dissect your family and feed it to the sharks. I am your worst nightmare. I will be the end of you," I say, and inside the dim glow from his navigation panel, I can tell my words affect him. I can tell by his face they've at least invoked some degree of fear.

He swivels his head back to the wheel as we approach land. "Who are you?"

I laugh, the mean kind of sarcastic cackle. "You're asking that now? Too late. The damage is done. You. Are. Finished." At his hesitation, I realize this might be an out. "Unless you drive me back to my sailboat right now. Before anyone knows I'm missing. That's your only chance."

"If you're that important, you're worth more than average. I'll take my chances," he replies in Portuguese. "Now shut up, or I'll put you to sleep. You're annoying me, and I need to focus."

At least what he's saying does confirm my kidnapping-for-ransom theory. They'll have to keep me alive. Not by much, I remind myself.

I did research about this during my preparations. They'll keep me alive without harming me. Bianca will make sure not a hair on my head is touched if they want a top-dollar exchange. They aren't so uncivilized that I'll be raped and pillaged. This is a large operation to fund terror, from what I understand gathered by the boat and equipment they used to trap me, and truly, I mean nothing except a payday to them. They'll piece out my boat, part by part, for sure.

A pang of grief hits. I've lost so much already, and who knows what's to come.

I realize the irony of my damn life being in Bianca's hands because of something she deemed a stupid idea. If I live through this, I'm never going to hear the end of it. I'm going to make these assholes lives a living hell as retribution.

"Where are we going?" I ask again when I remember my phone, still on in my pocket, my dad living his worst nightmare as he listens to this unfold in real time.

I had to shoot people. I know he has made it to his computer by now and will be using the phone to see my exact location. The knowledge he gains will make a difference in my being found. I continue to pester in hopes of gathering information that will help him.

"Tell me. I demand it. Where are we going? Where is my boat? What are your plans?" The questions spill out of me like a toddler seeking the answer to why.

"I told you to be quiet," he replies, dropping his right arm behind him, then swinging it.

A needle lands in my thigh hard and sharp before I have a chance to inch away from him. He presses the plunger before I can wiggle back, and the blackness overtakes me in seconds.

"Toward Madagascar," I say out loud so the phone will pick it up. Looking at the stars, I try my best to remember my celestial navigation course, but the dizziness sweeps me away, and my eyes close without permission.

The last thing I remember is the deep vibrating hum of the engine as the boat slows, and my kidnapper's voice as he talks to someone named Raza on his radio.

## CHAPTER FOUR

*brody*

"AND YOU'RE sure you'll be able to complete the operation without blowing everything and yourself up?" Commander asks, a brow raised.

He's nervous, and I can't blame him. It's the first mission of its kind in the SEAL Teams, and I'll be doing it solo. It requires some acting and skills that, honestly, I'm not sure I possess, so I'll have to ad-lib. It also doesn't have a definitive start or end date. It's a *however long it takes to get what we need and out of there safely* kind of situation.

We plan for many different scenarios when we're preparing for missions, but this operation is something we can't plan for.

"I'm not worried about your infiltrating the pirate camp and extracting the hostage. I'm worried about the in between, McCoy. When no one is supposed to know who you *really* are. The hostage can't know you're an operator, either." He looks at me sideways. "Can you blend in?"

I nod.

"I know I'm an asshole who can't hold his tongue, and I'm quick to react in real life when dealing with idiots, but this is work, and I will be able to fulfill everything needed of me. I know it," I tell him, laying a hand on my chest.

I feel guilty for the poor idiot being kidnapped in the first place, but it was also part of our plan, so I don't feel *that* bad. It had to happen for my part in this to be possible.

"This can't be a traditional mission where we all storm in there, guns blazing. It needs to be covert. I'm the man for this job," I say, shifting in the uncomfortable seat in our naval ship's office.

The air is stale and always has a metallic, oily scent. If I think about it too much, it makes me want to throw up.

"I can blend in."

Even as I say it, I think about tactics I'll use to keep my true identity from the enemy and their captive. *Act like Nolan,* I think. He's the only other person I know as well as myself. I already look like him. I just need to act like him—have the patience he has. *Is that even possible?*

My teammates left muster several minutes ago after it was declared that I was the man for this particular job. Not just because of my tenure, but mostly because of my sparkling personality.

"I know you are a man who can give people hell, McCoy. You know the hostage is female? We didn't plan on who the hostage was going to be. It was just her unlucky day."

I blow out an annoyed breath.

"I can deal with females. Why does everyone think I'm this Neanderthal without any social graces?"

He chuckles under his breath.

"You kind of are, no offense. I didn't say anything in muster, but we got a little more intel about what kind of female this is. She's from one of the wealthiest families in the States. All we knew when we jammed her navigation system was that it was extremely high-tech and suspicious given her coordinates. There was no reason for us to believe that was a civilian boat. We aren't in the wrong here, but we weren't right either. As such, her family is demanding her back unharmed. They're demanding it pretty emphatically too. You must succeed."

Hissing out a breath, I close my eyes.

"Fantastic. The Coast Mafia knew exactly what they were doing when they took her then. We needed a kidnapping for ransom to get in. We didn't need *this* one, though," I say. "At least we know her family will pay if things don't go according to plan. If I need to get her out of there quick, for say, medical reasons, her family can be a backup plan if I need to stay there longer."

The way Commander is looking at me tells me he hopes it doesn't come to that.

"Hey, we have no idea what's going to happen when I get there. There could be more than one organized crime syndicate in play if she's worth that much. The crime rings don't all operate the same. You know that." I pause. "How much are we talking for ransom?"

Commander grunts and shakes his head.

"Millions. The mother demanded to talk to the captain of our ship because she thought that he was in charge, and they let her believe that. The FBI put her through because I guess she's got a screw loose and hollering about who she knows on the inside. But McCoy," he deadpans. "If, when you get there, she's unharmed, you have to make sure she stays that way just to be on the safe side."

"I get it. That was always the plan. What's her profile?" I ask.

Commander shifts the stack on the desk in front of

him and hands me a cream folder with paperclips sticking out.

"She's a talented sailor in her own right. She won the America's Cup. That is an incredible feat," he states.

I open the folder and see a photo of her holding a silver bowl-shaped trophy with a wide smile. The picture is black and white, but I can tell she's blonde and thin. Basically, she's exactly what I thought she'd look like. A fucking moron who sails alone in dangerous waters.

"She is twenty-eight and has a degree from Columbia," he says.

Okay, maybe not a fucking moron, but still an idiot.

He goes on. "She is unmarried and owns more real estate than a monarch. Her dad served in the Navy for ten years while having a trust fund with nine zeros at the end, so not all typical stuff in here. She works as an engineer at the family company. Wyndham is the last name," he says as I scan the words, trying to soak everything in that may be of any importance to me.

What makes her tick? Does she have pets? What can I say about her world to have something in common with her?

I meet his gaze when it registers.

"Like Wyndham Technology?" I ask, unable to keep the shock from my voice. "That family?"

"Same family," he replies, tone low. "So when I say keep her safe, it's less of a suggestion and more of a direct order." He laughs as he finishes his sentence.

They developed the software that created AI, along with a laundry list of cutting-edge technology the military uses daily. It is the biggest tech company in the world.

"The mom really meant she knew people on the *inside* then," I remark, reading over the rest of the notes.

She has a sister, I notice, and store that information for later.

"I'm going to take this with me to look over tonight."

I tap the file on the desk, and it makes an echoing noise.

"You picked the right guy, Commander. It's going to be great to finally nail these assholes to the wall and dismantle this."

Another kidnapping-for-ransom band will more than likely pop up, but taking apart the criminal ring that is being funded is our end goal.

Commander grabs my shoulder.

"I know you'll make me proud, McCoy. I think putting you outside of your comfort zone is going to be good for you, for our squadron. You've been on the Teams a long time. This is exactly what you need to propel you to the next level of development. Something that challenges every part of you."

I nod, unable to let his words sink in. "Thank you, sir."

Commander tells me when I'll set sail, and hands me another file with all the details about the sailboat I'll be on and the coordinates where I'll sail to—not far from where our target was captured, honestly.

They'll implant a chip under the skin near my wrist tomorrow morning before I take off. It's undetectable by the naked eye, and I can trigger communication by a combination of hard presses to let my Team know it's time to come if need be. He talks me through the process, and I nod along, a little freaked out because I've never had one before. When he's sure I don't have any other questions, he tells me a phrase to use if necessary, and then he leaves, the door shutting behind him like a can of tinned meat.

I jolt at the noise and take all the information back to my berthing, where I immediately pull up my secret laptop and go down a rabbit hole to find out as much as I can about this family. I want to know things the file doesn't have. Take a peek to see if she has social media or other professional accolades I should know about.

Ah, so the black-and-white photo doesn't do her justice. She's attractive in the conventional way. Symmetrical face, perfectly balanced features, and big blue eyes. I shudder at what's possibly happening to her at this very second. Hopefully, by this point, the captors know how valuable she is, dictating them to keep their bodies and weapons to themselves.

Clicking an article with the Wyndham last name in it brings me to an exposé about her. Saylor Wyndham. Not only isn't she a fucking moron, but she's also incredibly intelligent. I've used some of the technology her team helped create. Her most recent project focuses on neural transmissions. Essentially, your brain is syncing with technology, so you can control computers and technology with your thoughts, thus bypassing the keyboard or touchscreen. A tiny chip implanted on the back of the neck reads the neural waves from our brains and talks to the computer. It's similar technology I'll have implanted tomorrow, but not as nuanced and brilliant, if I'm being honest with myself.

The commonalities I share with the captor's family are unexpected. Her dad went to the Naval Academy, just like me. He majored in mechanical engineering, just like me, and their main US residence is near where I live, but that's where the similarities end.

The Wyndhams have real estate all over the world, and the mother, Bianca, supports so many charities and foundations that I don't even read them all. The list is too long to scroll to the bottom. The sister, Bronwyn, is a philanthropist who runs an art museum with her husband. The laundry list of Ivy League degrees and accomplishments goes on and on. I want to hate them on principle, but I can't. Not fully, anyway. I email my brother before I go to sleep.

*Nolan,*

> *I'm setting off for a side quest tomorrow and won't be able to email or call for a while. Please tell Mom and Dad I'm okay. You would be happy if I could tell you what I have to do and how uncomfortable it's going to make me. Happy in a good for you way, not a torture my twin way. I hope the new location isn't tanking too hard. Kiss Grimace for me and tell him I'll save him from your merriment as soon as I can. I'm sure he's seizing from the joy he's surrounded by. I hope no one has touched his feet.*

*Your brother,*
*McBrode.*

When I fall asleep, my mind plays a dreamscape of the Wyndham family across my eyelids. They're like fictional characters come to life. Saylor Wyndham isn't just all of her accomplishments and her last name. Now she's *my problem.*

The wind is whipping my face as I fuck with the sails to make them do what I want. While I'm sure brute strength isn't the right way to accomplish this, it's my way to do it.

Another ship dropped off my sailboat for the mission, and I set off for my intended destination in the afternoon because I need to arrive at the Mozambique Channel by nightfall, when the pirates hunt. They typically kidnap on a schedule, a week on and a week off, so we know they'll be out here trying to catch another bounty after the Wyndham woman.

I drop the anchor and curse when it doesn't do what I want the first time. I don't have the finesse to enjoy sailing as an actual sport, and I can't let the pirates see that. This is supposed to be my hobby. I need to look like a lost, dumb sailor looking for help.

"Damn it all to hell. Who the fuck does this for a good time?"

I'm all for suffering for fun, but this is another level. The rain hitting my face sideways feels like pinpricks and the damn sails have a mind of their own. While I have my captain's license, it isn't something I sought out. It was a check in the box. A requirement for my profession in this area. Most SEALs loathe the fucking water—detest being on a ship and would rather skin themselves alive than spend long periods of time at sea. My stomach tips and heaves as the boat rocks.

When the anchor release finally works, I'm a second away from breaking something. If this were a normal mission, I'd have a wetsuit, and I'd be under the water, using a rebreather system called a Draeger. I'd swim through the ocean undetected at night, and sneak onto the beach to overtake the enemy. That's what I've practiced hundreds of times. What I'm good at. Some may even use the word perfect as a descriptor.

The wind blows a gust of sharp raindrops into my left

eye. *Fuck this kind of water.* Fuck this. I rub my eye using a fist, and I wait to be *captured*. The thought makes me sick. I plug in my coordinates and send them back to the naval ship, where Commander and my teammates are tracking my every move.

I wish they could see me. I throw both middle fingers up to the sky and growl like a damn grizzly bear. *You signed up for this*, I remind myself. I sit down in the small seat that barely fits my ass and cross my arms for warmth. It's a bit chilly. One more thing added to my growing list of discontentment. I'm cold *and* wet. My boat isn't nearly as nice as Saylor Wyndham's technical dream—there were images of it in the folder—but it's fine enough to entice a pirate to look twice. That's all I need.

It would be fantastic if they could hurry up and steal my boat and kidnap me already. Let's get to the gritty part.

I use my radio to send out a distress signal using a channel that isn't secure, but also not the main emergency channel. The pirates will be listening and plotting, if they aren't already. The lights of both shores of Mozambique and Madagascar are visible through my telescope. One side looks lively, a bustling city filled with life, and the other side looks like a ghost town with dim, sparsely lit areas.

Rubbing my wrist where the new implant itches my skin, reminding me that I won't be alone, I relish and curse this assignment. I decide to go below cabin to get away from the rain when I see the fucking telltale flashlights in the distance. A boat is approaching from the side.

*Game time.*

I toss my hand up in the air and wave it left and right in the direction of the boat.

"Come and get me, motherfuckers," I say, grinning to myself as the boat gets closer.

I can tell from here that they're from the sector that took the Wyndham woman. There are differences between the factions: how nice their boats are, what they're wearing, and what direction they're coming from. They're closer now, and I can see what they're wearing: black hoods. That's a tell.

*Take me to the promised land,* I muse. *Take me to her.*

When they raise their guns, it takes everything inside my damn soul not to decimate them. It takes a few seconds to swallow the lump in my throat. Not because I'm scared, but because I have to let them do what they will with me.

I was told if they sense I'm a threat, they may not take me. I need to appear weak in will and musculature. I'm six foot four, so there's no hiding my height. My hands are in fists down at my sides, about to burst from the pressure of clenching them. When they get close enough, I recognize they're speaking Portuguese.

"Put your hands up!"

I comply after slamming the button to tell my ship I've made contact. It also erases the connection to them, so it can't be traced.

"Help me," I say. "My systems are down."

I know I'm not saying the right words, but I continue to blather on as they board my boat.

"I need to dock at Maputo," I explain.

I say the port name twice, so they know exactly what I'm saying. Feigning stupidity is not my strong suit, but I need to appear inept.

"No," the captain of the boat says. "You're coming with us."

Though I can tell he's hesitant as he looks me up and down.

*Sell it. Sell it. Sell this fucking charade.*

"Please don't hurt me," I say, nearly choking on the pussy words.

The sentence tastes so bitter and wrong that my voice actually shakes.

"I just need to dock at Maputo. I don't have a lot of money on me."

I might just make myself sick with this, but I lay it on thick, bringing my voice up, and sliding my hand into my pocket.

"I have some cash if that's what you're after," I say, bringing up a wad of Euros. "Here, take this. Please don't hurt me."

"Take him," one man says to the other. "Both of you," he adds once his gaze flits over my size again.

They board the boat, and I do my best to look scared, but I have a feeling I might look bored as I allow them to zip tie my hands and jerk me onto their little boat. I do protest and plead like a good civilian would, but I don't make their lives as hard as I could, given that I could kill them with ease right here and now.

I know they drug most of the victims, and while I hope they don't do that to me, I'm ready for it if they do. I've prepared my body and hydrated so it will get out of my system quickly. This mission has a lot hinging on the fact that I need to roll with whatever happens.

I speak in their language again, pleading with them to release me, telling them I don't have money for ransom. There's a whole story they prepared for me. It's imperative that I hide the truth about who I really am. So I tell these men my story—test out the waters of believability. I was willed the sailboat by a friend who recently passed away. I was taking this sailing trip because it was his dying wish. He wanted his ashes spread at sea in a particular spot I couldn't find. I don't have any family, as I was in the foster system in America. My name is Brody still.

I say it quickly, so they perceive it as nerves and trepidation. Overshare. That is what the normal person would do in a state of distress. I also say it in English, so they know that's my native tongue. Verbal vomit.

They ask me questions about my life and conclude that my ransom money will have to come from the government if it's going to come at all. I keep them talking the entire ride to their beach camp and continue prattling on about whatever I think sounds desperate and makes me seem terrified. There are lulls, but my adrenaline is off the charts, so time passes quickly. Finally, they pull into one of Madagascar's many bays. Even at night, I can tell how white the beach sands are.

They load me into a Jeep and drive through a tropical jungle. There are plateaus, valleys, and thick vegetation from what I'm cataloging on the drive. I'm being a top-notch captive, so there's no talk of using the sedatives, and I'm watching them like a hawk in case they try to deliver a dose on the down low.

The man in the passenger seat turns to look at me, and for the first time, I sense distrust. My stomach turns, but I remind myself they don't know who I am or what I'm capable of.

Maybe my lies just seem too practiced, too smooth.

"What will happen to my boat?" I say in their native language. "It's important to me. Will I see it again?"

That's a question a normal citizen might ask, I think.

What would Nolan say? I quickly decide to make that my new motto.

"Don't destroy it, please. I'll pay for it."

The man in the passenger seat narrows his eyes at me in the dim light.

"Should we destroy you instead?" he asks.

I shake my head. "I don't mean anyone any harm. Please, don't hurt me. I'll do whatever you say. I just miss my friend, and that boat was the last thing left of him."

The driver calms him, using his name, Raza. Raza seems satisfied, or maybe carsick from the winding roads we're speeding on. He turns back to face the windshield.

I notice he's fidgeting with something in his lap, and I shift uncomfortably in my seat, trying to get a better view without being obvious. My hands are zip tied behind my back, so when he turns back to face me and I see the syringe, I have a knee-jerk reaction to bash my head forward into Raza's. But the forward motion was perfect, and even though his nose is bleeding, the needle went through my jeans and into my thigh.

The sedation seeps over my body like a web. Fuck. Fuck. Fuck. Fuck. It's begun. The part of this that will be the hardest. The unpredictable nature.

Raza is staring at me, fury singeing holes into my soul as blood trickles down his face. "I told you he was holding back," he says in English.

He wanted me to hear. So he knows I know my act sucks.

"He's not who he says he is."

Before I drift completely, I'm hit with a profound sense of failure. I fucked this up before it even began—didn't even make it to second base.

When I open my eyes, two men are dragging me, legs dangling, to a door that's built into the side of a craggy, mountain-like feature. The drugs cause me to process everything in a foggy dream state. I hear them grunting as they maneuver my limp body across the sand, but I know the second my thoughts crystallize.

*When I hear her scream.*

It's not the scream of fear or panic like you'd expect. No, no, this woman is fucking furious, incensed beyond all recognition. Then she comes into view, hands wrapped around the bars she's encased behind, blonde hair wild, hanging loose around her face, mouth open as she devastates our goddamn ear drums with her war cries.

"Put him with asset twelve. Maybe she'll kill him and make light work for us now that we know he's not worth much."

I recognize neither of the men carrying me are the men I know from the drive here.

One of them laughs. "Maybe it will calm her down. She can take out some of that aggression on him."

We're close enough now that the burning torches are illuminating her face. Her blue eyes meet mine, and maybe it's the sedative, or possibly exhaustion, or maybe it's because I told myself I'd be more like my brother to get through this, but all she looks like is trouble.

Saylor Wyndham locks her gaze with mine and lets out the most feral scream I've ever heard in my life.

# CHAPTER FIVE
## *saylor*

THEY CALLED ME CRAZY. They called me an insane woman. They said that I belonged in an insane asylum. All for what? Asking to use the toilet I know they have in their building, instead of the hole in the ground that's attached to the back side of my mountain *cage*.

I see Nery and Ravelo dragging a monstrous man toward me, so I decide to show them what crazy really looks like. Screaming until my voice physically gives out seems to be the only thing they respond to. Nothing else gets their attention.

I hear them laughing about something, but their voices are low, so I can't make out their words.

The man looks up, and I recognize the confusion. He's coming off the drugs, the jab, and must be a recruit for our island in paradise, sans the paradise. Ravelo laughs again, and I know he's said something about me because the captive man meets my eyes. Mostly, I look at him long enough to know if he's someone I can trust or someone who is going to complicate my life further.

When I decide his vibe is not passing the first check, I

| 53 |

yell as loud as I can, and as wild as I can manage with a sore throat. Gripping the bars, I shake the door as hard as I can, to no avail.

Ravelo drops the man and comes forward.

"Your roommate just arrived. Move back if you don't want a jab," he says in English.

Interesting. Usually, they speak in Portuguese. This must mean the man only speaks English.

"This cage isn't big enough for both of us," I scream. "He can go somewhere else," I say.

Nery drops the guy's other arm, unable to hold him up on his own. He's big, muscular, nothing like the two scrawny men trying to hold up his weight.

"He's going here. Rain is coming, and it's the only room that doesn't flood."

"It always rains here," I wail. "Every day it rains. How could you engineer something so simple so badly? How? You guys are a bunch of damn morons. I swear to God above, you're going to kill me with your ignorance before you get your money!"

I suck in a deep breath.

"Let me out of here, and I can fix it for you. I'll improve this whole island prison, so it's more habitable. For you. For me. For the damn ogre you're lugging around without a home."

My gaze drops to the man who is crawling away unsuccessfully. Ravelo drags him by his boot back to my door.

"And you! Just knock these bastards out and let me out of here. Do your muscles even work?"

I'm seeing red and breathing fire at this point. They've left me alone all day. I haven't seen a soul until now. I'm grasping for anything at this point.

His eyes are blue. They flick up to meet mine, and a hint of disdain flashes like a bolt. He doesn't speak.

"Asset twelve, move back."

Nery pulls a fucking syringe out of his pocket and loads it into his blow dart gun. I swear they think it's a carnival game. The jab.

"Move back," he says again, then repeats himself when I don't move.

I take a step back, then another, keeping my eyes trained on the stupid blow dart gun. Ravelo pushes the man into my cage, and they lock it behind us.

"He takes up more than half the space," I say. "This isn't fair!"

Nery lowers the weapon and smiles with crooked, grimy teeth, black outlining each one.

"This isn't a hotel, princess. This is captivity. This isn't about fairness."

I blow out a breath.

"And who is this?" Nodding to the man on the ground in a fetal position. He's facing the wall.

"How do you know he's not going to kill me? I'm not worth a cent if I'm harmed. I know Bianca has made that clear." I use her name because they're all terrified of her.

Like I suspected, Bianca came into negotiations like a hot lead pipe. Fired up and ready to crash through everything.

"How do I know he's not going to kill me in my sleep?"

Ravelo shakes his head.

"We don't know. Maybe he will. You aren't worth all the noise you cause."

Nery shakes the brown blow dart gun. I should be thankful they don't have real guns, but somehow that stupid brown pipe is just as terrifying. I killed two of their best men, and they are making me pay. That's what this is. It's retribution in any way they can.

The men leave, their pants dragging across the dirt, getting peppered by rain. They grab one of the torches on their way back to their main area of the base, leaving us with one outdoor torch and a small lantern I have on the floor opposite the man. When they go out, I'll be in pitch blackness with a stranger.

"Who are you? I know you can hear me. The injection puts you out quick, but you wake up quickly. I saw your eyes. I know you're back."

He rolls over but stays on the ground, lacing his hands behind his head. I move my lantern to see his face a little better.

"Has screaming got you anything except a blow dart, or is that a viable tactic to get things around here?"

So smooth. So calm. So unlike me when I woke up in this dirt-lined prison. I exhale, sitting down by the lantern.

"Who are you and why do you give off...those bad vibes?" I clear my throat. "Are you going to hurt me? Let's get down to facts right now, before anything else."

Might as well keep with my neurotic persona. It lends to an illusion of control—when I have zero.

"Name's Brody. Pleasure to meet you," he deadpans. "Vibes? What does that even mean? Some esoteric description for not being able to label something correctly using intelligence?"

He presses his lips together into a smug line. He lets his gaze slide over to meet mine.

"If what you mean by bad vibes is ambivalence, then yes. I don't care about you or anything except getting the fuck out of here. So, no. Hurting you isn't something worth my time or energy."

ALL THE WAY UNDER

He raises one infuriating brow as he surveys my absolute rage. Why are men patronizing, witless monsters?

"What? Not used to men not caring about you?" Another smirk. "So...back to the important *facts*. Does scream baiting work to get their attention? What do you know about them and their schedules?"

I lick my lips. They're chapped and just as angry as I am.

"No. Screaming doesn't do anything but make me feel better about making them uncomfortable."

Pulling my knees up to my chest, I watch Brody carefully as he sits up, brushes off his pants, checks his pockets, and seems to miss something that was there before.

"They take everything while you're out," I explain. "Even though you present as an absolute jerk, I'll answer your questions because I think if we work together, we'll have a better chance of getting things done."

He looks at me, and I can tell he's nervous. His breathing is still slowing, and there's a quiet unease in his blue gaze.

"Ravelo and the blow dart dick, Nery, were the men who brought you in here. The status of their hierarchy is questionable, but Raza, another one, is somewhere above them. They bring food in the morning, and that's it. I'm almost fluent in their language, so I understand things they say to each other."

I'm proud of that. I bet this moron can't translate.

"What do they say to each other?" Brody asks in Portuguese.

I roll my eyes.

"Of course you speak it too. Do I have any advantages here?"

All of this is overwhelming, confusing, and downright disgusting. I spent the morning trying to wash myself with the bucket and sponge they brought with my food, and I was humbled down to my very soul.

"You have muscles, a bad attitude, and you speak their native language." I throw up my arms.

He looks me dead in the eyes. "Hey, don't be so hard on yourself. You can scream."

"You have something worse than a bad attitude. You have an awful personality. Is this due to the bad night, or do you radiate negative energy like it's your job twenty-four hours a day?"

Brody wipes his hands on the sides of his jeans.

"What do they say to each other?" he asks again.

When he asks it in English, it doesn't sound like an optional question. He ignores every mean thing I just said, almost as if he didn't hear me.

"They talk about everything, even though they know I can understand. My ransom, my mom when she's being belligerent in negotiations. They talk about their food, my ass, the new house-type thing they're building. It's made from bamboo and has a thatched roof. It's on stilts to avoid the flooding, unlike the shelters here, which flood constantly." I pause. "We aren't in the highlands despite this mountain cage," I say, sniffling as I readjust my legs. "And by my calculations, I'd say we're close to the beach where they store their boats."

Brody listens intently, shaking his head, like what I'm saying matters, and for a moment or two, I feel validated. Like something I know matters.

"If they're already talking to your family about ransom, did they say how long this process will take?"

Closing my eyes, I try to ward off the wave of exhaustion.

"It's political, so it's not as cut and dry as they give

them money, and they give them me. What's a kidnapping for ransom without a little suffering?"

I tuck my face down into my arms and try my best not to fall asleep.

"The criminal groups who are taking a cut of the ransom have to align, and evidently that's something that doesn't happen with any regularity."

"How long have you been here?" he asks.

I raise my head, setting my chin on my knees.

"A week, but it feels like a month."

"Have they...hurt you? Other than the darts, I mean. Are they violent?" he asks.

I narrow my eyes. "Don't think you can take them?"

He shakes his head. "I'm merely trying to figure out what makes them tick. I was sailing the channel, so I wasn't completely blind to the risk and knew some things going in to my sail, but seeing this firsthand is something else entirely."

"They haven't taken advantage of me," I deadpan. "Nothing but the blow dart. By all means, you tell me what you think makes them tick."

Brody stands, and it's a little surreal because he has to duck to keep his head from hitting the ceiling. He is the epitome of a man, which begs the question.

"How the hell did you get captured? You're double the size of them."

"Money and power make them tick. Obviously. Look at where they live," he replies. "And I'm just a mechanic who likes to lift weights. Who the hell expects to be kidnapped? I didn't think that's what was happening to me until it was too late."

I smirk. "I killed two of the bastards on my way out."

I slow blink once and again.

"It's why they hate me, and I scream a lot. Have to act like a crazy killer to keep my reputation intact."

Brody's eyes widen, and it's satisfying to watch the shock cross his features.

"You killed two men? How?"

"With my bare hands and pure female rage," I joke. "And a gun, *obviously*. What was I supposed to do when they tried to board me with black masks and rifles?" I give the same word back to him.

"I shot them. Were you sailing the channel without a gun?" I ask, dumbfounded that a man who looks like this didn't prepare. Brody looks like the kind of guy who is prepared for anything.

"I didn't anticipate sailing the channel. It was a backup plan when my GPS went offline, and I wasn't sure what to do next."

So he's not a great sailor. Maybe not even a good one. I won't hold it against him.

I fire back. "Where did you leave from?"

"Lisbon," he replies.

"What was the purpose of your sail?"

He leans back on his elbows.

"Why the interrogation?"

"I just want to learn," I say. "Plus, no skilled sailor doesn't bring some form of self-defense, especially when you're solo. Trying to figure out what you were thinking."

His gaze flits to the bars of our cage door.

"I was heading to Australia to spread my friend's ashes along the coast, and I'm sure you know how strict their laws are. Sailing in general is a fucking dreadful pastime. I was merely doing what was asked of me." Brody's gaze turns wistful. "What are the odds they let us out of here if you stop screaming? Not free us, completely, but perhaps put us to work while they figure out the politics. They could use help building, I bet. That's the angle I'll use."

I hold up one hand.

"Wait, wait. You said, *I'll.* So I'm not invited? This is just your plan?"

Brody tilts his head to the side, his jaw working back and forth as he lets his eyes cut down to my legs and back up to my face.

"I'm not sure you're worth the risk. What are you good at other than screaming and eavesdropping?"

I can't help it. My eyes flare.

"What have I done to deserve automatic disdain other than give you information to form your escape plan? You are so barbaric. You haven't even asked me my name!"

"What's your name?" he says, smirking.

I can tell I've caught him off guard. Like I tripped him up in some way. It's exhilarating.

I don't even want to tell him, but that feels too juvenile given our circumstances. If I'd met Brody in the wild, I'd have walked away from him without a word the first time he opened his mouth. I'm not his type.

"Saylor." Then I spell it, because that's what I always do. My mom had to spell it a *special* way.

"Like a boat?" he asks, amusement lighting his face. "Like your hobby? Am I adding lying to the list of things you're good at, or do your parents hate you that much?"

Scowling, I let my mouth open.

"You will not speak to me like that," I snap. "There's no reason for you to be this hateful!"

"Getting taken from a boat I hate, riding in another boat I hate, landing here at a place filled with bugs and whatever that animal is that won't stop screeching, I also hate, being put in a cage that anyone would hate, and being trapped with a woman who thinks she knows it all, but also got captured, isn't a really great place for my personality to shine. Admit, at least, it's ironic you were named after something that will lead to your death."

"I can't believe you said that." I shake my head, wondering if he was dropped as an infant.

He might be the single most awful human I've ever met, and let me tell you, I've met a lot of people.

"My father named me after his passion. The one thing he loved other than my mother. I love my name even if you deem it ironic. I don't plan on dying here with a man who has no manners, class, or intelligence."

I whiffed on the last one, because it's obvious Brody isn't a run-of-the-mill idiot. He's educated. I can tell. That makes it a little worse.

"Your parents must be so proud that you treat women like this. I bet they brag to all their friends. And the screeching, it's a lemur," I say smugly.

He has the good sense to appear mildly embarrassed. Ah, so he does care about his parents. Noted.

"You're right," he says. "I shouldn't have said that." He doesn't apologize, though. "If we have to share this space, we should be cordial."

His gaze wanders back to the door of the cage, where the last torch is almost burned out. The walls and floor are made of a hard mud substance, which makes me think it could cave in any second.

"Is there a bathroom in here? I have to take a leak."

I grin. "Let the fun begin, roomie. Behind the half wall behind me is a hole in the ground. Our gracious hosts did put a roll of the thinnest toilet paper known to man in there. They told me I should be grateful."

Brody stands, stretching his arms over his chest, and pulling his knees up and down. The sedative causes soreness, and I feel a little bad for him that he's experiencing it for the first time, but he's barely even human in his conscious form, so it's hard to express that.

"Figure out where you want to sleep," he says, stepping next to me and back behind the mud wall. He laughs when he sees the hole and makes a joke about digging out of the side of the wall.

"The whole structure would collapse, suffocating us. It was the first thing I thought of. We need to work on the other plan of being released during the day so we can explore and see where we are and what we can do to get out of here. Maybe I can find my satellite phone they stole off me when they drugged me."

I lay down with my head on my balled-up rain jacket.

"Maybe I can kill a couple more of them while I'm at it, really make some noise."

He zips up his fly. I hear it, and then he says, "We aren't killing anyone. That's counterintuitive to getting them on our good side." He pauses. "Actually, you go ahead and kill people. That will make me look that much better, and not only will I get free time, but I might also get my own cage. They'll be worried you'll kill me too."

"Were you born this annoying, or is *works poorly with others* on your report card?" I ask. "It was a joke. I'm not going to kill anyone else, and especially not you, even though you might deserve it at this point."

He steps over me and lies down, propping his head on his hands. He exhales noisily, but keeps his eyes open, focused on the metal bars of the door.

"*Gets shit done* is on my report card, baby. Now go to sleep. We don't need a cranky, screaming Saylor."

"Was that a joke?" I ask. It would be a step up from an insult at this point.

Brody smacks his lips. "I wouldn't joke about something so serious."

"Did you just call me baby?" I say, roasting everything he just said because it wasn't offensive.

He turns his head to look over at me. We're probably two feet apart.

"Baby suits you more than Saylor," he says.

"Why?" I return.

"Because someone needs to put your ass in the corner."

He laughs, his white teeth sparkling in my lantern light. I hate that he's attractive. I hate that he makes jokes and is sardonic to a fault. I hate that his body looks to be a perfect specimen too.

But part of me is glad I hate everything about him, because if I didn't, if he was polite, and mannered, and kind on top of the exterior package, something completely different would be happening in this dirt cage, and that is *positively evil* to even consider.

# CHAPTER SIX
## brody

THERE'S no fucking way I can sleep. The ground is rock hard, and there's no way to anticipate when these guys will be back. There are torches lit in the distance, near the stilted building they're using as a main gathering area. I'd guess that's where they sleep as well. I'll have to sleep eventually, but that can't happen until I've formed some semblance of trust with the woman sleeping soundly next to me.

I glance over to check on her to find her hands tucked under her chin as her lashes flutter gently. I wonder what she's dreaming about—who she thinks about when her mind takes over unconsciously. I bet she misses her mansion and money, her soft bed, and the butlers at her beck and call.

Surprisingly, Saylor did not come off as I thought she would. There's no sense of entitlement to be found. Something about this experience has stripped her of everything except her fire, which is unmatched, honestly. I can't be like Nolan when she's like that—so witty and sarcastic. It's like she's speaking to me, the real me, and it's strange.

I've offended her, sure, but perhaps not as much as I'd offend a random person off the street. She takes my blows with ease and gives it back tenfold.

Saylor knows a lot for the short amount of time she's been here. She's observant beyond measure and knows the exact intel she needs to benefit her overall standing in this village. There's a hole in the fucking ground as a toilet, and as cruel as I am with my words, she doesn't deserve to suffer like this. I vowed to protect her, but I'm going to go above and beyond now that I know she's a worthy teammate. I will be able to count on her. While surprising, it's welcome. Gathering intel and figuring out the hierarchy alone would have been difficult, but not undoable. She has done that task for me.

Saylor pulls her knees up, shivering in the night air. She's using her jacket as a pillow, so choices were made. I take off one of my layers, a half-zip sweater, and toss it on top of her shoulders. Settling in under the warmth of the pullover, she sighs in contentment.

I bet, in the real world, it takes way more than a sweater to make this woman content. It's a gross thought, because this isn't the kind of woman who would ever look at me twice, but I allow myself the thought merely because she piques my interest in a way most women cannot.

I still have a thick long-sleeved shirt on top of a T-shirt, and a tank top under that. I was thoughtful in my approach, considering that this situation might arise.

Saylor exhales long and hard, and her breathing evens out again. The sound lulls me into a false sense of security.

There's fuck-all secure in what's happening though, and I remember Commander's words about going with the flow and letting the circumstances dictate my next move. I didn't fight them too hard, and I ended up exactly where I needed to be. In some ways, it felt too easy, as if they knew who I was and who I was here to find. I know that's not the truth, but it's still something to consider.

I fold my arms across my chest and look at the roof, tracing the lines in the red, muddy material. I read that it cracks during the drying process. This looks pretty similar to what was in the file. Saylor was correct in her assumption that this will cave in if the supporting structure is impacted in any significant way. The most common way these things collapse is weather incidents, tropical cyclones being the main one, and we're at the end of that season.

Saylor's breathing lulls me into a twilight sleep. I can still hear the tropical noises, lemurs howling, and insects chirping in a rhythmic cadence. After the harsh reality of setting forth on a mission of unknown length, I feel a strange peace in the calmness.

Even though I'm hungry and cold, there is an essence of something I don't have in my life in the form of expectations. There are none.

I rub the spot on my wrist that itches because it's healing over and think about my friends back on the boat. They're probably laughing, thinking about what kind of trouble I'm getting myself into. I glance at Saylor and think it's not the kind of trouble they think I'm in. For once in my life, I want my insides to match my actions.

What if I didn't have to hide? What if I could be myself here?

I bob in and out of sleep, only woken when the chirping insect noise silences. I sit upright in time to see a new guy walking toward the cage, pushing a motorbike that's missing parts. It's before dawn, yet an inkling of light broaches the horizon in a pink hue. I stand, careful not to wake Saylor. She's wrapped in my sweater, blissfully unaware of our visitor.

"I need food. Please let me help you with that. I can fix it," I whisper, letting my gaze catalog the pieces that are missing and what he needs to get it running.

I run down the list in his native tongue, so I'm sure it's not perfect, but he seems interested in what I'm saying.

"I promise. I'm not a threat." I try to hunch down, to make myself appear smaller and avoid direct eye contact.

"They didn't give me anything to eat last night. We can let her sleep," I say, nodding to Saylor behind me. If she's in here, she's safe.

He looks hesitantly at the sleeping dragon on the dirt behind me.

"A real bathroom too? Please. What's your name?"

Mako is his name, and he pulls out a damn dart gun as he unlocks the cage and lets me slide free. He locks it so quietly, I'm not surprised Saylor didn't stir. Mako forces me to walk in front of him with the dart gun pressed to my back.

"You can fix my bike?" Mako asks when we've rounded the corner and we're out of earshot of our cage.

There are a few other cages like ours, but smaller and empty. There are a couple house-looking buildings on stilts that are on the back side of our cage that we can't see. That's where they're watching us from.

"I think someone stole parts, and I'm not sure what it needs. I don't know how to fix it."

"Yes, I can fix it if we can find the parts it needs. I'm great with machines."

His face lights up when I start pointing at the engine and explaining what it needs and the process of installing them. I keep him busy with my explanations as I get the lay of the land. It's hard to tell how far the ocean is without daylight.

"Can I have something to eat?"

"Yes," he says, bringing me to one of the houses.

We climb rickety stairs that creak under my weight, and each step is followed by a slight sway in the breeze. This isn't sturdy by any means. When we get to the house, he opens a door made of bamboo that's been tied together. Mako leads me to a table where there are half-empty plates of food. My stomach growls the second I see it.

"You can eat anything here," he says, eyeing me warily. He took a risk letting me out, and I can tell he's weighing what would happen if I went rogue.

Raza appears from one of the couple of makeshift doors, and Nery and Ravelo are behind him. They don't look surprised to see me. It may mean my plan to get out of that cage didn't even need to be a plan.

I apologize to Raza for the black eye he's sporting and thank him for the food. He's in charge. When the others are in the room, it's obvious by the way they watch him and their submissive stances. I've taken so many classes on this that there's no question except who is above Raza, and is this all a ploy to confuse the captors?

"He's going to help with my bike," Mako explains. "He is good with machines and building things back up."

"Is he?" Nery says, twisting his dart gun between two dirty fingers. "Or did asset twelve force him to say anything to get out of that cage?"

I could play it up right now. I could make her seem crazy and solidify their assumptions, but she'd stay locked up, and it would be easier for me if she had some freedoms when it's time to extract.

"You are fetching a handsome ransom," Raza says. "And it was agreed upon quickly. Almost too quickly." He raises one bushy, black brow.

"The government doesn't play around with American hostages, right?" I ask. "I know that from the news."

I try to play it calm while also establishing respect. Give to get.

"How long until I'll go home if it's already been agreed upon?" It's the only rational question.

I shove bread into my mouth and barely chew before swallowing.

"These things take time. Sometimes the ransom goes up if we play hard to get. Or if we get new information about an asset," Ravelo answers, winking when he says the last part. "A month or two, maybe more."

My stomach sinks. I've never been a particularly good liar. There's no possible way for them to find out about my background unless I tell them. There wasn't anything tracing me to the military on my sailboat. There's nothing outwardly damning. No telltale tattoos, nothing. My language skills and clean body were part of the reason I was chosen for this task. We were thorough in our planning, but doubt creeps in.

"And the woman?" I ask, even though I have no right to know anything about her.

Nery answers, "Asset twelve is worth more. That one will be here for a while, I think. Even as bothersome as she is, her ransom is going to fund many things. Probably double your hold length. Maybe six months."

Fuck. If that's right, I won't be leaving here without her.

"The other two hostages on the other side of the base are leaving in a fortnight. They have a lower ransom, but we're holding out for more."

I try not to look interested. How big is this base? Who else are they holding? How long have they had them? All questions that weren't answered in the files.

People go missing all the time in these waters, but I'm surprised the Teams didn't know about the other hostages. *Go with the flow,* I remind myself. I eat more scraps and find a piece of untouched bread. I secretly slide it up my sleeve. A bargaining chip, depending on Saylor's mood.

The men are talking among themselves, worried about me being loose, no doubt, but also weighing how much I can help them.

"I can help stabilize those stairs too. So you don't sway in the fucking wind every time there's a storm. I saw everything I needed to fix that on the walk here."

Ah, was that too observant?

"I think," I add on.

"We don't let assets walk around and pretend they're guests at a resort," Raza says, opening the same door he came through to let other men in to clean.

I count them, cataloging their faces to memory. I grab some more food before it's whisked away on primitive wooden trays and try to save as much as I can without anyone knowing.

"We let you out today to talk to you about asset twelve. Because she's going to be here for a long time, it would be better if we could trust her out and about."

"And her mother is crazy," someone says under their breath.

I think about Bianca Wyndham's information and try not to laugh. Of course she's pulling strings from the other side of the world.

"If asset twelve can be free during the day without causing harm to our men, it would be better for everyone."

Nery still has his weapon aimed at me, unsure of what I'm going to do next.

Raza doesn't look phased by my presence any longer.

"You have size on your side. If you agree to help keep her under control, you get this"—he waves his arm to the tables—"and freedom during the day. We will keep two guards for you every day as well."

How is this all falling into place so effortlessly? Without a challenge.

"She's too much for you?" I question, moving toward a plate that hasn't been cleared yet.

There were twenty-two plates. I counted them seconds after I entered. If I agree quickly, they'll question me more than they already are.

Raza looks at me in that knowing way, and I stand a little taller—a challenge I subconsciously take.

"She killed two of my men." She wasn't bluffing. I'm impressed. "They have placed different rules for this asset due to her social standing. I'm merely giving you a better way of life in exchange for another set of eyes on her."

So...no one wants her harmed. This must be humbling for these motherfuckers. They kidnapped a woman, and not only can't they harm her, but they must also give her things to satisfy the ransom guarantee. If they don't, some of the money will be held back. This isn't how my ransom will work. Not at all.

"Yes. Fine," I say.

"Put the food back. We will feed her a proper meal," Raza says, eyeing my sleeve. "Unless you're still hungry."

I nod, embarrassed they caught me red-handed.

Ravelo comes back with a meal and motions for me to exit. Nery follows me with the always looming threat of sedation.

The sun is up, igniting the tropical landscape surrounding us. I don't hide my appraisal. The dirt paths converge to a pebbly road in the distance. The ocean is through the trees, perhaps two hundred yards from the trail we're following back to the cage. There's a grouping of motorbikes and two vehicles. One was the one we used to get here from the beach. Others are lingering, barefoot, watching curiously as they lead me. Not only do they not let assets walk free, but it also seems to be unheard of. I swallow down the uneasy feeling of being somewhere foreign and dangerous.

When we get back to the cage, Saylor is up, clutching the bars. She's not screaming, though. She *is* wearing my sweater. It falls to her mid-thigh. When she sees me, she sneers.

"You got out and left me," she says, when I'm close enough to hear.

Nery appears from behind me, and Ravelo slides her a sack of food.

"Let's calm down," I say, hoping she doesn't go full feral and make things more difficult.

It's a new day. One in which I don't have to be a sarcastic prick if I don't want to.

"I have good news," I add, flaring my eyes so only she can see.

Saylor takes the food and backs up so they can let me back into this damn hole. After they lock it behind them, I see the tears. Fuck. I do not know how to deal with any emotion, but this is the kind I've run from in the past.

"I'm so tired of being in here. You could have woken me up," she whispers, eating the oatmeal-looking slop in a dish.

My stomach rumbles in hunger. I won't be able to eat even a fraction of what I'm used to.

"I know we don't see eye to eye, but think of things from my point of view," Saylor says while chewing. "What if they let me out and not you?"

Fat chance. I wouldn't be sleeping to begin with.

"I made a deal. We'll be able to get out of here during the day. They said you're such a pain in the ass, and you'll be here for so long that part of your ransom agreement states you need freedom throughout the day."

"How did you manage that?" she asks, big blue eyes staring into mine.

I shake my head. "By not screaming," I say. "And by not killing people."

The irony in this sentence isn't lost on me, and I can't resist flashing a little grin.

She notices and looks away. Saylor wipes at her face with the sleeves of my sweater, and I feel uncomfortable.

"Bullshit. It was my mother, wasn't it? That's who gave the terms of the ransom. How did you get involved?"

Stretching with arms against the bars, I ignore how seeing her in my clothes makes me feel. It looks like she's naked underneath, and it's been a long time since a thought like this has crossed my mind. The proximity of her doesn't help, either.

"They wanted to make sure I wasn't a flight risk. We're going to have to work," I say. "Don't get too excited. We're not going to be sipping cocktails in a lounge chair."

Saylor narrows her eyes. "Who said that's what I want to do? I'd literally lick the ground and roll in a mud puddle if it meant getting out of here for any amount of time. To pee somewhere other than a hole would be enough."

She finishes eating and pushes the bowl away with her foot.

"When are they letting us out?" She stands, grabbing the bars next to me. "Thanks for the sweater, by the way. I'm going to assume I can keep it."

The urge to say something scathing bubbles, but I hold my breath and keep it buried. I nearly choke on the next words.

"You're welcome." Even though I feel her gaze, I don't dare turn my face to see it head on. I'm too out of character right now. "They didn't tell me what time. I think this is where patience comes into play."

Swallowing down all the vitriol on the tip of my tongue, I back away from the bars and her and sit down, stretching my legs in front of me. I need to work out. That's what is wrong with me. I have too much pent-up testosterone without an outlet. Women have never been a focus of mine, especially because of how much trouble they always seem to be.

Saylor lifts my sweater over her head, and her shirt underneath rides up, exposing her black lace bra. I look away, but she's in my peripheral. There's no escaping her. I take this time to remind myself who she is and how she lives outside of these dirt walls. She ties the sweater around her waist.

"Brody," she says, spinning to face me.

I look her way now that it's safe, but I don't respond to my name.

"Tell me everything you saw out there. I need to be prepared."

This is safe. This is work. I tell her all I saw, and she listens intently.

"I bet my sat phone is in the stilted house where the food was," she says, sitting in front of me. "They weren't hostile. Did you see any women?"

I shake my head. "They do have two other assets. There is another side to this base, or that's what they said. I'm leery of believing everything all at once until I see things for myself. I offered to help fix a broken bike engine, and they seemed to like that skill."

"I can fix things too," Saylor chimes in. "What else?"

She listens like it's the most interesting bedtime story in the world. When I've given all the facts, she looks at me quietly for a beat or two, just looking into my eyes. It makes me uncomfortable, but I allow it, and I'm not sure why.

"You're different today," she says. "The vibes are different." Saylor smiles widely, challenging me to offend her *vibes*.

I hold the eye contact. She has flecks of lighter blue inside the deep blue. They may be the most unique eyes I've ever cared to notice. Nolan and I have blue eyes, but it's the standard color everyone has.

"I had a good night's sleep," I lie. "It's a new day. Don't worry, I'm still cranky and mean at heart. The prospect of exploring has issued a temporary halt on sardonic insults."

She smiles wider, and *now* it's time to look away. I pick a spot outside and stare diligently.

"What can you fix?" I ask.

I need her to tell me more about her so the things in my head don't accidentally come out and make me a liar. The fact is, I know practically everything about her life without knowing who she is as a person. I find it surprising the two things don't match in any way, shape, or form, or perhaps the stereotype I labeled her with is dead ass wrong.

"Everything, pretty much. I'm best with computers, but my dad can fix anything, and I helped him since I was a little girl."

At the mention of her dad, her voice changes.

"I miss my family so much, which doesn't make any

sense because I'd still be sailing right now and still not seeing my family. Something about being trapped here and not knowing when I'll see them again really makes me sad."

If she only knew how long they were intending to keep her, she'd probably start screaming again. I'll keep that fact to myself.

"These groups aren't notorious for torture. They just want money. You can fix engines?" I ask to distract her from her emotions. Selfishly, I don't want to deal with them. "What do you do?"

"Why do you care about who I am and what I do now?" she fires back, laser gaze homing in on mine to see if I'm lying.

Her trust is what I need the most at this point. It would make my life a whole lot easier.

"I need to know what skills you have other than sailing and having a name to match that. These guys have some form of trust in me that they do not have in you, killer. Either you're with me or against me. How am I selling you, Saylor? What do you have to offer other than voice pipes that annoy the fuck out of them?"

She winces. "There it is. There you are."

I open my arms up. "What do you want? I'm trying here."

"Trying to be an asshole?" she hisses.

"No, that comes naturally. I need to figure out how you can be useful and non-threatening outside of this. When I ask what you can do and who you are, it isn't because I care, it's because I'm trying to save your life."

"You just said they don't torture. Which is it? Now you're trying to save my life?" Saylor asks.

I groan. "Do you want to stay locked in here? If you do, just say so."

"Maybe I don't want to share who I am with an absolute asshole stranger. Did you ever think of that? Maybe I find it weird they just bust you out while I'm sleeping and return with some magical deal where we can both be free outside of this cage. Maybe you're one of them. You look like a warmonger. You present like some backwoods killer who has no regard for societal norms. You seem like you belong here with them, Brody." Saylor says my name like a curse. "If that's even your real name."

Rolling my eyes, I decide this is going to be a pain in the ass. The whole thing.

"This is why they want me to help them. You are difficult, and you killed their men, so you can't be trusted. This is fairly easy to understand. You stay here, and I'll go out alone. I don't care, but I feel bad for you."

She scoffs. "You feel bad for me? I was fine before you got here, and I'll be fine if you leave."

What a stubborn, jagged pill. This is why I avoid women—why I haven't had a girlfriend for years. Why do they have to be so spiteful? I'm trying to help her, but of course, she assumes I have ulterior motives.

Don't I, though? She's seeing my lies without seeing them.

"Sounds like a plan," I say.

"Why can't you just be a kind human?"

"Why can't you?" I counter.

She huffs and stands. "Because you're incorrigible, and you can't be trusted. The first moment I laid eyes on you, I knew something was off. What's off, Brody? Tell me."

"I'm not going to bend over backward for you. That's what's off, I guess. I'm not one of those men who keeps trying to help after you push them away and refuse. You tell me once you don't trust me or want my help, that's it.

This is who I am. I'm selfish and self-serving. I'm kind when it's deserved and earned. I'm not going to blow smoke up your skirt or say things I don't mean."

I see Ravelo and Nery heading toward our cage, but she's staring at me while I speak, so she doesn't see them yet.

"If you don't want my help, say that. I figured you'd want out of this cage, seeing how I hate it already, and you've been here longer. By all means, Saylor, make yourself at home. Don't trust me." I stand up and wait.

She nearly falls trying to stand up when she sees them.

"They're letting us out," she says to herself.

One guards and one unlocks, like usual.

"No, baby, they're letting me out."

Saylor shakes the bars when they let me out and go to put the lock back on. She nearly yells.

"I'm a software engineer. I can improve any computer systems or GPS devices you have here. I helped invent the high-tech software that was on my sailboat. I can show you how to use it. I know you've stripped my boat, and I know you probably don't have any clue how any of it works. I can help you. I won't hurt anyone...else. I promise."

Her blue eyes flash to mine. Ah, so I'm excluded from that little promise then.

"I can also work on engines and build anything you can come up with." She said it all in Portuguese, so it sounds like she means it. I wonder if she did that on purpose.

I smile at her as she pours her heart out not only to me, but to our captors. She'd rather do it the hard way, then. Noted.

"I do think she'd be of help," I add, then smile when she looks at me like she's trying to strike me down dead.

Ravelo lets her out, and she looks like some sort of cave-dwelling animal seeing the sun for the first time. She shields her eyes and looks up at the sky.

"Thank God," she says, wincing against the heat as she takes in her surroundings.

It's the typical tropical climate. Hot during the day and cold at night, but the cave always stays a little cooler because it's semi-underground.

"Thank God," she repeats, taking in her surroundings, immediately eyeing the roads and paths. "I'll do anything," she says, looking at me, dark circles more apparent in the sunlight.

They lead us in a different direction from where I was this morning, and we walk side by side.

"Anything?" I ask, smiling.

"Anything," she replies.

I whisper, "How about trust me?"

She lets out an exasperated breath.

"Yes. Yes. I trust you," Saylor whispers.

# CHAPTER SEVEN

## *saylor*

IF THIS WAS any other circumstance, this would look like the beginning of a porno.

Brody lifts his shirt and tank top over his head, tosses them, and his abs—*damn near ten of them*—flex and glisten as he stoops down.

"Pass me the mallet," he says, holding out his hand. I stare at it for a few seconds, unable to look at anything else without feeling scandalized.

Brody is not like the men in my circles. He doesn't look like them, talk like them, or act like them. I can't help it. I look once more at his torso, and he chuckles.

"Do you know what a mallet is, or did they not teach you that in school?"

I shake my head and hand him the mallet. It would be weird if I didn't bring up my insane behavior.

"My dad has a garage filled with tools and can fix practically anything in the world, so I know what all the tools are. I just have a question. Do you live in a gym? How do you look like that?" Another head shake to clear my mind. "I don't know if I've seen that many abs on one person.

Don't flatter yourself. It's like looking at a weird zoo animal or something, not like a physical attraction."

He laughs again. It sounds like velvet coated with honey, the expensive kind, but maybe that's because I haven't been in the real world in a while. I'm jaded. His biceps bulge with each whack of the tool. Definitely don't see that kind of show in the real world.

We're repairing a bamboo bridge that crosses over to a stunning waterfall. Hence the porno thoughts when they mix with Brody. Not that I've seen many, but the ones I watched with Archie always begin in a lavish destination with the couple trying to accomplish something other than sex. It's always an unsuccessful quest, so they just do it instead.

"Do they not have gyms where you're from?" he asks, holding out his hand for another nail. I drop one in his palm, careful not to touch his skin.

"They do, but not the same kind you go to." I pause. "Do all car mechanics look like this under the prison jumpsuits?"

He stops hammering and holds out his hand again. I oblige.

"I don't know. Are all software engineers this deprived of a true male body?" He says it coyly, wearing a half grin.

Jesus, this is borderline flirting, and I started it. Nery and Ravelo are on the bank of the lagoon below us. They glance up every once in a while, but for all intents and purposes, it's just Brody and me.

I watch him tie pieces of bamboo together with skinny rope and pull them tight. More muscles move and twitch. After he binds it, he lets his gaze flick up to meet mine.

Chemistry. Pure and simple.

Probably because he's mean and nasty and out of my league. Men like this don't look at brainy women like me. If he met my family, he'd run far, far away. But why am I even thinking about this? There is no purpose or endgame to my thoughts. Except when he wipes the sweat off his brow and slams the mallet hard, my stomach tips and spins.

"I wasn't deprived of the male body. I was deprived of ones that look like yours," I say, answering honestly.

He raises one brow.

"The weird zoo animal kind of male body? Gives off those bad vibes?" Brody says, hammering in the last nail.

Standing to his full height, I make a point to look away after I notice his jeans hang low on his waist.

"Makes me scared to think what you've been accustomed to before now."

"Yeah, I guess I did put it that way," I finally reply.

The men in my circle are long and lean. They have a little belly pooch from drinking too many Negronis. It perches perfectly on top of their wildly expensive belts. There's nothing else to say that wouldn't make my ogling less awkward.

"I designed this repair, your manpower finished this work, now are we allowed to go swim in that waterfall? Is that too forward for our first day of freedom?"

"It's easier to ask for forgiveness than it is to ask for permission," he says, kicking off his boots and heading down the embankment, sliding on his heels in the sand.

The men stand and rush over as soon as there's movement. Brody takes off his pants and dives into the water before they can reach him. Nery stands at the edge of the water watching, his dart not even raised. It only takes a couple of beats before I realize this is an opportunity I may not get again soon, and I take off my socks and shoes while they watch Brody and enter the water on the opposite side.

The temperature of the water is frigid, causing my entire body to go rigid for a few seconds as I adjust. I don't know what could possibly live in this water, but for the moment, I don't care. Let the rare tropical fish eat me alive if they want. I feel clean, washed free from the sweat that's caked my body since I got here. I take my time under the water, scrubbing at my hair and body. I wait until my lungs burn before sliding above the water.

Ravelo and Nery are watching us, hands on their hips, like a pair of mothers watching their naughty toddlers. I don't see their weapons, so I take that as a sign they aren't going to punish us yet.

Swimming over to the waterfall, I pull myself up onto the ledge behind it and slide off my clothes so I can wash them. The water is too cold for bacteria to grow, of that fact I'm confident. But I still let my eyes dart around to see if there are any obvious creatures as I ring out my clothes.

Brody pops up in the water the next second, causing me to squeal and jump.

"Where did you come from?" I shriek.

The moving water splashing against the still creates a loud, constant whir, so I have to talk loudly.

"I'm trying to clean my clothes," I explain, sliding into the water to conceal my black bra and panties on display.

His blue eyes look extra blue next to the sapphire water of this lagoon. His long lashes stick together as he focuses on my face. I blink once and then again, shaking off this haze he's put me in.

"A little privacy?"

He grins, biting his lip.

"Just checking out the zoo animals," he says, then

disappears under the water like some sort of marine creature, swimming away.

Swallowing down the moment, I roll my clothes on the rock, trying to get the dirt out of my shirt and his face out of my mind. Some soap would help, but I'm not complaining. This new freedom feels exhilarating in comparison to the cave I've been encased in.

I hear yelling in Portuguese, so I dress quickly and swim under the waterfall, letting the water pressure push me under further as I kick toward the embankment. When I surface, I see Brody talking to the men. He's only wearing a pair of boxer briefs, his jeans hanging over one arm. I guess he washed his clothes too.

I stand when I can touch, my feet visible against the stark white sand.

He's trying to convince them to let us come here daily. He's selling our skills for time outside of the cage. He must want this as much as I do.

Remaining quiet seems my best route after all the screaming I did, so I let him work. Brody seems to have taken courses on negotiations or manipulation, or has some other quantifiable skill I'm not versed in, because it works. We have to work on the motorbike when we walk back to the base camp, but they've gathered all the parts needed to repair it.

Slowly, I exit the water, dripping water from my clothes and hair like a drowned rat.

"Do we have our next project?" I ask, keeping my tone low.

"Yes," Nery says. "No more running off like that without permission."

I nod furiously. "I'm sorry," I say, telling him I couldn't resist a bath after so many days.

"You can come here daily to clean if you finish the

tasks given to you for the day," Ravelo adds. "There's a lot to get done around here and not enough talent to do it. We need to use you while you're here."

Brody seems pleased, with a smarmy look on his face.

Letting my eyes wander down to his wet boxer briefs is a mistake now that he's turned toward me. He's hung. Closing my eyes, I put my hand over my mouth to stop myself from saying something I'll regret. Turning, I face the other way and exit the water without turning around once.

Hung like a zoo animal, my subconscious whispers.

Unfathomable is the only word that comes to mind when I can't get the image out of my head on the walk back. He's fully clothed now, the bottom of his jeans filthy from the dirt path we're on, and I just want him to take them off so I can confirm what I think I saw.

In the real world, I'd call a friend and gossip about it. In the real world, I'd probably never cross this guy, though. I walk quickly to fall in stride next to him.

"How does this base function without people with skills?" I ask, trying to keep the conversation about work.

Brody looks down at me, smiling, eyes glinting in the sunlight.

"You killed them, Saylor." He chuckles.

That forces me to eat my words.

"I didn't realize I was dooming an entire evil civilization by defending myself," I whisper.

"It might end up being a good thing because it means they need our help, but it's why they don't trust you."

I squint, turning behind me to look at our captors. They're holding a decent distance between us.

"It's not like I have weapons, or muscles, or anything that I could defend myself with," I say.

He licks his lips. "I wouldn't be so sure of that," he says.

I try and fail to keep the wonder out of my eyes, then ask, "What does that mean?"

Brody exhales a tired breath. "It means they fear you."

"Why wouldn't they fear you? I saw what you looked like without clothes."

Damn it. It just slid out so effortlessly, like my subconscious was chomping to make me look like a horny, idiotic woman.

He laughs under his breath. "Because I haven't given them a reason to fear me, which is lucky for you. It doesn't matter what you look like sometimes. It matters who you are."

"And who am I?"

He looks uncomfortable, swallowing hard before replying, "Someone with a ransom larger than mine. I'm guessing you have connections by what they've told me."

The pit forms in my stomach. He knows who I am.

"What exactly have they told you?" I ask as we round the last bend before we get to the makeshift parking lot for the vehicles. Our cage is close by, and it gives me shivers for more than one reason.

He shakes his head. "It's why I wanted to know what you did and was asking questions. They said you had a high ransom. That's all. It's easy to leap from that to having connections," he explains, stooping down when he recognizes the bike that's missing parts. "I want to go home and see my family and my dog, and have this in my past. It doesn't matter what they say. We shouldn't believe it, anyway. They're crooks."

Other men bring a large, heavy, balled-up tarp and open it next to us with a bunch of stolen parts. Brody blows out a breath when he makes the connection. There are bits and bobbles from a lot of different technologies.

My hand immediately darts out when I see a screen that looks like it belongs to a GPS. It's smashed, but I bet I could get it working if I can find the right makeshift tools.

"Are you married?" I ask, questioning just what he means by family. He used that word to be intentionally misleading, goading me into asking more questions. I think. Or maybe he doesn't share things about himself often.

I roll wires in my hand, testing the ends to see if they're sharp.

"I'm not," he deadpans, picking up spark plugs and a carburetor.

"Kids?" I return.

He shakes his head. "Nope."

"So who is your family?"

He turns his head, annoyed with my line of questioning, I bet.

"My brother and my parents. I have a guard dog too."

"Where do you live?" I ask, handing him a wrench. It feels oddly like being in my dad's shop, and a pang of grief hits me square in the chest.

My dad has to be sick with worry and guilt for allowing me to go and do this. Talking to Brody, even as square as he is, helps.

"The North East," he deadpans, then lets the wrench clank down against another tool. "Near Sag Harbor. Anything else?"

"We live close to each other in real life," I say. "Do you have a girlfriend?" My voice gets irritatingly high on the last word.

He sits, facing me.

"What about me would make you believe a woman would want to be committed to me long term?"

*Your abs* is on the tip of my tongue.

"The way you present yourself to me doesn't have to be the way you are to other women. Even people like you can be nice to the right person," I explain. "We're trapped on an island. You said it yourself that it doesn't bring out the best in you. I don't think it's that far-fetched that you have a girlfriend or a situationship back home. Whatever it is that men do these days."

One of his brows shoots up. "I am not a man who does situationships. I do work."

"You do gym. You do moods," I say, cracking myself up. "Seriously, you don't have anyone?"

"That's hard to believe?" he asks. "Do you?"

He's just throwing my question back, but it makes my stomach flip.

"I don't. He broke up with me before my record-setting sail. Now I'm setting different records, I'm sure. Not the good kind either."

Examining my nails, I smooth my fingers over my cuticles. Bianca would die if she saw them.

"I have family waiting too. My parents, my sister, and friends."

"You're disbelieving that I don't have a ball and chain, and you don't either?"

I clear my throat. "Well, it's different for you, I'm sure. It's not so easy for me to date."

I need to be careful about what I say. The last thing I want is to have to tell him about the circles I have to stay inside of and the type of people who are deemed acceptable.

"I don't check the normal boxes as a partner. I like odd things like sailing and software. I don't deal with typical male bullshit either, so it makes it hard to find someone who...appreciates me." I scrunch up my nose when I realize I still said too much.

"How is that different for me? Are you assuming I don't have high standards and enjoy dealing with typical female bullshit? It's hard to find someone who appreciates you no matter what. If anything, it's even harder for me. I like the gym and mechanics. Those things don't attract a lot of ladies."

He begins wrenching again, but drops it out of nerves. His hand shakes as he picks it up. I'm making him nervous or uncomfortable.

"You don't talk about this kind of stuff often, do you?"

Brody shakes his head once. "Never."

"What's your type?" I soldier on, needing more info to figure him out.

It's the most fun I've had since before the sail.

My mom's spring soirée was enormous, and all my friends were there. We dressed in matching flowy maxi dresses, drank champagne, and made plans for more partying when I returned from my sail. I don't remember laughing so hard in my entire life. Of course Mom invited prospects for me, her friend's sons. They all have the same bland personalities, with the same insipid style, with the same degrees and ambitions. I tried to engage with them, but they all reminded me of lying, cheating Archie at the end of the day, and I don't want that.

"I don't have a defined type, and if I do, I've never thought about how to describe it," he says, pouring gas into the bike tank from a black makeshift can. The bike doesn't start when he bypasses the starter to try to see if what he just fixed is working.

"Let me," I say, moving him out of the way, taking the

wrench, and redoing what I saw him mess up. "Describe it," I order while I focus on the task. "Think about your type and describe it."

"When I think about something, it's not going to be this instantaneous ah-ha moment. It takes time to sift through my thoughts," he says.

I peer over my shoulder, and he's watching my hands with narrowed eyes.

"I don't want to be bored or bossed around," he replies. "I don't need to think too hard for those."

"Okay, same," I reply, switching wires out with ones that I found when they first put the tarp down. It cranks immediately when I try. "But it's hard because I'm a woman and men want to tell me how to live and who to be."

He shakes his head.

"Good job," he says as he moves my hands out of the way to finish the job. "I'll put it back together now."

At the sound of the bike starting, the men guarding us from a distance clap and whoop.

"We keep doing this, they're going to crown us leaders of the pirate tribe," Brody remarks, grinning. "The right man won't tell you how to live and who to be, but it feels like you know that already. You're fishing for someone else to tell you that."

I scoff. "I'm the leader of pirates now. I don't need anyone to tell me anything."

I brush my hair over my shoulder. It's stiff from drying in the sun after being wet.

"I take it back. Maybe I need someone to tell me where to find some shampoo and soap."

Brody tries to hide a smile, but I see it before he turns back to work.

"There's a large garden east of the main building.

| 91 |

There must be stuff growing that can be used for soap," he says. "Do you know anything about herbs or mixing things? I don't know much in that regard. I know leaves of three let it be, and if it's shiny and red, you could turn up dead."

Clearing my throat, I say, "I do know a few things. I studied all the different countries I sailed to as a kid." I regret telling him that fact, so I bluster on, "We need to get into the garden. I'd kill...I mean, I'd do anything for a fresh vegetable, too."

Brody picks up a different, smaller tool and stands to get a better grip.

"You think you can use whatever manipulating skills you have to get us into the garden tomorrow?"

"Manipulating?"

"Yes. I mean, they took to you immediately. There has to be some skill you have that made you trustworthy so quickly. To them."

"To them? Not to you?"

Brody starts the bike using the button, and it roars to life on the first try. He's better than I gave him credit for after the first wiring mistake.

"I didn't kill people, Saylor, and you said you trusted me."

"I do now. It's not like I have a lot of options. But you have to admit, even if you had killed people, they'd still trust you over me."

He offers the bike to the guard, pushing it toward the man with his eyes aglow, then walks back to me.

"I can't say, because I didn't do anything to make them hate me, and you did." Brody pauses. "What's your type, then?"

"That conversation was done and over, and you're

bringing it back up. See? It is entertaining and interesting to talk about it, right?"

He picks through the parts on the tarp, examining each piece and part, rolling them in his hand to catalog them.

"You won't believe me when I say this, but I don't know. Really, I don't. I know my exes weren't my type just because they're my exes. My sister fell in love with her first boyfriend, and it was game over. She's married now. I guess I expected the same thing to happen for me, and when it didn't, I sort of gave up trying...too hard."

"Someone at your job? A man who has the same talents and hobbies? Someone who likes sailing?"

He's spitballing, trying to see if anything lands as a response.

"What was your last ex like?"

I raise my brows. "All my exes have cheated on me. I've come to expect that as the norm. Archie cheated and lied, but he was charming when he needed to be and had a good job."

I almost say, a good pedigree, but I stop myself.

"When he broke up with me, he said it was because I wasn't serious enough about life, because I wanted to do this sail around the world." I exhale noisily. "That's how they caught me, you know? I was trying to sail around the world, and my AI system went down. I needed to dock to fix it before I continued on my journey."

Brody narrows his eyes. "You expect men to cheat on you?"

I'm flustered now that he's turned the questioning back on me, exposed in a way that I never am.

"They always have, so either that's what I attract, or that's how men are, and I'd hate to think it's a *me* problem."

"I have never and would never cheat on a woman."

Brody takes out the junk parts and closes the tarp, so the weather doesn't destroy anything more.

"When I find the right woman, that will be it for me. The men who have cheated on you aren't men. They don't deserve your time or energy."

My stomach flips. "Was that a compliment?"

He shakes his head. "An observation about basic human nature. If humans cheat, they aren't in love. I've seen it a lot with my friends. Some are faithful and some aren't, and the common denominator with the men who step out on their wives isn't their wives, it's them and their own issues. It's fucked up."

"You seem to know a lot for someone who doesn't talk about relationships often," I counter.

"Here is a compliment. You were right. Talking about this is entertaining. I may learn something about myself," Brody says, raising his face to the sky. "The rain is about to start. Do we ask them for food before we go back?"

Ravelo waves us over and brings us to the stilted house that has the tables for eating. We eat, and I watch Brody carefully. He seems to be deep in thought and avoiding all eye contact. I correct my first impression of him in my mind. He's not bad vibes, he's hard to get to know vibes. After seeing him nearly naked, he's also hot vibes. He fixes things. He's educated with a skill set to rival my own. He has blue eyes. Biceps. Abs. A deep voice. A section of hair right in the center of his forehead that forms in one perfect curl. He is loyal. He has a dimple on one side—the left.

I'm staring, and I only realize it when he turns to look at me. He licks his lips and grins. He knows what he's doing to me. He has to.

"I have another question," I blurt.

Brody juts up his chin and bites into a chicken leg. "Ask it."

I run my hand through my dirty hair and say, "If we were in the real world and you saw me out on the street, would I be your type on looks alone?"

"Oh, this is a fun game," Brody replies, rubbing his hands together. "Tell me what you're wearing in the real world."

"This. I'm wearing this," I reply, erasing my smile. "Be serious. I need to test my theory. Am I your type physically?"

He swallows a bite of food, and I take a bite.

"I am physically attracted to you. If I saw you on the street and knew nothing else, yes, I would find you attractive."

"Would you approach me?"

He rubs his chin with his thumb and forefinger.

"I don't ask women out. My last relationship was a long time ago and lasted for a year or so. But for the sake of your theory, I'll say yes. I'd ask you out." He tilts his head. "The question is, do you say yes to me? In the real world?"

I'm dirty, still hungry after eating, and staring at a man who is equal parts unnerving as he is gorgeous, and all I can think of is sex.

"Yes. I'd say yes."

"Ding. Ding. Ding," he says, pressing his lips together. "I think we have a winner. You've found your type."

He palms his chest. "Happy to be of service, baby."

I swallow down the last bite and continue staring at him. He's acting smug, but he's covering for an insecurity. I'm sure of it. I lean back in my chair.

"Looks like you've found your type too." I lean over and tap him on the nose as I say, "Me."

# CHAPTER EIGHT
## *brody*

I'VE LOST count of how many times she's tripped me up today.

Saylor just touched my nose, and my whole body broke out in an electric shock. From a fucking boop on the nose. The crackling attraction between us is undeniable and visible to anyone.

She's looking at me now like she wants to devour me whole. I know, because I've been trying to hide that same look all day. I saw her in her black bra and panties, soaking wet, and wanted to take her right there—the guards standing on the shore be damned.

Herein lies my unexpected new set of problems. How to stop myself from falling for a woman, whom I am likely to be spending every waking moment with, and still keep a pulse on my job and the end goal.

"This isn't the real world, though. We're trapped without options."

She shakes her head, blue eyes staring into my soul.

"I would still say yes," she deadpans, face expressionless. "Are you saying you want me here, but not in the real world?"

Leaning to the side, I peek over her shoulder to where the guards are. They aren't watching us closely, and there's no way they know what we're talking about. It still makes me uneasy.

I say her name once, hoping to break the spell, but it does the opposite.

"Look around. This is not the place for our entertaining conversations."

I cough to cover a laugh. There have been very few times in my life when I've dealt with a woman coming onto me. Mostly, this happens at a bar, and it's easy enough to make a joke, laugh, and walk away because I'm not interested or attracted.

I am living with Saylor. Sharing everything with her for an undetermined amount of time. What would happen if I gave in to my desires? How sideways would this go if we fuck, fight, and botch this? I wouldn't be able to convince her to do anything if she's pissed at me tinged with scorn.

Saylor leans toward me across the table, her breathing speeding. Fuck. This wasn't in *any* of the plans. Is this what my commander thinks I need? This sort of nuanced, illogical problem I'm supposed to fix or succumb to?

"I was asking a yes or no question," she says, breathing heavily. "Yes, or no? You and me, in the real world?"

I'm about to say yes when the scene behind her piques my interest.

Ravelo and Nery are looming several tables over, speaking to two men I've not seen yet. They have to be the other hostages.

"We aren't in the real world," I hiss. "The other

hostages are behind you. You need to focus on our surroundings, Saylor."

Something about me saying her name snaps her out of the whatever lust haze she was in.

"Two men, and they're speaking English. We need to talk to them." I'm not sure why they're here now, but this may be our only chance to figure out who they are.

Saylor looks over her shoulder, then spins back to me.

"You have to talk to them. They like and trust you," she says, her demeanor changing on a beat. "Try to get their attention."

"That's something you can do," I reply, winking, now that I'm safe from her sexual desires.

She smiles and shakes her head subtly. Saylor turns when the guards leave and signals for them to come over.

They look to be in their twenties or thirties, and they've been through it. Their clothes are worn, and their skin is mottled with dirt. It's easy to tell they haven't been afforded the same luxuries we have. The one on the right looks terrified, but he stands and approaches our table, sliding in next to Saylor.

"You have to help us. We've been here for months. They said we aren't worth much, and they may kill us if they can't get anything for ransom."

I swallow hard, deciphering how this new complication affects my initial plan. Surely the pirates are just telling them they're going to kill them. They're trying to get a higher ransom from the government.

"Please help us," he says, low voice shaking. "I'm Turner, and that's my younger brother, Collin. We don't have family, and I think they picked us up by accident, thinking we were someone else. Rich people of value or something. We're nobodies, and I just need to get my brother out of here. Please."

Turner's voice turns to a whisper on the last plea. When his face lands on mine, I see a brief flicker of recognition, and it sends a trill of warning down my spine. I try to place him, but can't.

Saylor palms her chest.

"We are also being held in the cage across the way. Are you guys in the one on the other side? I'm Saylor, and this is—" Saylor says, laying a hand on my arm.

I cut her off before she could say my name. "What skills do you have?"

"I'm a math teacher," he says. "A high school math teacher. My brother is a real estate agent, and he's good at...video games."

I exhale a breath, showing my irritation. I don't have much time. "How well can you lie?"

Turner looks around erratically, eyes wild. Not well, I think to myself before he replies. "I-I don't know," he stutters. "To save our lives, I can."

"You know woodworking and carpentry," I say, lowering my voice to a growl. "We will need your help soon."

Turner looks at his brother, then turns back to Saylor, then me, nodding. His gaze finds mine.

"I know you," he says. "Where do I know you from?"

From my periphery, I can see Saylor narrow her eyes at him and then me.

"You've been caged for a long time. We're just the first Americans you've seen. We don't know each other, but we will soon if you do what I say."

I don't know him. That's for sure. What are the odds that he knows me from back home? From college? He teaches math, so he must hold a college degree. From the Naval Academy, though? He looks the same age as me, but I'm also weathered from a rough and tumble life.

"Tell your brother to man up if you want to live."

He's across the room, shaking without his big brother by his side. Clearing my throat, I let my eyes dart to the guards returning, the bamboo door making a swishing noise as they enter.

"You saw how the stairs needed to be fixed, and you know woodworking. They let us out because they found out we have skills they don't. Specialize in something. We'll be fixing the stairs sometime this week, and we will need help. Tell them that."

As soon as Nery sees Turner at our table, he blows a dart, hitting him in the bicep. Saylor screams. Not her blood-curdling, annoying screech, but an actual scream because she's terrified, and that dart missed her by mere centimeters.

Turner falls to the ground seconds later. His brother, Collin, runs over, tears streaming down his red, dirty face.

"You aren't allowed to communicate." Nery hisses.

Collin puts his hands up, making goal posts with his arms.

"We didn't know. Please, we didn't know. Don't dart me," he pleads. "I'll carry him back. Don't hurt him more."

His words shake because his body is trembling so hard. They have broken them down.

Nery prepares another dart.

Even if I shouldn't care, I step in.

"I called the brother to talk to me," I say in their language. "I overheard them speaking about the stairs here. He has woodworking skills and can help us with our project tomorrow," I explain, saying tomorrow, even though they haven't said when to put a time frame on the order. "He will be helpful to us."

Saylor grabs my wrist, gaze wide and pleading. She stays silent, willing me to read her face.

"Both of these brothers are useful. He gardens," I say, nodding at the shivering shit kneeling on the ground. Him gardening sounds like a lie they'd believe. "He said he noticed a blight on the arabica beans. He wanted to know if we saw it."

The lies keep coming because Saylor is looking at me like I'm a superhero who can solve the world's problems. Why does letting her down feel like a mortal sin?

"Yes," Collin says, barely believable.

Great, they both suck at lying. Good in most cases, bad when it comes to saving their own life.

"Yes. That is correct."

I close my eyes because I'm getting secondhand embarrassment from this show.

Nery orders Collin to carry his brother back, and I make eye contact with the younger brother. He nods at me. This is the charade he needs to play.

Saylor stands from the table, shaking herself, planting one hand on the bamboo surface to steady herself.

"They are unpredictable," she says, hushed, as Ravelo walks us out of the room.

Collin is struggling with Turner over his shoulder, but I don't dare help. I need to protect Saylor. She needs to be the focus.

"They weren't supposed to hurt us."

They won't hurt her. She's worth too much, but a dose of fear is good to keep her in line. She looks up at me, and tears pool in her big blue eyes.

"Thank you for standing up for them. You didn't have to because I know you don't care."

I care. I do. In my own fucked-up way.

"We can use them as tools," I say instead.

She huffs, standing closer to me now than she ever has as we walk toward our cage.

"Can I use the bathroom over there before we go in?" Saylor's question is laced sweetly as she points to the shack we can see from our cage.

Ravelo seems to think about it for a moment or two and agrees. Since we're over here anyway, he allows me to go as well. From this new angle, I can see where the other hostages are being held. From the second floor of this stilted structure, they have a bird's-eye view of both our cage and theirs. They can also communicate with anyone in the other stilted structure we eat at. The lineup of their buildings is tactical in nature.

He locks the door behind us when we're back in our cage, and Saylor throws herself onto the floor.

"Could this really go on for months?"

"It's how they drive a higher ransom," I explain, then realize this is information a car mechanic probably wouldn't have.

I'm being too honest with her, and I'm slipping up.

"That's what I read before my sail, anyway."

She nods but also sobs. Saylor sits up.

"I know that, but I really need to get out of here. I'm losing my mind already, and they've been here for months. It's impossible to think about a long timeline. I acted like a complete psycho today because you're my only company."

Pressing my lips together, I try not to smile.

"Psycho is a strong word," I reply. "It's okay to be attracted to me."

Saylor groans. "There's the attitude that ensures I'm going crazy instead of actually being attracted to you."

"I'm attracted to you," I say. "And to answer your question, yes, if we were in the real world, I'd still be attracted to you. I can separate what's happening to me at any moment from my emotions. Those are separate things, and I know I would want you in the real world. Even though I doubt you can separate your situation from emotions. I don't think you'd want me in the real world. I'm not your type. This is where we should be talking about stuff like this. Not in crowded areas with our captors around. I guess that *was* a little psycho."

If they heard that conversation, they'd surely cage us in different areas, and as uncomfortable as this proximity is for my willpower, it's what's best for the mission.

I chance a glance at her. She's staring at me, eyes intense.

"Why don't you think you'd be my type in the real world?"

*Careful with how much you say, Brody. Careful.*

"From what I know about you so far, I think we're from two different worlds." Perfect. Leave it at that. "Which doesn't mean much for relationships, I suppose, because a lot of times opposites attract, but I think my being the person who is making your life better earns your affection in my favor. I'm your only convenient, viable option. I'm sure men are clamoring over you outside of here."

"I admit, most men are nicer to me, but I don't think it matters what world we're from." Saylor pauses. "That almost sounded like a compliment—the other guys wanting me part at the end there."

She just glazed over the different worlds thing there. She rubs her hand, the center of her palm. "It's sore from all the hammering."

She's close enough to touch, and my fucking intrusive thoughts win. I grab her hand, flip it over, and rub her palm with my thumbs. She allows it. Watching our hands, her face a mask, hiding all emotions now.

It feels electric to touch her on purpose. I want my hands all over her tight body. Mostly, I'd love them on her hips so I can direct her on my dick. *Yes*, I think. That would fulfill this intrusive need that began the second I saw her.

"In your world, you don't hammer a lot, then?" I ask, hoping my double entendre hits.

She clears her throat. "I don't. Operating systems don't have handles or require brute force."

I work my thumbs into her hand, feeling just how fragile she is. Her fingers are half the size of mine. I've crossed the line. Why stop now? Moving my thumbs up in an illusion to massage her wrists, I feel her pulse. It's beating against the thin skin in a wild tempo. Even though it's her heartbeat, all I hear as it thuds against my thumb is fuck. Me. Fuck. Me. Fuck. Me. Over and over, quicker and quicker, as her gaze penetrates mine. Fuck. Me.

I clench my jaw to quell the storm inside my chest, and her blue eyes dip to my neck, then back up to meet mine.

The sun is almost set, but her eyes shine with the last bit of sunlight, and looking into the depths of her gaze pulls me deep. She has me rapt in the moment—something ripping open inside my heart.

What is it about this woman specifically that does it for me? Is it the half-love, half-hate? Hate and love are two sides of the same coin.

Saylor is infuriating and beautiful. She's intelligent, yet soft. The pull is magnetic in a destined way. I would have called bullshit if you told me these thoughts would cross my mind.

"Are you going to kiss me?" Saylor asks, licking her lips.

A knot twists in my gut.

"I'm thinking about it."

She exhales, her lips pillowing open to expose her teeth.

"What's to think about?"

My dick is hard. Everything about this moment screams forever, and yet, what comes to mind? My fucking commander. My mission. Duty. Honor. Respect. I deflate. Literally.

Cradling her face in my hand, I take one last breath before I let my brain, the big one, rule my body. The sun sets, and the light just illuminating her blue eyes goes out. It's like she reads the decision straight from my mind before I've fully made it.

I lean in and inhale the sweet scent of her skin. Her hair still smells of something sweet, and being this close forces a visceral reaction from my body. Leaning toward her a bit more, I commit the scent to memory as my guts tighten in response.

Kiss her. Make her mine. Be a man and do what's right.

I default to my usual misanthrope. "When's the last time you brushed your teeth?"

Saylor jerks back, pulling her arms away.

"That was insanely rude!" She aims a finger at my chest. It's small and pointy. "You feel this. Whatever this is between us. It's not because we're trapped here together. It's not even because you have a perfect freaking physique. It's more than that. It's deeper. We have chemistry."

She says the last three words slowly, an eternity passing between each one. It feels looming, like a threat promised that I won't be able to stop.

It's like a weight pressing down on my chest. A foreign twist of a knife as the truths spill from her fucking delectable mouth. I release my breath, trying to hold it together.

"Saylor, stop. This can't happen. Chemistry or not, it doesn't make sense to complicate this."

From the light of the lantern, I can tell she's furious.

"Use," I say, pausing for effect. "That energy to figure out projects and ways we can do things to keep us out of this cage."

Saylor lifts her chin and scoots away from me as far as she can.

"You're right. Absolutely right. I've lost my mind. Obviously, I've lost it completely for thinking someone like you would want someone like me." She clears her throat and sighs long and hard. "You're right."

I feel like an absolute prick. Don't I always feel like a prick when I say mean things? This time I care, and it's confusing.

"I do want you," I say, tone low. "More than I should, and more than I've wanted anyone else before. This isn't an ideal situation for wanting anything except getting out of here alive."

Shifting, she looks at me dead in the eyes again. A soul-searing look.

"What happened to you? Why are you the way you are?" She shakes her head. "It's not just because you're stuck here. Something happened to you. Was it the death of your friend? The one you were going to spread the ashes of?"

My breath catches, and I cough quietly. How does she see through me when I've been able to hide my past for so long?

My past is charred with a tragic incident that didn't

change me, per se, but it did solidify less-than-desirable traits that weren't set yet. I don't think about it. I don't talk about. Friends and family don't mention it. I'm not even comfortable with lines of questioning that dredge up memories. Like this. Right now.

She's targeted the pain point with incredible ease. It doesn't have to do with my fake dead friend. It does have to do with death and the interminable distrust that sprang from it.

"I hate to disappoint you, but I was born this way." It's not a full lie.

"I don't believe it," Saylor says, shaking her head. "I don't believe it for one second. You are holding onto someone or something that was done to you for dear life. Life is short. You think there's time, and I'm here to tell you there's not. You just try to find simple pleasures in life, like sailing is for me, around all the other crap in life. I have been forced into a box my entire life, and I was angry." She pauses. "Maybe not as angry and mean as you are, but I know trauma when I see it. I'm surrounded by people trying to mask as people they're not. Lie to me all you want, Brody, but you can't hide from the truth forever. Mean people are always mean for a reason, and they're mean until they realize it's not worth it anymore."

The pit in my stomach turns to dread. How long will I be able to keep this charade up?

"Go to sleep. We have a busy day tomorrow," I reply, lying down, folding my arms behind my head.

I know damn well I'm not going to sleep tonight. I'm going to think about the words she just said and compare them to the words Nolan always says when he's trying to reason with me. The sentiment is the same. I can't even bring myself to respond to her statement.

Saylor zips up the sweatshirt and rolls away from me.

"You're going to be giving me a full-throated apology. Mark my words."

I readjust the hard-on that, by some witchcraft, is still there, and nod to myself. For the first time in my entire life, I may consider being less of an asshole. Not because the pleading from my brother, whom I love dearly, has finally resonated with me. No, because this woman, whom I've just met, has spoken to the hollow place inside me.

Maybe it is time to face my past and forgive myself for my mistakes. Maybe it's time to move on.

I glance over at her when her breathing evens out. She sleeps so quickly and soundly. She sleeps like a human who knows exactly who she is and what she stands for. Maybe, just maybe, I'll allow myself to give in to her while we're both trapped. I could learn something about myself and give her what she obviously so desperately wants.

Nothing is easy in life, though. I'm not naïve. Like the SEAL creed goes, *the only easy day was yesterday.*

## CHAPTER NINE

### *saylor*

## THREE WEEKS LATER

BRODY'S ARMS are folded across his chest.

"You're doing that wrong," he deadpans. His face is dirty from the soil smudged across his cheekbone. "I told you the irrigation output levers needed to be twenty inches apart because of the weak water pressure." He nods at my dirty ass hands and the contraption I made myself. "That's about twenty-five inches, so the water won't flow."

"Brody," I chide.

It's a warning. I'm exhausted. I'm hungry. My shoulders are sunburnt, and my spirit is nearly broken.

"It will work." He's right. I know he's right. "What? Do you have a ruler in your brain? How can you look at this and know how many inches it is? There's so much dirt. My eyes are crossing at this point."

They are letting us eat the veggies and fruit that fall off the plants in exchange for the irrigation system we've developed and are installing. Even with the extra food, it's not enough. I don't need a scale to tell me I've lost weight, and the gaunt hollows in Brody's face let me know I'm not imagining things. I also think he's gotten new abs. If that's even humanly possible.

"Let me have a turn. We're almost done, and then we can head to the waterfall. Mako is on, remember? He lets us stay as long as we want."

His tone when he speaks to me is different. It's no longer *I told you so*. It holds actual empathy.

I stand up, dusting my hands on the sides of my pants I found in the junk pile, and catch my breath. The skort wasn't tactical enough for the work we've been doing. The sun is beating down on me, and I haven't had water since the late breakfast they gave us.

I run the back of my hand across my forehead. "I need water."

The irony of us laying irrigation is that it's not potable. We'd get sick if we drank it. I tried last week and ended up vomiting for two full days. It was miserable.

Brody looks up after burying the nozzle at what I'm sure is the perfect twenty inches and exhales. He can read my face easily now. That's the thing with spending every waking second with someone.

I see Turner and Collin coming back from the waterfall, clothing wet, with smiles on their faces, and get wildly jealous. They're on a different project thanks to Brody.

He stands and walks over to Nery, gesturing over his shoulder to me. I'd swear Brody was one of them for how much they seem to respect him. He's treated better than I am, but I don't complain because it works in my favor.

He comes back with a flask and extends it down to me.

"He said we can go to the waterfall now. I told him you weren't feeling well."

"And he cared?" I hiss before uncapping the jug and chugging the water until my stomach is full and painful. I hand it back to Brody, and he walks it back to Nery.

I watch as Mako appears to walk with us to the waterfall. I pick up my satchel that holds extra veggies and a bar of soap I was able to make from shea butter and wood ash.

Mako told me the soap-making process after I promised to make enough for the base if I could keep some for myself. The same goes for toothpaste. I explained that it would be better for everyone involved if we stayed healthy, and washing our bodies and brushing our teeth was part of that. I was sure to figure out a way to brush my teeth after Brody brought it up the first time.

"It's taking so long, Brody," I say, trying not to break down, but tears brim at the corners of my eyes. I feel them, like hot traitors ready to ruin my tough persona.

I'm the strong sister. The one built like my dad. I should be able to deal with this, but doubts creep in. Will they hold me here longer because I'm useful to them? Has my mother given up hope that I'm alive? Will I die on this base from an infection that can't be cured because antibiotics would be impossible to obtain?

I don't know how much longer I can take of the manual labor day in and day out. There's no way to calculate time because every day is the same. There are no weekends to break up the weeks. Or lunches with friends. Or dates with a boyfriend. Sure, I get to look at Brody daily, but he has the self-control of an armored vehicle.

He looks at me like he wants me. He touches me here and there, and the touches are filled with more. The chemistry is something from my mom's romance novels. Like, I know this man would rock my world, and I'd go as far as to say I could destroy his, but he holds me at arm's distance.

He's been kinder, and his approach is gentler, understanding. Professional. Even when I nearly attack him at the end of the day.

It's our usual song and dance. He knows it's coming. I plan what tactic I'll try to see if he can resist. Aside from stripping down naked and forcing myself on him, I've tried every pickup line, corny or not, every flirt, suggestive smile, and seductive conversation I can muster. He knows I'm protected from pregnancy with an IUD, and how I have a come kink. I want it in me and all over me.

Nope. Nothing. Shot down.

Does he want to? That's a thousand percent affirmative. His reasons for not are what I need to discover. Today, though? I'm exhausted, my body weary, sore.

He lays a hand on my shoulder.

"We're almost there," he says. Then I swear he says, "I almost have everything I need," under his breath, but I'm so tired I'm probably imagining it.

"The work is done for today," he adds.

When the waterfall comes into view, my mood immediately improves. Mako takes a seat next to a tree in the distance and folds his arms behind his head before snoring. He truly is the worst guard ever, but we've also never given him a reason to believe we'd do anything wrong.

"Thank God it's Mako today," Brody says, and I notice for the first time how exhausted *he* looks.

I have a routine at the waterfall. I sit down, take off my clothes, grab my soap and toothpaste, and swim behind the waterfall to clean myself. After, I sun myself on a rock, but I won't today because I've had enough damn sun.

Brody takes his turn, then joins me near the shore on an adjacent rock. We don't do much chit-chatting while we're here. It's sacred.

The only time I feel normal is when I'm here. In the

open air, where I can hear the tropical birds singing and the water rushing. I'm not caged or working when I'm here. I can just be.

Today, as I pull myself up on the rock behind the waterfall, strip down to my bra and panties to begin my cleaning process, Brody follows me.

He lumbers up next to me, water dripping off his skin onto the rock and my legs.

"Hey, you feeling better?" he asks, pitching his voice louder so I can hear.

"Careful, Brode," I say, using the nickname I coined when Brody felt like too much. And it rhymed with chode, which drives him bananas. "That sounds a bit too much like caring, and you wouldn't want to give me the wrong idea."

I smile, looking over at him. A small smirk plays on his lips, and I hate how my stomach flips.

I close my eyes and exhale loudly. "I am now," I reply. I look at him, placing my chin on my knees. "Are you doing okay?"

He nods, and his square jaw draws my attention. "Yeah, I'm doing okay."

His blue eyes melt into mine. It's another of those moments where he completely dismantles my insides with a mere look. It's happened hundreds of times, and each time, I'm shocked he still has the ability. There's never been anything else to compare it to in my past.

"I do care about you. You know that, right?"

I mock choke. "Did the man, myth, and legend finally cave and admit to owning some sort of emotion?"

Brody grins, and it causes an actual riot inside of me. My stomach flips, and my skin electrifies. If a feather touched me, it would be enough to send me to another dimension.

"Guess I'm more tired than I thought, then."

He didn't refute it. This is monumental when it comes to him and his lack of anything, except rude wit and avoidance tactics.

We've been close to breakthroughs when we talk about our lives back home, but he won't ever delve too deep. I know he has a twin he has a soft spot for, a dog that lights up his entire universe, but he doesn't talk much about his job or friends. It's as if there's a place in time where he won't or can't go past. A stamp marking a period obsolete.

"This is huge," I say, pulling the bar of soap out of my bag and lathering it on one arm. "You're admitting to emotion *and* that you're tired."

I lather my other arm, neck, and chest. He watches my hand as it moves over my chest.

"I don't think you've complained about being tired once yet."

He shakes his head, watching me wash my legs and feet, dipping them in the water to get them wet. Brody clears his throat, drawing my gaze from my toes to his face.

"It's less of me being tired, and more of me being worn out. Worn out from resisting this." He clears his throat again, jutting his chin up at my body. "It's ah, getting to be a lot."

I lose my breath at the sheer honesty in his shining eyes, and the breath stays lost when it turns to something more sinister.

He stops my hand holding the soap when it's on my thigh closest to him. I freeze at the contact. He's touched me here and there—my shoulder, my face, my wrist—when he loses himself, but this time it feels different.

Taking the soap from me, he runs it over my leg. I

startle at the touch. Not just because it's been so long since I've been touched like this, because it's *him*.

I don't dare say a word for fear of him stopping. The waterfall in front of us shields us from Mako and anyone on the bank of the lagoon. It's a private lush oasis.

He slides his hand between my thighs, and I gasp, but he pauses. He continues washing me, setting my skin ablaze. He stops before his hand brushes between my legs and spins me to wash my back, pulling me back between his legs, my back against his chest. His hands are rough, calloused, but somehow feel soft against my skin.

He unhooks my black bra and slides it down my arms. I toss it on the rock next to me, reveling in the fact that this is finally happening. It doesn't matter that I'm bone tired. His touch gives me a second and third wind. It's a craving nothing has ever matched.

He reaches in front of me with lathered hands and clutches my breasts, pulling me to lean against his chest between his legs. I exhale, rolling my head back against his shoulder, tipping my chin up. Brody rolls my nipples between his fingers before sliding his big hands down between my legs, pulling my panties to the side.

"Is this what you want?" he rasps in my ear.

It sends a shiver down my spine as the heat grows from the touch of his hands, his voice finally giving me what I've wanted since I laid eyes on him—validation that I'm not crazy. This. Is. Something.

"Spread your legs for me."

I scoot back, until I can feel his cock against my back, giving him a better access, knees splayed open.

"Unfortunately, yes," I reply, my tone a breathy plea for more. "This is exactly what I want."

Twirling my clit between his fingers, a flood of wetness pools between my legs.

"The question..." I ask, breathing heavily, turning my head to glimpse his face, "Is this what you want?"

His square jaw works. I can feel it against the side of my head.

"I want to be rough because of what you put me through for the past three weeks. But I'm also tired." His voice is a low growl, edging me closer to the brink. "Tired because I don't sleep while I'm lying next to you."

Brody's heart is hammering against my back, and his slick skin warms. My own heart pounds in unison, hearing him say words I've only dreamed of.

"Lying close to you only makes me want to be inside you. Eviscerating you. Taking everything from you that I haven't been brave enough to take."

His breathing is jagged against my ear as he presses his lips against the rim.

"I'm not sure I have the energy for what I've dreamed about—the need I have inside me. There's no way I can wait another day."

He licks my ear, sending shockwaves throughout me.

"Another hour," Brody growls, then bites my lobe. Hard enough for me to know he means business.

"Or another second," he finishes.

I do too. I come apart, arching my back as his thick fingers work my clit to an oblivion. The rapture is immediate. I close my eyes and ride the orgasm as the waves pulse.

Brody whispers into my ear. "You like that?"

I nod, unable to form full sentences.

"You. Are. Mine," his voice rumbles against my neck.

He bites the skin gently, inhaling deeply, like he's trying to consume me. His words are more powerful than the orgasm. It's the first time I forget where I am and what I'm enduring because of who I'm with.

Turning my head, I angle my body to the side so I can kiss him.

He beats me to it, grabbing my face with both his hands and crushing his lips into mine. It's aggressive.

This has built for weeks, the chemistry we've buried with jokes and teasing.

Brody bites my bottom lip and pulls away. It hurts. It will leave a mark, but I want more. I want him to mark my body inch by inch. This is the first time in my life I want a man to *own* me.

The kiss slows, his tongue languidly brushing against mine as he opens his mouth, tasting me. I can smell his scent mixed with the lather of the soap. It's intoxicating. If you could bottle it, women would clamor for miles to give their life savings for a bottle.

Being this close to him makes my head spin. What's going to happen when he's finally inside me?

I catch his bottom lip between my teeth and give it back to him. Pulling away from the kiss slowly, I let my gaze find his. His lids at half-mast, he is wildly turned on. Brody's blue eyes hold a soft intensity. There's a depth I've seen before, but never like this, never just for me.

Releasing his lip, it pops back into place. We stare at each other for a few breaths without speaking, letting the heat simmer like a volcano. The water rushes down around us, encasing us in this mind-altering moment.

I whisper, "But are you mine?" I finally ask.

Something flashes behind his eyes, and I wonder if I've ruined it, if he's retreated to the place where he hides.

I hold my breath and press my lips against his in case this is it. If this is all I get, I'm going to make the most of it right now.

Brody takes the soap that's sitting on the rock next to

my thigh and rubs it over his chest, ignoring the question that seems to have shaken him.

It was easy for him to call me his, but when the roles are reversed, it causes a riot inside him.

Taking the soap from his hand, I wash him all over, lingering on the rippling abs and the V that peeks out from his boxer briefs. He slides them off, and I continue my assault.

Brody's dick is even more magnificent than I thought —thick, veiny, and long. Taking it in both hands, I lather it. He lets a moan slip, tipping his head back to stare at the rocky top of our secluded cave. While he was rough with my body, I'm careful with his, letting my hands slide over his balls softly.

Leaving his cock, I wash up to his neck and straddle him to wash the top of his back.

"Give me that," Brody says, tone cracking on the last word as he takes the soap. Then he rolls our bodies into the cool water below us to wash the soap off.

I slide off my panties and toss them on the rock. Our bodies are slick, pressed up against one another. The temperature of our skin offsets the cool tropical water splashing behind us.

He pulls me to stand on a stone that's next to the rocky cave wall so we can both stand. The water is waist deep, but he pulls me up his body slowly, a crawl, so I rub against first his dick, then every rippling ab, until I'm able to wrap my legs around his waist, and his lips are taking mine.

He cups my ass with one hand and holds my head with the other, taking possession of my body in all ways. He groans, pulling me closer. My clit is sensitive. I circle my hips so I'm rubbing myself against his abs.

I pull away from the kiss, my hands on the sides of his rough face, and look into his eyes.

"Brody," I whisper his name, my lips brushing against his as I plead my case. "I need you."

There's another flicker of something, but this time it vanishes quicker than before.

"I need you too," Brody replies, kissing me slowly in between each word.

I leave my eyes open because there's something about this action that feels like I'm being worshipped.

Sliding from my mouth, he kisses my neck and lowers me down his body, pushing me toward his dick. My heart hammers with anticipation and need. The moment seems surreal. The location. His body. His words and actions are so tender and pure that it almost feels as if he's someone else entirely.

I close my eyes when I feel warmth, his hard tip at my core.

"Open your eyes," he growls.

I obey.

"I want to see the moment you know."

"I know what?" I ask, squirming, trying to get him inside me. I clutch his biceps and watch his muscular body as he holds me at bay.

"The second I become yours," he replies, finally allowing my hips free.

I slide down, letting him feel me. I cry out, forgetting where we are and who is on the other side of the wall of water. Brody puts a hand over my mouth as he starts fucking me, long and hard, his blue gaze locked on mine as he slams into me.

I add to my memory bank. This is a porno.

He closes his eyes as he fills me for just a moment, relishing the sensation. The ecstasy blankets my body as the cool temperature of the water dissipates from the fire burning between our bodies. My core clenches automatically when he thrusts into me deep and holds.

"Fuck," he whispers.

Brody kisses me and slows his pace. It's a leisurely fuck, and he releases my back to hold on to my hips. I float back on top of the water, my arms out to the sides. My ears are under water, so I've lost that sense, the roar of the waterfall.

He watches where our bodies are joined, then raises his eyes to my stomach and breasts, and his gaze catches on mine, and what I see there takes my breath away. More than possession, more than lust, this is obsession dipped in love, wrapped with a chemistry so pure, no one else would believe it exists.

We lock eyes as he moves my body on and off his cock. He hits my G-spot with each slide, and he knows it—a beautiful smirk transforms the carnal haze playing across his face.

Brody's grip is firm, and with me floating, he's controlling every move. I envision what we'd look like from above, and it forces me to creep even closer to the brink. This big, stunning man, fucking me slowly, surrounded by paradise. He's taking what he wants, and the thought gives me a thrill.

My whole body tightens as the tingles begin and slip over my body, beginning at my throbbing pussy. He slams into me one more time, forcing my face under the water, and I come, bubbles escaping my mouth as I scream out in pleasure. It's the oddest sensation, coming around his massive, hot cock as my body is enveloped in cool water. My heart hammers as the waves of the orgasm wash over me.

Brody's hands pull me up out of the water, and he

doesn't give me time to catch my breath. He fucks me hard, his mouth covering mine as I pant out in protest, but also relish being fucked with our bodies pushed together.

He comes inside of me before my breathing evens. His face buried in my neck, his teeth sliding across my throat. He pulses inside me, the thickness hitting the walls with each jerk. We stay entangled, our lips languidly kissing each other's lips, neck, and face. It's tender and caring. Words that I never would have used to describe anything to do with Brody. Chancing speaking isn't even something I'd consider, because this feels like a love spell—it feels like magic.

He's still inside me when his head whips to the side. I follow where he's looking and notice a bird. It looks to be an Ibis of some sort. It has dark eyes and creamy feathers. It turns to the side and looks at us intently. I smile, licking my lips when Brody's gaze flits back to meet mine.

"We are the zoo animals on display," I tease. The bird spreads its wide wings and turns to swim away from us.

"I'd be an animal on display if it meant fucking you all day," he deadpans, eyes roving my body. "I honestly don't know how I'm going to get anything done knowing this is what I could have instead."

There it is again, that worshipping, so un-Brody-like sentiment. All it took was mind-blowing sex.

"I have to know. Is it always like this for you?"

His face shutters, and he swallows hard.

"Yes and no. It's been a while," he finally replies. "Not like this, though."

Brody exhales long and hard, causing his stomach to ripple like the wake from a boat. His abs are unreal. Literally.

"Fucking you was something out of a fever dream." He stutters. "Doesn't even feel real now."

I nod. "I feel the same way."

Seconds pass and we just live in the moment, his dick softening inside me.

"We can't let the guards know. What if they separate us?"

Another flicker in his blue eyes. It's as if he has modes or settings, and things I say trigger them.

"We won't let them know. We shouldn't do this in the cage," he says. "Only here."

Sliding out of me, he hisses.

"It's cold," he whines. "It's going to be hard for me to hold myself to that, but it's what will be safest."

Standing on the rock below us, I go up on my tiptoes. He seems unsure of what to do, so I pucker my lips. Smiling, he leans down and indulges me with a fiery kiss. My lips are swollen and feel bee-stung when he pulls away.

"If we do any more of that, I'm going to need a second round, and I'm not sure we have time for that."

God, do I ever want more of him.

"We could push it and see how long we can stay. If Mako is sleeping, we could stay here until dinner. We won't be missed. I want more."

My heart bangs on my chest, knocking, reminding me who I am and what I'm doing, but Brody takes precedence, somehow. He is more than my final puzzle piece. It feels like we were always meant to be here together.

I was put here to save him.

I FUCKED her one more time, leisurely, doggy style, on the rock behind the waterfall, to just drive the point home that I'm done for.

It's hard to recognize myself next to this need for her. Especially given the situation. She called my name when she came, and I lost my mind completely with emotion.

Saylor is extraordinary in a way I can't describe. I'll never get over her. Ever. If I lived a hundred lives, I'd look for her in each one. When this ends, and the façade becomes reality, it's going to sting worse than anything else. Maybe even worse than the aftermath of the incident that blocked the emotional part of my damn life until now.

Saylor walks in front of me, and even though she has clothes on now, all I can see is her naked body and the indent at the bottom of her spine that I came all over. We're in the dining building, being led to a table in the back. I'm so caught up in my thoughts, I don't realize Collin and Turner are here eating until we're basically on top of them.

"You'll eat here," Mako says.

Nery and Ravelo come in, eyeing us peculiarly. Or maybe it's just because we disappeared for the last half of the day. It's hard to tell, but one thing is certain. I have all the information I need to deconstruct this terrorist group. The inner workings are laid out in my mind, and the plan to dismantle them will be effortless with what I've learned over the past weeks.

We sit down and wait for them to bring us food. Saylor wrinkles her nose when she sees what they're eating.

"Again," she whines, keeping her voice low. "I may skip," she says, mostly to herself.

Seeing her naked confirmed how thin she's gotten. I wouldn't call it unhealthy yet.

"You can't skip," I reply, swallowing down the lump in my throat.

The food has progressively gotten worse, which has been fine with the supply of the random vegetables and fruit we've been able to eat.

"You have to keep your strength up, even if it means eating this."

Nery sets down two trays, and the sound ricochets off the walls. When he leaves, Turner looks me in the face, and I see the recognition. It's terrifying because I don't understand it or reciprocate the feeling.

The guards never put us together with the brothers. Why today? What does Turner know?

Turner shakes his head, eyes locking with mine. "Took me forever to figure it out. It kept me up at night, but when I saw you earlier today, it hit me where I know you from."

My stomach turns to lead, and Saylor drops her fork

to stare at the men on the other side of the table. We stare, her in confusion, and I, in fascinated dread.

"Where?" I ask, unable to recall any diversion tactics I learned in all my training at this moment. This is so far from an actual mission that it has me fucked up five ways till Sunday.

"We live in Maryland," Turner says. "When I was in high school, a girl who graduated a few years ahead of me died in a car accident. It was all over the news. You were the driver of the car she was in. I saw your face plastered all over the news articles. You were at the Naval Academy with her, out on a date."

It's exactly as bad as I suspected. He knows who I really am, but maybe that's all he knows about me, stuff from back then. Because of her. Because of the incident that screwed me up.

"Jocelyn," I say, swallowing hard. Forgetting for a moment that Saylor is watching my every move and studying my words, I go on. "She was my girlfriend."

There's no sense in lying now. I shake my head and slam my eyes shut, knowing the nightmare will play across my lids. The hot, steaming wreckage, the scent of charred flesh. Her body.

I force my gaze to Turner's. "So...what of it?"

"Small world, I guess," he says. "I always remembered your name because it was tied to Jocelyn's. It hit me hard. I followed your career," he adds. "I know who you are, Brody. It is weird how we are tied to the things that happen to us as kids. The things we remember, the need to look up old news stories over and over, to search on the internet for the other people involved."

I hold up a hand.

"Enough. That's enough. We don't need to talk about

any of this. Especially here, surrounded by ears," I explain, trying to get him to shut up before he blows my cover.

God, what a fucked-up mess that would be if Saylor finds out I'm a SEAL.

Wait, no, if the guards know I'm a SEAL, this will be over. They'll try to kill me right here and now. There's no way to offset that accusation other than to fib more or accuse Turner of lying, and somehow, I don't think that's my best option now that we're so intertwined. I can't stop thinking about Jocelyn.

"It was an accident, and it's in the past. I've moved on."

If moving meant doing everything in life for the sole purpose of forgetting it happened, punishing myself, and then stewing in the memory until the bitterness oozes out of me any chance it gets. Then yes, I've moved on.

Saylor clears her throat and then asks, "But have you *actually* moved on?"

Her voice sends a chilling threat into the air. The threat of having to tell her more...the truth.

Of course she connected the dots. No one has ever read me so well.

"Yes, of fucking course I've moved on. It was a long time ago, when I was in college. I was a kid."

Jocelyn was my first real girlfriend. My first love. She was also a midshipman at the Naval Academy, two years younger than me. We had a lot in common, and she had a wit far superior to mine. We'd been together for a year when the accident happened—long enough to plan my future with her, and long enough for her to break my chest wide open and give me something else to live for.

Saylor's blue eyes widen as she stares at the side of my face. I don't dare look at her. She shovels a bite of food into her mouth, and I can see her wince in my peripheral vision. This conversation with her isn't finished.

Turner leans over and whispers something to his brother, and I don't even try to listen in. Our conversation has drawn looks from all the guards who have their gazes poised on us in a way I'm not used to. The distrust I see on Ravelo's face gives me pause. I aim a lopsided grin his way, trying to let him know there's nothing to see or hear over here.

Collin is the one who speaks now, aiming a finger at me like a weapon. "Get us out of here. There are no excuses now."

My breath hitches. It makes sense that in their minds, I am the police, merely here to swoop in and save them. SEALs are known to come in and save the day. They aren't supposed to know that about me. Heat crawls up my neck as my gaze dances between the brothers.

Saylor stands up loudly, grabbing her tray.

"I need to go tell Ravelo something I thought of with the irrigation system in the vegetable garden. I just thought of it."

She leaves, without saying another word, walking toward the back of the room, toward the group of guards.

"We know who you are. Why haven't you gotten us out of here yet?" Turner hisses, a confidence I've yet to see from him. When humans are desperate, they resort to behavior that is unlike their norms. I can confidently say that's accurate. To a fault.

I watch Saylor talk to Ravelo and Nery closely while deciding which way to go with the brothers. Gaslight. Manipulate. Reverse.

"You don't know motherfucking shit about anything. I was kicked out of the Teams," I say, my words sharp as a razor blade.

I watch their lips drop, and then the light dwindles from their eyes.

"I got rolled up by these motherfuckers spreading the ashes of my friend, because I'm a shit sailor, and I ended up here instead of Australia. I didn't know the waters well enough. I can't help you." Shaking my head. "I might have been someone back when you read a news article about me and Jocelyn and the accident. When I graduated from the Naval Academy, I did go on to try out to become a SEAL, but I didn't make it all the way through training. I got hurt and was sent to be a mechanic. I use my damn engineering degree now. I've had no training for this."

I wave my hand around the room. I know enough to know that there's nothing about me online after I became a SEAL. Operational Security forbids it. Turner saw a graduation announcement posted by the Naval Academy and took a leap that I made it through training. This is the hill I must die on.

"You're saying you don't know how to get us out of here? I call bullshit. You got yourself out of that cage in record time. You know something we don't."

It's true. During my time on this base, I've learned nearly everything there is to know using my keen sense of observation and just by listening when no one thinks I am. I know how many guard shacks are on this base. I know how many men are in those shacks at any given time. I know that there are two men above Ravelo who run things here. I also know where they sleep and what they look like. I also know I might have to kill them to get off this island with Saylor. Now, I realize, duty binds me to getting these jokers out of here too.

"We've been here a long time. You have to get us out of here."

Sometime during my half-convincing charade, I

realize Saylor left the room, and a wave of panic sweeps over me. It's an odd feeling to feel this protective over another person. I haven't left her side for more than a couple of minutes here and there, and she's always been in my line of view or my peripheral.

Collin notices my shock.

"You are having a little island romance in this hell-hole?" he says, shaking his head. "You're sweating."

My gaze flicks to all the doorways, and somehow, I know she's no longer here.

"He's sweating," he says to Turner.

"Listen, fuckers. She's our only hope of getting off this island, so yeah, it does make me nervous," I say, trying to spin another story. Admitting my feelings for her isn't something I can comfortably do. The thought of having a conversation about my feelings with her makes my stomach tilt and flinch.

"Who is she?" Collin asks.

"She's rich. Richer than both of you can imagine. Her family is why we'll get out of here. If you both don't fuck it up before then. It will be on you if you keep blabbing," I add the warning because they've pissed me off. "If you want me to get you off this island when we leave, keep your mouth shut." I swallow hard. "About me and my past and everything you think you know."

They nod. I grab my tray and try to be casual as I walk up to a guard.

"Where is asset twelve?" Too casual? Who knows, but the terror I feel is building its way from the bottom of my feet to the top of my head. The need to see her and be close to her is the only thing that matters right now.

"Ravelo had business with her," Nery says.

Tapping my fingers against my jeans, I try to rein it in. The emotions are wild, licking up my spine, twirling from my heart and mind like a dance. A dance with the fucking devil. One in which I'm damned to an eternity of this absolute mire love has caused.

Love. I admitted it to myself.

Not only is this a chink in my armor, but it could also mean my death. Because doesn't it always for me?

Right now, I want to pummel his face until he tells me where she is, and that would cause chaos. I'd be tased and tranquilized immediately.

"Oh, business in the garden? Is she showing him the improvement to the irrigation line?" I say it in his native tongue because if I said it in English, it would sound like a threat. There's no keeping my cool.

He shakes his head. "You're going back to your cell for the night. Asset twelve has business in the main office. Raza is going to take you back now."

He looks over to Turner and Collin, narrowing his eyes in suspicion.

"Did they tell you anything of significance?"

This is where I need to lie to keep him on my good side.

"Only that they don't have anyone to pay their ransom," I reply, and then, because I need some predictability, I say, "They mentioned trying to make a run for it tomorrow morning. They know Saturday mornings are when the fishing boat docks at the west dock to deliver the resupply to the base."

That's extremely specific information. For them to know that would imply the brothers are at risk of fleeing. It's my information, though, and there's a lot more where that came from.

"I'm not going to allow them out anymore," he replies.

Exactly as I knew he would.

"Thank you." Nery nods, and Raza appears, leading me to the exit.

I don't try to make conversation with him as we head back. I keep my eyes peeled, desperate to make sure she's not at the garden or the junk pit where the bikes are being fixed.

The sun hasn't set yet, but with each passing second that I can't see Saylor, the rare feeling of vulnerability rears like an ugly monster I have no chance of defeating. Raza unlocks the rusted padlock and opens the door. I'm slow to go in, and he notices my hesitation.

"Asset twelve will be staying in another holding cell for the remainder of her time here. You have this one to yourself."

The next question comes without my permission.

"Why?"

Even I hear the panic, so when he raises one brow before he responds, I'm not surprised.

"She requested it. You'll have more space. She's a wild animal. Ravelo was doing you a favor by getting rid of her."

I don't like the implication of his last sentence. In fact, it makes me want to kill him and find her immediately, but I must stay cool, calm, and collected.

Do I know how to do that?

Walking forward, I allow myself to be caged. The lock makes a clanging sound against the bars.

"You will still have to work with her during the day," Raza admits, eyes downcast. He thinks I don't want to be around her. I guess I should mark that as a win.

"I'll do whatever I have to do," I reply. "Any word on my ransom?"

Keep him talking. That's all I can think will help me figure out where she is. There aren't any other holding cell cages on this base save for this one and the one the brothers share. They must have her in the main building structure, which all the guards have access to.

"There will be soon," Raza replies. "You keep your ears open like you always do, and I'll be here for you early tomorrow."

I rub the chip under my skin, eager to press my finger down, eager to end this in all ways, because I can't think straight.

Why wouldn't she want to be in here with me? After the magical afternoon, I can't see a couple of sentences from strangers about my past throwing her this far off course.

I replay the conversation at least a hundred times in my head before I finally allow my eyes to close. Sleep won't come, though. No, not after the trajectory of the day unfolded in such a haphazard way. Maybe it's good she's not next to me for a night. I'll be able to think clearly about the next steps I need to take.

Her body. Her lips. The way her laugh catches on a low note before it cascades into a melody that calms me.

Saylor has thawed my cold, dead heart. I feel the change, and it hurts as much as it injects me with excitement because these circumstances aren't valid. This isn't real. Our time together won't transcend. This cage and this tropical swampland paradise will be a mere memory tainted by suffering and plagued by the unknowns.

She realized it. That's why she wants distance.

I lost Jocelyn in a horrific way, and somehow, I understand losing Saylor like this will be worse than death. I'll know she's out in the world being loved by someone else who doesn't deserve her. It's an agonizing thought.

*Think of the plan. It's almost time, McBrode,* I chide.

My brother comes to mind, and I let myself be sad

and wistful while I go through the sand table plan that lives solely in my brain. I miss Nolan. He'll be there for me when I get home, I remind myself. If I live through what needs to be done. This isn't a situation of only the good die young. This is uncharted territory in a mission that has too many variables to predict what will transpire when I say go.

When sleep eludes me, I shuffle over to the wall adjacent to the toilet. I move a few rocks out of the way that I've carefully chipped away and pull out the gun I stole from the old parts-and-pieces junk pile.

They haul in new things every Saturday on the fishing boat, and I couldn't believe my luck when I found the loaded gun and random bullets inside what looked to be a dismantled glove box. It probably came off one of the boats they stole, and no one opened it up to see the contents.

I hold it in my palm, feeling comforted by the familiar weight and shape. Eight bullets. If the gun doesn't misfire, I have eight lives to take if need be. I didn't anticipate having this luck, but now that I have no idea where Saylor is, I don't feel as fortunate. I want to use it now to get what I want.

I tuck the weapon back behind the rocks, adjusting them so that, to the naked eye, nothing is amiss. Saylor knows I have the gun, but has no clue I know how to use it well.

Lying back down with my hands behind my head, I try to drift again, but this time I'm haunted by the car accident.

Jocelyn was in the passenger seat of my dark green 4Runner. She was wearing a bright red dress because we were heading back to college after dinner out to celebrate our first anniversary. It was a big deal. I bought her a necklace with a diamond inside of a water drop to represent the fact that we met at a naval college. It took me a month to pick it out—I agonized over what would be a perfect gift. Too much and I'd scare her away, but too little and she might not know how much she meant to me. I was a careful driver, always following the rules, never taking chances, especially with her in the car.

Jocelyn was telling me how she picked out the wallet she got me, a wallet I still use to this day. She said the man at the leather store told her his whole life story and his divorce drama as he was engraving the brown leather with my initials. She debated putting her initials and mine, so I'd always remember this was an anniversary present, but decided on just mine in case *life had other ideas*. She still wanted me to use it.

I looked over at her, my eyes directly on hers, and replied, "Life only has the ideas I give it, Joci. And any life I live will have you in it. I promise."

She smiled, lips glossed, and a megawatt smile shining. That's when the headlights transformed the side of her face.

Her green eyes turned to the windshield at the same time mine did. A large delivery truck swerved into our lane, and I decided right then I'd carry this regret for the rest of my life.

I jerked the wheel right to try to avoid a head-on collision, and the passenger side of the car slammed into a large oak tree. The mail truck hit the tail of the left side of my SUV, ripping the 4Runner in half.

I don't remember anything after the collision until I woke up in a hospital, Nolan leaning over me with worried eyes. My parents were there too. Jocelyn wasn't.

Nolan knew what it would do to me. I think that's why he wasn't the one who told me Jocelyn was dead. It was my dad who said it very bluntly because that's the only way to deliver news that doesn't seem real. You have to say it outright in as few words as possible.

"She died on impact. The delivery driver had a blood alcohol level six times the legal limit. He lived...barely. You escaped with some scrapes and bruises. A concussion too. The delivery driver shouldn't be alive for how much alcohol he had in his system."

"It's my fault," I whispered.

Dad shook his head. "It was the delivery driver's fault, and he's going to pay for deciding to drink and drive for the rest of his life."

He didn't pay. He killed himself in prison after his trial. That's why it made broad headlines.

"The tree. I should have pulled left."

It was all so crystallized in my mind and still is. I could have saved us both if I had jerked the wheel the opposite way. I visited the site of the accident dozens of times over the years, thinking about how things could be different if I'd saved her and made a different decision that night. Maybe if I wasn't so fucking in love with her, I would have kept my eyes on the road. Maybe I could have thought more clearly.

It was an open casket service, and she didn't look anything like *my* Jocelyn. The makeup was too heavy, and they had to do some weird patch jobs on her face because of the damage from the crash. Her parents buried Jocelyn wearing the water drop necklace. I saw it in a new light as I stared into my first love's coffin. It was indeed a fucking teardrop, not water. Fuck the diamond. Fuck everything that meant anything.

When I said goodbye to her that day, I said goodbye to the last remaining good part of myself. Sure, I was surly and dark as a child, but losing Jocelyn solidified my nature in a way that twisted into disdainful in a cruel way. There wasn't anything I could do to fix it except become a SEAL and save people. As many as I could. It will never be enough to make up for that night, but for every life saved, I keep her in my life. Like I promised Jocelyn.

If I lose Saylor—if I can't get her out of here alive—I don't know how I'll recover, if I'll ever recover.

One thing is for certain now. I want her in a way I've never wanted anyone before. What I feel for her is real and deep, and even if I get her out of here alive, I'll lose what's left of my heart.

I'm still awake when the sun rises, and I have to blink rapidly several times when I see Saylor on the other side of my cage. She's alone. Her clothing isn't *her* clothing. She's in men's clothing, and she has a new bruise riding high on her cheekbone. Saylor looks left and right before inserting the key in the door, setting me free. I scramble to my feet, nearly tripping from the shock of seeing her.

"Grab the gun," she whispers. The sunlight glistens off her blue eyes and her smile. "We're getting out of this zoo."

This woman has me fumbling on the ground as I reach for the gun.

"What the hell are you doing, Saylor?"

When I'm standing in front of her, the cage door wide open, she grabs the center of my shirt. Pulling me toward her and down, she presses her mouth against mine. The sensation makes me feel like I'm fucking floating. I hate that I love it. Hate that I don't want it to stop.

Her lips move against my mouth, lingering. "I'm getting us out of here."

She tucks her hair under an old Yankees ball cap she found somewhere in a junk pile, I'm sure. I tuck the gun under my waistband and readjust my fucking hard-on.

"Unless you have a better idea? The fishing boat leaves in thirty minutes, and we have to go get Collin and Turner."

Unless I have a better idea.

Is she kidding?

Fuck.

*Here we go.*

## CHAPTER ELEVEN

### *saylor*

HE'S FUCKING BEAUTIFUL. He distracts me from the most important job I've possibly ever had, which has a time limit.

Thirty minutes. We need to find Collin and Turner and get to the west dock before the top of the hour.

Right now, all I can think about is how much I missed Brody when I wasn't next to him. I considered if this chemistry and attraction was some twisted kind of trauma response, but looking at him now, feeling my heart pound against my chest at the sight of him, I confirm this is real. I pull him to me and kiss him, slowly so I can taste him, and relive making love to him at our waterfall.

Looking into his deep eyes, I keep my mouth against his, weary to pull away. "I'm getting us out of here."

Pulling a ball cap I found out of the back of my pants, I try to tuck my hair into it so I'm less conspicuous. He has the gun and secures it. He hasn't said as much, but I can tell he's comfortable with the gun. He holds it like my dad does. Like he's unloaded millions of rounds with precise accuracy. It's something you can't hide. At least he can't hide it from me. I know there's more than meets the eye with Brody, but now isn't the time for anything other than the matter at hand.

"Unless you have a better idea? The fishing boat leaves in thirty minutes, and we have to go get Collin and Turner."

He stares at me, mouth a little ajar, gaze questioning, and he shakes his head, but then he follows me out of our cage into the cool, wet, dusky morning.

We run, me setting the pace with my short legs, him staying so close that his arm bumps mine with every stride. We both know exactly where we're going, even though no one has outright told us where the other bunker cell is.

Turner and Collin are asleep when Brody snarls at them—and it is an actual snarl too.

"Get the fuck up," he growls as I fumble with the ring of keys that caused my black eye.

We have a finite amount of time before the guards wake up from the darts I peppered into them while they slept. Nery grabbed my wrist and slammed me into a wall because he was last, but he wasn't quick enough. I darted him three times to make sure he'd be out for a while. Ravelo is the only one not accounted for, but I'll take my chances with a gun against him.

Collin and Turner are the definition of shellshocked as we pull them out of the cage and tell them we're heading to the west dock. We rest in a copse of dense palm trees on a sandy path. The brothers are behind us, stooping down, hands on their knees. This is more exercise than they've gotten since they've been here.

"Ravelo wasn't darted," I explain to Brody. "The rest are down and will stay down for a while."

Brody glares at me, mouth open.

"You darted all the guards at the same time? How?"

Giving them a taste of their own medicine, which I learned how to concoct in my free time after noticing what herbs they pulled to make it.

I lift and lower one shoulder. "Like it's hard?"

"Saylor, this wasn't planned out. How can you be this careless? What happens when the fishing boat captain shoots us between the eyes?"

I wipe the sweat from my brow.

"My parents paid him off. Don't ask me how, because the only words I have for you are Bianca Wyndham."

There's no sense hiding my last name at this point. It's why we're getting out of here.

"The captain was in the main building last night, taking orders for what he needed to bring back this morning, and he got me alone." I exhale and inhale deeply, still tired from running. "He told me to meet him at the boat this morning, and he'd take me to Maputo, where my parents are waiting. Evidently, my mom got sick of trying to negotiate with the government. They were taking too long for some reason."

Brody looks away, shaking his head. I must admit he seems far more flustered than I thought he'd be for getting the hell out of here.

"She found out this captain's name, I don't know how, then she paid him a lump sum at the dock, like a damn mobster or something, and he gets the other half when I'm delivered unharmed."

"And us?" Brody asks, waving a big, lumbering arm to the brothers who seem to be fighting over something. "I didn't hear anything about us in that story. What's this captain going to do when he realizes you're arriving there with a troop of us?"

I shake my head as I watch Brody move his thumb over his wrist, up and down like he has a cramp.

"The fact that this worked out up until this point is kind of crazy. The captain said he was going to leave me a key by the cage last night if I couldn't get out."

The brothers' argument is heated now, their voices picking up in the wind.

Brody hushes them violently, and they shut up.

"What is this captain's name?" Brody is asking weird questions about things I didn't expect him to care about.

"It was something with a Z," I say. "The names here are hard to remember because they're so different from back home. You know that! We had a conversation about it."

"Zafy?" Brody barks, both brows raised. "Captain Zafy?"

I nod, pressing my lips together.

"Like Daffy Duck. That's right. Yes. That's him. How did you know his name?"

Brody's body stiffens. His shoulders are rigid with tension.

"Because he's one of the leaders here, Saylor."

He paces, only a few steps each way, putting a finger to my lips when I try to talk.

"I must figure out which angle to play. Maybe he wants the ransom all to himself, and he's willing to part with you at the sake of his community suffering."

He shakes his head. "No good leader would do that. It doesn't make sense."

He messes with his wrist again, and when he paces back toward me, I grab him, holding him to the spot with my gaze.

"You have the gun. Kill him if you must, but get us to Maputo." I grab his shirt. "We all know how to drive a boat. We can get away from here and back into the real world and give this escape a real shot."

His lips twitch as his lashes drop, and his gaze lingers on my lips. I shake my head. "It doesn't have to be complicated."

Brody kisses me, and it may be the worst time for the most perfect kiss the world has ever seen, but that's what makes it memorable. There was defeat in his eyes as he leaned down to take possession of my mouth. He leans away from me.

"We're going to have some help here in a minute or two, and I need you to know I didn't tell you because I needed to keep you safe."

I narrow my eyes and tilt my head to the side.

"I am the slow military government that's been taking too long to get you out of here."

I widen my eyes, though it's not shock. It's something akin to puzzling the pieces together.

"Almost everything I've told you is true. I'm a Navy SEAL, and not only am I to bring you back alive and well, but I also needed to gather intel and take this faction down." He shakes his head. "I can't kill Zafy, so that complicates this. My Team—Actually," he says, pausing to look at the sky, craning his neck to the side. "More than my Team are heading to the east base and far fields right now to take over this compound. We need to do this my way, Sweet Pea."

He fiddles with his wrist again.

"I have an implant under my skin that called them here."

I stutter, but try to compose myself. He's a Navy SEAL, and he's kept me here for over a month. He has inside information. That name could have only come from my dad. What is going on here?

"You could have pressed your little button and gotten us out of here the day you arrived and didn't?" The anger simmers, right at the surface, waiting to lash, but as my dad would say, the past is past. Focus on the future.

He looks away, ashamed. "This is why I couldn't tell you. I needed to make sure I had all the information before we left, and then, well..." he whispers.

"Well, what?" I retort.

He looks at me. "Then I figured out who you were to me and what that meant."

"Stop dancing around it. What did you figure out about me, and what did it mean?"

"Admittedly, I just found out the last connection I needed to ensure we're able to close this kidnapping-for-ransom ring down for good. It's only been a few days of stalling because I enjoy spending time with you."

I press my lips together and plant my hands on my hips. The helicopters are in the distance. They're chopping the air at a breakneck pace that echoes in the humid jungle air. The animals chirp and scream as the foreign noise breaks their usual stillness.

"Spending time with me is really vague, Brody."

He looks away and up, clenching his jaw, then turns back to me. The time for talking is dwindling. Neither of us knows what comes next.

"What do you want me to say? That I fell for you? My target? Someone I'm meant to protect at all costs? Am I supposed to just put it all out there so you can destroy me the second you realize I'm a military employee who doesn't have an endless bank account and connections all over the world?"

"That is not me, and you know it," I snarl, aiming a finger at his chest. "I don't care what you do or how much money you have. I care about your heart and the truth." I tear my gaze from his. "And right now, it sounds like I only have your heart, seeing as we don't have time for the truth. Where should we go?"

Brody picks me up with one arm, and he slams me against the tree forcefully. Then he lifts me. My cap falls off from the force, but he catches it with his free hand smoothly and slips it backward on his head.

*Shit.* My stomach flips and flutters.

"Now that that's out of my way," he growls against my ear. Without any care for the fact that we're in danger, Collin and Turner are watching, or the helicopters chopping the air, he presses his lips against mine.

Brody's lips feel like a drug. Even though I have nothing to compare it to because I don't partake in party drugs like most of my friends, I know addiction when I taste it. His tongue slips into mine, and I swear I feel his pulse, his desire, the chemistry buzzing from his body into mine.

Opening my eyes to watch him turns me on even more.

"If we weren't in grave danger with an audience, I would take you right here and now." He grins, leaning in to kiss my collarbone, then my neck.

I exhale loudly. Brody kisses me once more, pulling back to look me in the eyes. They're blue and pure, and for maybe the first time, I don't see a shield. Nothing separates us.

Maybe I don't know the whole story about his past, but in his eyes, I can see forever. As corny as it sounds, and as insane as we must look right now, given the circumstances.

"If this were a movie, we'd be about to die."

Turner yells. "We are about to die," he says, panting loudly.

Brody swivels his gaze.

"Aren't we?" Turner asks now that he has Brody's attention. "Answer her first question and stop thinking with your dick. Where do we go?"

Collin shakes his head. "This could be our only chance. Our last chance. This has to work. We need to get home." The sentence is desperate. A plea. Brody lets me slide down his body and places me on the ground.

"You have both. You know the truth," he whispers, shaking his head. "You've known it all along, Sweet Pea."

I swallow down the ball of emotion in my throat and merely nod.

"Promise me we will make it through this. You'll find me."

He nods sternly once. His face shutters.

"Let's move to the water. The docking area we came to when we first arrived. It's not monitored like the west dock or the beaches. It's where they'll expect me to be once they see the lay of the base from above. That was agreed upon before I set out on this crazy mission. Follow me," Brody says, loud enough for the brothers to hear.

He takes my hand, and we run again. He pulls me, running quicker than my shorter legs can handle.

I listen to my heart pound in my ears and try to focus on his hand in mine. I didn't get enough of this version of Brody, and even though it's insane that he could have gotten us out of here days ago, I agree with the reasoning. The waterfall wouldn't have happened. I wouldn't believe love could grow so strongly if we hadn't had the extra time.

A gunshot ricochets from behind us. I don't turn to look because Brody does. I focus on keeping my footing.

Another shot. Then another.

I can see a matte black helicopter on the sand at the

end of the trail we're on. It's a funnel, though. There's nowhere to hide unless we go inside the jungle on the left or right. Then Brody pulls me to the side, entangling us in the wild brush and thick green plants. He pulls the gun from the waistband of his pants, lunges out of our hiding spot, and shoots. My cap is still on his head, backward, and it takes a full second for the thought to clear and for me to realize this is bad.

"Collin is down," Brody says. "Stay there. It's Ravelo. He's hiding. I need to take him out."

I don't have time to protest. Brody leaves me in a wet bush that probably harbors three types of insects that can kill me and one snake that wants to make me dinner. This is the only alternative to being on the trail.

There are more gunshots what feels like minutes later, but rationally I know only seconds have passed. I'm sweating, my clothes are covered in wet mud, and nothing feels real anymore. It's hard to remember who I used to be and what I found important. It all feels trivial after enduring this.

Brody's teammates, in full camo uniforms with guns and helmets, run past my hiding spot, heading toward the sound of gunfire. One of them notices me. His eyes go round, and he looks like he's terrified of me for a beat or two.

"I'm Commander Orwell. We are here to save you. You are safe."

Seeing other people who have no ill intentions is baffling.

"Okay," I say. "I'm Saylor," I say, extending my hand.

He shakes it, then pulls me out onto the trail. Brody jogs up, and the radios on the other SEALs are making so much noise that I know they must not be worried about being quiet.

Brody looks at me, then his commander. Brody has blood splattered on the left side of his face and neck. There's some on the hat too.

"I'm so glad you're okay," I say, wrapping my hands around Brody's waist.

Commander Orwell looks at Brody oddly. "Good to see you alive, well, and covered in blood, McCoy," he says, then clears his throat when his gaze drops to me. "Why don't you take her to the bird, and we'll get the other two."

I pull away. "Are the brothers okay?"

Brody's face looks grim. "Ravelo shot Collin in the leg, and Turner is not handling it well, but we have a medic with him now." He shakes his head. "It's going to be fine. They'll be okay. Don't worry about them."

He wraps an arm around my shoulder and walks me down the path to the helicopter.

"The kind of fine when women say, 'I'm fine?' Or like, he's actually going to be fine?"

"Too soon to tell," Brody answers honestly, helping me up the rungs on shaky, tired legs.

I sit in one of the seats in the back, and the shock sets in. Brody watches me closely.

"Saylor, you're going home. You should be happy."

How do I tell him my happiness is tempered with the unknown? I don't know how to go back to my normal life after this. I don't know who I am after the spell we spent here. My time on this island changed me. I don't know how to wake up alone or work alone. I don't know how to be without Brody. Without him, what does tomorrow look like? A year from now?

The sweat slips down Brody's face as he looks at me, one eyebrow jutting up when I don't answer whatever question he asks.

"How am I supposed to do life without your mean, sarcastic mind and body, McCoy? Is that your real last name? He just called you that."

A crease forms between his eyes.

"It is. Everything will work out how it's supposed to work out," he says. "Don't worry yourself with that. Focus on the fact you're leaving, and you'll be reunited with your parents in Europe soon."

"Where will you go?" I ask, hearing the hysteria in my voice. How far I've fallen to become this kind of girl. The clingy type.

He lifts one shoulder up and down quickly.

"Back home, I think. Sag Harbor to see my parents, my brother, and dog, and then back to work."

"That's it?" I ask, feeling my breaths come faster. "What about the details?"

Brody's face changes, and he turns away to look out the door at the mob of SEALs swarming the beach. He looks back at me.

"I care about the details," he replies. "I care. Maybe I haven't for a long time, but I do now." Brody's jaw works as he thinks. "Tell you what. You go back to your life and settle back in. If you still feel the same way about me after some space and distance, here's my number."

Shaking his head, he grabs for a pen and rips a piece of paper off the corner of a paper map. He jots down his number and gives it to me, crunched up. His hand lingers inside mine.

"I want this to work, but this is my life." He waves a hand next to him. "You are in shock, and this is far from your normal."

"This isn't your normal. Come on," I argue.

He widens his eyes. "It is, though. This or something like it."

He takes a bottle of water from a cooler between the cockpit seats and hands me it. I open it, marveling at it for a second before twisting off the cap and guzzling it down.

I notice he doesn't drink one. He's worried about me.

A SEAL pops his head in.

"Mark," Brody chirps, grinning. "I didn't die," Brody proclaims. "Ta-da, motherfucker!"

Mark looks at me, then back at his friend, a half smirk playing on his lips.

"I don't know about that. Commander said otherwise." The grin widens. "A different kind of death?"

"Well, you going to get us out of here then?" Brody asks.

Mark introduces himself to me, slowly, like I'm a child just understanding language. It's then that I realize I am indeed in shock, and they knew it before I did.

"I don't want to leave her. Can you give me the radio, and I'll send a quick debrief and give pertinent details?"

Mark detaches his radio from his chest and thrusts it into Brody's waiting hand.

I watch him closely, as if I'm seeing him for the first time, and in a lot of ways, I am. He speaks into the radio, first introducing himself to whoever is on the other end and then using abbreviations and acronyms for things that I don't understand. Which is a feat.

Not to flatter myself, but I know a little about a lot of things, but watching him, with the dang backward hat, relay information I have no clue how or when he collected, forces me into a realization. He is so much more than I initially gave him credit for.

I'm enamored. I've fallen for this man in all ways.

Even through the shock of everything around me, his face and his voice ground me.

"I love you."

I blurt it out like an absolute psychopath. In front of his teammate. In front of God and country. Not my country either.

Brody stops talking, but he doesn't look at me. His neck works as he swallows, and beads of sweat drop down his face.

Then he slams his eyes closed as if my words inflict absolute torturous pain.

I realize swiftly, maybe they do.

# CHAPTER TWELVE
## *brody*

WE TOOK the choppers to Maputo, then flew from there to Portugal. There were certain protocols we needed to adhere to before returning to US soil.

I first need to decompress. As a witness and the only SEAL with firsthand information, I'm not included in the aftermath and cleanup. The rest of my Team is on the enemy base, sorting through the remnants of guards and evidence.

I saw Saylor briefly in the lobby of the hotel, but she was with her parents. There is a security detail protecting the Wyndham family because they're here together, which is a large risk. I watched her for a moment or two before exiting out the side door before she could see me.

She isn't mine to protect anymore. The whole thing feels like a dream.

The longing I feel is annoying. I want to kill off the part of me that longs. I mean, what the fuck is that, anyway? It's a useless feeling. It doesn't ever evolve into anything fruitful. I'm in the hotel gym jacking the lame ass steel they have here. I was told I was lucky there was even a bench to begin with. I spent the last few days in here trying to recoup what the island stole from me. That, and eating. Anything to distract. Anything to get her out of my mind.

I'm not a moron. I know a relationship with Saylor in the real world isn't reasonable.

*We live close together*, my mind whispers. *It could work if you tried. The connection is real. She wants you.*

These thoughts float through while sweat drips down my chest. I have on black issued workout shorts that are a little shorter than I'd like, but Mark packed my shit, and somehow this is what I ended up with.

My phone rings, and I startle, with heavy dumbbells in my hand.

I'm not used to noises that don't come from the jungle.

"Fuck," I hiss, hitting the green button.

"Brother," Nolan whines out, then, "McBrode. My main man. The big gun killa."

I cut him off. "Enough. You're making my ears bleed." Clearing my throat, I say, "I talked to you last night. What can you possibly have to talk about now? I'm in the gym trying to gain some semblance of myself back. I could pass for McLan right now, and it's embarrassing."

As kids, people would mix us up constantly. In high school, I took his language arts exam for him, and to this day, no one knows. As adults, I've always had at least twenty more pounds of muscle.

Nolan chuckles, then I hear a woman's voice in the background. It's late at night where he is.

"You'll be back in town next weekend, right?"

A glance at my watch, and some fuzzy math later, I reply, "It's one in the morning at home. Why aren't you sleeping?"

I already know, but I need my damn brother to be honest with me. Honest in a way that he thinks is painful for me.

"Catherine and I are going to the lake house, and we want you to come. If you're ready to see people that soon." He adds the last sentence as a brotherly jab. "Just us. The guys aren't going."

"Wouldn't that be intrusive if it's just you two?" I ask, then decide to polish the edges. "I want to meet her and spend time with you, don't get me wrong, but that sounds a bit romantic?"

What I love most about Nolan is that we can go a long time without speaking or hanging out, and we fall back together as if no time has passed at all. There are not many people who have that.

"Bring friends then," Nolan replies. "It's not romantic at all. We go basically every weekend now. Sometimes friends come, and other times it's just her and me. Mom and Dad came last weekend. I bought a few jet skis to leave out there too."

A pit in my stomach forms when he talks about a life without me in it. "I'll be there. I want to meet her. Is she there now?"

"Yeah, she's been staying at my house." I can hear the smile in his voice. "Guess who loves her?"

"There's no possible way. He hates women."

Nolan laughs, and Catherine joins in. "Grimace is in love with Catherine. He's ready for you to have someone special in your life. She prepped him for you to finally get a girlfriend!"

"I told him to be sweet. I didn't think he had it in him, though," I explain, immediately missing my dog. "You'll bring him to the lake house for me?"

"Of course." Nolan gets quiet. "How was it? Will you

be able to talk about your trip, or will we dance around truths? You know I don't care either way. I'll just prepare everyone ahead of time, so we know limits."

Oh, do I have things to talk about. Things I can tell him for once. This is going to be the most interesting post-deployment debrief yet. How much do I tell him? I'll have to form some sense of how I'll craft the tale before I get back home. It's going to sound even more unrealistic than a normal combat deployment would sound to a civilian. It's going to sound like fiction.

"Brother, I'm fine. This was an easy pump. I told you already. I'm back in record time too. I'll tell you every gritty detail. Catherine too." He stays silent. "No need to prepare anyone. I'm feeling good."

"I thought you sounded different. It's hard to tell without seeing your face, though. Your malcontent doesn't seem to be as sharp. How is it possible that living on a remote island with the enemy for over a month improved your overall disposition? Was it like a Reverse Uno card? I mean, it doesn't make sense."

Saylor's face enters my mind. Blue eyes, ocean deep, with a smile that takes my fucking breath away.

"Yeah, it just wasn't what I expected. I'll tell you everything soon. And Nolan?"

"Yeah?" he replies, eager.

"Tell Grimace he's a fucking traitor, but thank him for doing what I told him."

Nolan laughs, tells me he's petting Grimace, then says, "I miss you."

My throat bobs with a hard swallow, and I clench my fist. *Don't be a pussy, Brody*, say it. *Fucking say what you mean.*

"I miss you too."

Silence. For one beat. Then another.

"I love you, Brody."

"I know," I reply quickly. "But I probably love you more, motherfucker."

He laughs, but his happiness is contagious. "Doubt that."

Another pause, but it isn't awkward.

"I'll see you soon. Kiss the dog for me. Say hi to Catherine for me too."

"You're out of your mind, McBrode. I'll kiss the dog and tell her hi. Call me tomorrow if you take a break from the gym."

The moment I say goodbye and hang up the phone, the gym door swings open. Roger Wyndham walks in, looking behind him and both ways as the door clicks closed behind him.

I'm star-stuck, honestly. Half human, half puddle. I look at the man who people thank for reinventing the wheel, creating technology that changed the world forever. Some people might feel this way about celebrities, but at the end of the day, they don't do anything to deserve it except pretend to be someone they aren't. He's also Saylor's father, and the need to make a good impression weighs on me.

"I'm sorry to burst in here during your workout, son," Roger says as he extends his hand. "I'm Roger Wyndham. I'm Saylor's dad. I wanted to thank you in person. I hope you don't mind me interrupting, but my security knew you were in here, and I wanted to talk to you alone."

Staggering, I take a couple of steps to clasp my hand in his.

"It's no problem at all, sir. I'm honored to meet you. Brody McCoy."

The way he shakes my hand tells me this may be more about Saylor than saying thank you.

"Wyndham Technologies is changing the world. What your company has done is life-altering." I clear my throat when he looks down. "I was just doing my job, sir. Keeping Ms. Wyndham safe and getting her back to you was part of the mission. No thanks needed."

I roll my shoulders, shaking off the nerves. I hesitate, my words caught somewhere between my chest and my throat.

"Saylor is a wonderful woman. You did one heck of a job. She held her own on that base with those men." I wonder if he knows she killed two people. "She really can figure out anything."

His smile is coy. "Not to toot my own horn, but I think she may have gotten that from me." He backpedals. "Don't get me wrong. Her mother, Bianca, is resourceful and wise, but I fear Saylor got her engineering mind from me, which is good and bad, because she also got her free spirit from me. Which is why we're here to begin with."

Roger frowns, but then meets my gaze.

"Saylor told me you're more than a Navy SEAL. More than a friend too. She also used the word wonderful, among others, to describe you as well."

I feel trapped in my own skin. Conversations like this are the antithesis of what I'm good at. Perform under pressure, I remind myself. This isn't any different than a debrief where I lay out the facts and give the truths. Not all the truths, though.

"She told you that, did she?" Real smooth, Brody. "Sir, I don't think either of us expected—" I begin, but he waves me off.

Roger shakes his head. "You don't have to explain anything to me. Your resume is impressive, and because Saylor and I are so close, I trust her judgment." He slips his hands into his pants pockets. "Thank you for taking care of her, and you have my blessing."

It's a vague statement, but what else could he mean, other than that he approves of me dating his daughter? My heart pounds as I rub a thumb over the edge of my jaw.

"Thank you, sir. I...I haven't spoken to her since we've been back here," I say, implying, I'm not sure what, if anything, we have between us.

Mr. Wyndham's phone rings in his pocket. He silences the call.

"She was in some shock, but she's coming around. I'm taking Bianca out to eat right now. The jet lag is hitting us hard. We're going to take most of our security detail, but if you wanted to go visit Saylor, help watch over her, I'd appreciate it."

There is a double entendre in his words. He knows she wants to see me, and he's offering it up as a task he knows I can't refuse. He's just as smart as Saylor, I realize.

"Of course," I reply, swallowing. I hike a thumb over my shoulder. "I'll hit the showers and head her way."

"She's in penthouse two," he says.

I already knew that.

"And Brody," Roger adds, his hand on the door lever.

I cock my head. "Yes, sir?"

"Saylor hasn't had the best luck with dating. There's been a lot of pressure on her from a young age, with standards she never agreed with. I need you to know we don't care about standards or wealth. We care about morals and ethics. It's hard to find *real* in our world. If you can't be real, please let her down gently."

He doesn't wait for me to respond. He leaves, closing the door behind him.

I stand in the gym, hands on my hips, staring at the

wooden door for far longer than is normal. I think about what he said and how many different meanings it could imply while I shower and change clothes.

I opt for a pair of shorts and a T-shirt because I lived in jeans for so long, my legs are chaffed and angry. I'm not sure when I'll willingly put on jeans again.

Raking my fingers through my hair, I realize how long it is. It's out of Navy standard, longer than it should be. I examine my face closely because a mirror still feels like a luxury. I shaved when we landed, but I have a dark blonde five o'clock shadow. I debate shaving before I see Saylor. I decide against it because it will take more time—time that I could be with her.

Sliding into flip-flops, I head up to the penthouse. A guard is standing there when the elevator doors ping open.

"Brody McCoy," I say, hoping this isn't going to be hard. I don't have it in me to deal with hurdles.

Saylor wants to see me. Her dad approves of me. It's almost like this is too good to be true.

The guard, wearing a suit, moves out of my way and nods at the door. "You're expected," he growls. "I'll shut the door behind you, locking you in. The room has been secured, and there are guards on the roof of the building across the street, monitoring from all angles."

His brows knit together. I can tell he didn't want to give me this information. It was forced to be given.

"She's safe here."

Well, I'm fucking glad someone is on the job when I'm not.

I give a short nod. "Thank you. I'll watch her six while I'm here as well."

He closes the door behind me, and I turn to a breeze from an open balcony door. The white curtains billow. It smells like a different version of her. A mix of her real shampoo and her inherent scent. The scent that I know. It's fresh.

A rush of adrenaline hits as my cock hardens in response. I fucking hate that it's immediate. Hate that I feel so strongly, but it's innate. I can't fight my head or my heart when it comes to her.

Saylor is wearing a robe, and her hair is wrapped in a white towel. She's leaning against a doorframe, one leg crossed over the other, watching me.

"I wasn't sure you'd come."

I grin at the same time I sigh out in relief.

"You sent your dad to fetch me. Did you think I wouldn't listen to that man? I'm an asshole, but I'm not stupid," I say, taking a tentative step toward her, then another. "I'm glad you're settled in and safe. How are you feeling?"

"Okay," she replies. "Missing you."

She's still as stone, but her grip on the doorway tightens. It's an immeasurable gesture I only notice because I'm trained in reading body language. She means what she just said, and she didn't want to say it.

"Slightly horrified when I remember what I went through. But I can't regret it because of *you*."

I cross to her, smiling, watching how it melts her just to be in my presence.

"What did you tell your father, Saylor? He implied you told him about us."

I pull the plush white belt of her robe. She jerks closer to me.

"Us in *this* capacity, not the captivity capacity?" I say, looking into her blue eyes, letting it drop to her lips.

Saylor has on makeup. It's the first time I've seen her like this—like she'd appear on the street instead of inside a cage. It's understated and fucking beautiful. Her lashes curled up, giving an even more perfect view of her eyes.

"I told him I wanted you," she says, swallowing hard. "If you'd have me, and if my parents thought it would be acceptable."

That makes my stomach sink. "Acceptable?"

She looks to the side but can't resist looking back at my face.

I pull on the belt until it falls open. I can feel the heat from her shower radiating from her smooth skin.

"The thing with my family that's not like normal families is that my mom has opinions on who I should end up with."

She huffs, licks her lips, and stares at my mouth.

"The good thing about being kidnapped and having you save me is that you earned a Bianca Wyndham pass. She doesn't care who you are or what you do because you saved my life."

Another noisy exhale exits her perfect pout.

"She saw you in the lobby yesterday and decided on the spot that you were acceptable." She grins. "I know how vain and classless this all sounds, which is why I didn't say anything before, but it means something to her, whether it makes sense to the rest of the world or not."

"But I passed the test? What did she like most? My face or my muscles?" I tease, but inside, I'm allowing the shock to roll through.

It's odd. But just because this way of dating doesn't make sense to me, I know that others live differently. My only concern is being *enough* for Saylor.

"I don't think you're like that, just so you know. You wanted me when I was cruel and a simple mechanic, remember?"

Her eyes widen. "I'm nothing like her. My mother

wanted me to get back together with the guy I dated in college, Archie. He cheated on me with multiple people, and she didn't care. Archie passed the test too. Don't flatter yourself too much. I think I'm merely being granted a hall pass because I could have died."

She takes off the towel on her head and drapes it over a chair.

I inhale the sweet, familiar scent of her hair.

"Hall pass. Is that what I am to you?" I ask, reaching between her legs.

She's soaking wet. Saylor squeezes her thighs together, trying to keep me from seeing the evidence. "You just want to fuck me?"

At the word fuck, she spreads her legs and lets my hand slide between them fully. I push the robe off her shoulders and back her into the room behind her.

It's a living room, with several chairs, a sofa, and a small chaise. The bedroom is too far. There is another set of French doors in here that are open, and I notice the building across the street. They're about to get a show if they're watching this room.

A flush creeps up Saylor's neck. She grabs the hem of my shirt and lifts it over my head. I take off my shorts. I hiss a sigh of pleasure when she wraps her hand around my shaft.

"No," she replies, shaking her head. "I want you to make love to me."

Leaning down, I press my lips against hers. "I love the taste of you. I want to taste you everywhere," I breathe against her lips.

I slide a finger inside her and crook it toward me, rubbing her G-spot.

It's odd having her like this—in the comforts of civilization instead of a waterfall. It feels brand new.

Saylor lies down on the chaise and teases her legs open.

"Taste me everywhere," she says, eyes on mine, smile deepening, slow and knowing.

Fuck. She's perfect. Don't fuck this up, I tell myself. You can't. You won't recover this time. You won't.

The negative self-talk only lasts a couple of seconds until I settle my face between her legs and lick her wet slit up and down. I savor the tang on my tongue and growl in delight.

Saylor makes little mewling noises, her knees wide, giving me full access. She's smooth from a fresh shave, and I try my best not to rub my scruffy face against her, but she's pulling my head to her, holding me.

I let my tongue fuck her clit, up and down while sliding one thick finger inside her tight slit to continue rubbing her G-spot. Saylor arches her back off the cream-colored chaise, and I follow her pussy up to keep my pace steady. She cries out, cradling my face, and her pussy grips my finger in waves.

"Come for me," I say, pressing my finger against her warm core harder.

She comes, screaming, gripping the sides of the chair with freshly painted nails that look like claws, fighting to hold the pleasure longer.

A sheen of sweat on her body creates more images of perfection. Like a painting in a museum, painted only for me. She's breathless from her orgasm, looking at me like I'm the only person on earth. The love is visceral and breathtaking.

"You going to come for me now?" she asks, licking her lips, gaze searing into my fucking soul.

She reaches between her legs and slides her fingers into the slippery wake I created.

"I'm wet for you. I'm only wet for you."

I shake my head as I watch. "I don't know what I did to deserve this, but there's nothing I've ever wanted more."

"I don't think we did anything to deserve this. I think we were always meant to find each other. This was always going to happen between us, one way or another." She slides one finger inside herself and moans. "How do you want me? Tell me what you've dreamed about."

My dick jerks at mere words. It might explode if I don't claim her soon.

"I've dreamed about being inside you in every which way you can think up, and even a few that are physically impossible while we're affected by gravity."

She pulls her pussy open with two fingers on each hand to give me a perfect view.

"Sounds like we need to find a way to get into space, then."

My hands find her hips before I realize I've moved. I pull her onto my dick slowly, kneeling on the chaise while her shoulder blades stay down on the cushion.

"Yes, Brody. Yes," she says, as I pull her tight pussy onto my dick.

She's so light, I can fuck her with my arms, without even thrusting at all. I pull her off and on, watching my cock sink into her and exit, glistening with her wetness. Saylor's arms are above her head, her hands holding on to the arm of the chaise, and her eyes are closed.

"I want this forever," she says, drawing a sharp breath.

My nostrils flare as my excitement takes over the moment. She's mine in all ways when I'm fucking her. When I'm making love to her. She belongs to me and no one else. Yanking her onto me, I watch her face wilt with need—and in satisfaction.

"I hate to be a pessimist right now, but forever won't be enough."

She smiles, a wistful look crossing her features. "Sit down. I want to ride you."

Delicately, I sit, my back against the chair while keeping her on me. She straddles me, her knees next to my legs. This angle gives me the perfect grip on her tits and access to her mouth. Every time she slips down, she pauses to kiss me, tongue tangled with mine, her hands in my hair.

Erotic torture is the perfect description. I feel hot and cold from the breeze at the same time. It's heaven and hell twisting together. She picks up the pace, her breathing speeding as I twirl her nipples between my fingers. Her chest is red, and she leans to one side, burying her face in my neck as her hips rock up and down in my new rhythmic obsession.

Saylor licks a trail from my neck up to my ear and back again, creating a trill of goosebumps down my spine. I grab her face.

"I want to look in your eyes when I come deep inside you," I snarl.

Her lashes flutter open, and the sight of her ocean eyes is all it takes to bring me to the edge and tip over. I skirt my hands down her sides to hold her hips still as my hot load seeps into her womb. She circles her hips, trying to get me deeper as my cock throbs against her soft walls.

The orgasm is so powerful it's almost painful as I come down from it, kissing her with eyes open, holding her chin with two fingers.

"Good girl," I chide. "I like it when you listen to me."

She circles her hips one more time slowly and stirs.

"I like it when you don't too."

Our teeth click as our kiss turns to big smiles.

"I do both equally as well," she says, biting my lower lip, then letting it pop back into place.

She licks my lips, tracing them with the tip of her tongue.

"If you can stay hard, I'm going to come again."

She slides up and down, my come dripping down my balls.

I grin again, raising one brow. "I'll be hard for twenty-four hours if it means you're coming on my dick," I reply, fucking her slowly as she kisses me while rubbing her clit against me.

Her hands rest sweetly on my cheeks, and it's intimate and personal and everything I never thought I'd have in my life. Someone so important that the world as I currently knew it ceases to exist. It's just about her and her happiness.

Saylor moves her hands to my shoulders, and her chest reddens as she moves closer to her orgasm, and I get to watch in awe as she takes exactly what she needs from me.

Letting her guide the pace is hard when all I want to do is slam into her like a barbarian. I held myself back for too long in those early weeks on the enemy base in Madagascar. Now that she's mine, there are so many things I want to do to her.

Saylor whispers, head hanging, "I'm coming again."

I don't dare move. She rides me, tilting her head back to the ceiling while hot whimpers gasp from her throat. Her pussy grips me, edging me closer to another fucking orgasm. When she slides herself down to sit and kisses me passionately, I'm renewed.

My heart catches and trips when she opens her eyes. "I love you," I say.

"I know," she replies, smiling against my mouth. "That was a bold exclamation for you."

In mock outrage, I press my lips together.

"I suppose I deserve the suspense, but I wouldn't have said it if I wasn't sure my dick just made you come twice. You must at least love *that*."

She sighs, and it's adorable and hot. Only she can accomplish that feat.

"I do love that," she whines, reaching between us to feel the base of my wet shaft. "And I do love you," she amends. "More than I thought was humanly possible."

My heart rate ratchets up, and I touch her face like she may disappear. I've memorized the way her face looks in every different scenario. When she's mad or sad, happy, or disgusted. But the way she looks right now is my favorite. Doubt creeps in.

"You think we can do this? Make this work back home?"

"One thousand percent," she whispers. "No question. That's how sure I am of you." Saylor shakes her head, her nose brushing mine as she goes. "We'll figure out the logistics. I'll move to where you live if I have to. You want to make this work as much as me, right?"

I find myself smiling like a damn lunatic.

"I do. I will, unfortunately, do whatever it takes."

"Why unfortunately?" Saylor asks, cocking her head to the side, hair falling into her face.

Brushing the hair away with one hand, unhurried, I hold her gaze.

"Because now I have this to lose, and it's terrifying to be willing to do whatever it takes to keep you."

I'd kill for her. Lie for her. Die for her. Send myself to hell if she asked me to disappear. Find a way to return to her if she wanted me back.

"You're looking at it wrong. *Fortunately,* we found each other and will do whatever it takes to be together."

ALL THE WAY UNDER

I swallow down the fear because every time she talks, my dick moves inside her.

"Agreed. Even if your positivity is alarming my sensibilities in all ways." I stand up, keeping her legs wrapped around my waist. "Saylor."

Her name is a drug. She's all I think about. It's baffling and scary.

"You say my name like you like it. You made fun of it, remember?"

I let her slide off my dick and down my body so she can stand behind a chair. I turn her around, guiding her hair over one shoulder to get it out of my way.

"I made fun of a lot of things before I knew you, and now you're the only weakness I'll admit to, but don't flatter yourself too much," I whisper, the last part, giving her words back. "It's only the biggest deal there ever was for me."

Saylor presses her lips together to contain a laugh, looking over her shoulder. Letting my hands run over her shoulder blades and down to the small of her back, I push her forward with my other palm, so she's bent over the chair. She spreads her legs, and I slide into her slippery cunt. Sighing, I tip my head back and let myself feel it *all*.

I'm so far under, I don't know how to exist here. How do I keep myself from drowning?

"PLEASE, the café is right around the corner. The security detail can be right around the corner if they need to." I clasp my hands in front of my chest, begging. "Mother, we're leaving tomorrow. I just want to have one real date with Brody in Portugal. We won't stay long. You know he'll keep me safe. It's a café, not a prison."

I must admit, it makes sense why my parents have so much trepidation in allowing me freedom. I got myself kidnapped, for god's sake.

"Saylor," she drawls. "We aren't far enough away from them for that much freedom. Why don't you have a date at the restaurant at the hotel? Better yet, room service, darling. I don't think you understand how dreadful it was for me while you were being held hostage."

Staring, unblinking, I wait for her to hear the hypocrisy in what she just said, but I don't hold my breath.

Dad butts in. "What your mother means is that this has been a lot. You're our baby, Saylor. You can go on as many dates as you want when we're back in the States. It's not safe here. For any of us."

I stamp a foot, irritated with my mother's attitude already and that they're making me feel like a child.

"I'm an adult. I can go if I want," I say, placing one hand on my hip.

"Just like you took a sail around the world like you wanted? Just like you got yourself captured and needed special forces to get you out? Did you want that? Just like that, Saylor?" My mother's words are laced with a promise to make my life miserable if I don't obey, but her voice shakes as she speaks, so it gives me pause.

I toss up my hands.

"This is a totally reasonable request. Food at a café," I huff. "Will I need security back home? Are you going to make these guys live in my house? Work out on the Pilates reformer next to me in class? The grocery store?"

Dad shakes his head, and I can tell he feels bad.

"It's a product of who you are. You've been through a lot. It's going to get worse before it gets better, Saylor. The news outlets have been following this story since you were captured. Think of how intriguing this whole thing looks to others. The phone calls for information have been incessant. You're going to have to talk to the media, and then your face will be all over the internet. Unhinged people will come out of the woodwork. Our friends will be asked if they know anything. Whether you want to admit it or not, this does affect all of us. We like Brody. We want you to continue that relationship. It's just going to have to be done in a more secretive way."

What he's trying to convey hits me square in the chest.

Dad goes on. "He must keep his anonymity for his career. What do you think will happen if they link Brody to the SEAL Teams? If the public finds out he's the one who saved you? And you're now in a relationship with him."

Dad's face looks weathered. It's my fault. The wrinkles around his blue eyes usually spark joy, but now they look haunted.

My mom sips a martini, and her cream-colored caftan billows as she exits onto one of the balconies in their penthouse. She has a stack of romance books on the table out there. Exhaling deeply, the gravity of the situation I'm in hits.

"They would never leave us alone if they found out. His life would be in jeopardy if they connect him with me."

Dad shakes his head. "Just at first. You know how these things go. Once some time has passed, no one will care about you and your situation, but at first, the spotlight is going to be on you."

I sit down in a chair and look at my watch. I have to meet Brody in his room in thirty minutes.

"I guess I knew I'd have to talk about the experience, but I didn't think it all the way through and what it would mean for you guys and Brody." I pinch the bridge of my nose. "I'm sorry, Dad. I'm sorry for getting us into the situation and that it's affecting you after."

A tear catches in the corner of my eye.

"If I could go back in time and never set sail, I wouldn't."

He sits on the arm of the chair, wrapping an arm around me.

"Yes, you would," he whispers gently. "You'd have to go to meet him."

We both sit in silence, him knowing me so well that my emotions overwhelm me.

"I'm sorry, still," I reply, lip trembling.

I can't keep it in. It was a lot, knowing my decisions affected others, but knowing my decisions are going to continue to affect those I love and care about is a whole different kind of pain.

"I won't do anything like this again. I might even be done with sailing. It proved I wasn't good enough."

"You stop that talk right now. Not only are you good enough, I think you should try again. Not soon, but you can do it. You can't control some things, but all the things you could control were handled perfectly."

When I told him I shot two men, his face iced over. He said we shouldn't tell Mom. Or anyone else, for that matter. I wonder if that's what he's referring to now.

Should I have just allowed myself to be taken easily? Without putting up a fight?

Now that my mind is clear, the whole kidnapping and my time in captivity feel like it was fabricated.

I look at Dad as a tear rolls down his face. I capture it with my finger.

"Stop, Dad. I do need to grow up. Mom is right. You stopped sailing."

"And it broke my heart. When you picked it up, it made me feel whole again. We can sail together. You won't give it up."

He nods, his chin on my head.

"We don't care what we must go through when we go home. We're just relieved you're okay, Saylor. I don't care about the noise."

He pauses.

"No one knows we're in Lisbon right now. Go ahead and go to the café around the corner. Be watchful. Take the full security detail. This is as much privacy as you're going to have for a while," he explains, thinking out loud. "When we get home, you won't be able to go out. Go," he commands, kissing the top of my head. "Let me know when you get back. I'll tell security."

Dad looks over his shoulder at the balcony.

"And your mom."

"We will go incognito, and I promise to be safe. Thank you, Dad. I'm sorry again."

"Stop apologizing, Saylor Jean. Go live your life."

I flee their hotel suite before he changes his mind, and before he tells my mother.

Three guards flank me as I take the elevator down to Brody's room. He's in the hallway waiting for me when the elevator doors slide open.

"There you are. I didn't think we were going to get out of this hotel, but he said we could go."

"With security?" Brody asks, raising one brow, peering behind me.

I nod. "I know, I know. I'm sorry. They'll stay far enough away." Exhaling in relief at the sight of him, I remember my promise.

"You washed the Yankees cap, right? Put it on, and a pair of sunglasses. I promised we would go in disguise."

He stifles a laugh, blue eyes sparkling with mirth. "I'm six foot four and two hundred thirty pounds, baby. It's not that easy to disguise me."

"Maybe I just want you to wear the hat, then," I counter. "Can you do it for me?"

Laughing, he bites his bottom lip, causing my stomach to drop and shimmy. He's so gorgeous. I still have a hard time believing he's mine.

"I'd do a lot of things for you," Brody says, scanning his key card to go into his room. I follow him in.

He has a nice room, not a penthouse, but it has a kitchen and a living room area. It looks like he's cooked.

"You're allowed to leave here? Did you go to the grocery store? I'm so jealous."

"We'll go to the grocery store together when we get back," Brody says.

The security guards allow us to be in his room alone, thank God. I wonder how that conversation with my father went and cringe.

He grabs the hat, which is sitting on the table, and a pair of Ray-Bans from the console table by the door. Then he kisses me long and hard.

"We'll do a lot of things when we get back."

My stomach goes from the floating in-love sensation to iron lead.

"There is a lot of sensation around my kidnapping and rescue. We won't be allowed to be seen together for a while. While the thought of picking out produce with you is sensuous," I smile, teasing him. "We're going to have to lie low back home."

Brody pushes his lips to the side, thinking about what I said.

"My brother sent me a few news articles. You are a Wyndham, so it makes sense. I'm stealthy when it comes to sneaking around. In the dark is my specialty. I have leave when I get back to the US. I haven't taken leave in a long time, so I'll have time to come up with plans to lie low with you."

Excitement replaces my dread. "You really don't care?"

"No, it's for your safety and mine. Commander would probably make me take leave if I didn't request it myself. When I said I'll do whatever it takes, did you think so little of my willpower that a little press was going to deter me from having you any chance I can?"

He snakes a hand around my waist, and the heat from

his skin soaks through my button-up blouse. Immediate attraction and need are what happens next. Pulling me to his body, he leans down and teases his lips against mine. An almost kiss.

"Whatever it takes," he says, licking his lips. "You are trouble," he growls. "I can't control myself when we're alone."

Lacing my fingers around his neck, I pull him in for a kiss, twining my tongue with his, tasting him, and relishing in the connection I crave whenever I'm not next to him.

"Control yourself. We have a date to go on, and we don't have a lot of time. When we get back here, I have a few things we need to try out."

The moment I tell him my plans for later, he shushes me with a head tilt and a wink.

"You say it now, and we won't make it to the café."

We exit his hotel room, him in a backward hat and a pair of sunglasses, me in one of his oversized black hoodies and a camouflage beanie he found in his tactical gear. We look ridiculous, and somehow it makes sense.

Brody doesn't hold my hand while we stroll down the street because he's on alert. It's hot to watch him protect me, but also disheartening because what if this is how it will always be? Never in my life have I wished not to be a Wyndham more.

Part of my security detail is wearing plain clothes a few feet behind us, and a few went ahead to scope out the café and the surrounding buildings before we get there. I can't tell if Brody is annoyed by the hired help or thankful for the extra sets of eyes.

I pull my beanie down a little further when we get to a stoplight because there's a group of people waiting. I slam the button to cross the road. Taxis fly by, and the scent of sweet pastries fills my nose.

Brody smiles down at me before letting his gaze sweep again. It's easy to play pretend when he looks at me like that. Like this is a normal date, without any hang-ups or qualifiers. Like I wasn't just held captive with him. He takes my hand when it's time to cross, and the buzz from his touch makes me blush.

It's a brisk walk, and his hand wraps tightly around mine until we're safely ensconced in the café. It's empty. I groan when I see security in the back.

"They bought out the café," I deadpan. "So much for a normal date."

"Why are you so hung up on being normal when you're anything but?" He pulls out a chair and extends his hand for me to sit.

The guard passes by our table and locks the front door.

"Your father's orders, ma'am," he says, obviously embarrassed, but duty-bound. I frown.

"Saylor," Brody chides. "This is safer. We aren't as far from Madagascar as you think. I'm not upset about a locked door and a couple of suits. You shouldn't be either. Your dad loves you."

He sits down and takes my hands in his.

"Imagine your child in this situation. What would you do? Especially if you have the means to *buy* peace of mind."

His eyes soften, and I lose myself in the moment, imagining having kids with him. Little blue-eyed babies toddling on the beach, fat bare feet kicking up water as they chase crabs.

Tears prick my eyes, and I hope he doesn't notice.

How would I explain how I've skipped several steps in my mind by merely looking into his eyes?

"I'd do the same," I finally reply. "It feels like a lot, and I'm afraid," I whisper.

The waitress hands us menus with shaking hands, and I feel for her, I do. But I know she's safe even if she's scared.

"Thank you," I say, meeting her eyes, sliding the beanie off my head and onto my lap.

Her brown eyes widen further as she looks at my face. Recognition. Shit. I clear my throat, and she scurries back to the kitchen.

"What are you afraid of?" Brody asks, also noticing the interaction.

"Well, for starters, nothing being the way it was before. I'm scared all the attention is going to scare you away. Your identity needs to stay under wraps for your own safety. What if I'm the one who spoils that? What if I get you killed for no reason other than being linked to you?"

He picks up the menu, shaking his head.

"You're spiraling. It's not that serious. We should enjoy our date. I'm going to have the pasta. What looks good to you?"

I stare at him, unflinching, then hit him with a slow blink.

"You really aren't bothered by the what-ifs?"

"Hell no. I'm ordering you not to be bothered by them either." He clenches his jaw.

I give him a mock salute with two fingers on my forehead.

"Yes, sir. Look at you with your clenched jaw. Am I annoying you?"

We're interrupted by the waitress asking what we'd

like to drink and if we're ready to order. I tell her what I want, literally the first thing on the menu—some sandwich because I didn't have time to look—and a bottle of sparkling water. Brody orders next, in Portuguese too, as he scans the window to make sure the coast is clear.

"I'm not annoyed," he muses. "I'm merely a curmudgeon. You know this already. I don't want you to worry about what might happen or will happen. Hell, I don't want you to worry at all, but I've dealt with some pretty heavy shit in my lifetime. Not just deployments where my brothers have died or I have narrowly escaped impossible situations, either. Normal stuff when I'm home. Being lonely or not knowing how to express myself without being an asshole."

I smirk.

"Are you sure you know how to do that last one?" I tease. "So you're saying dealing with a bit of notoriety isn't going to deter you from spending time with the kidnapped Wyndham girl?"

Brody presses his lips together and out.

"Abso-fucking-lutely not. You're underestimating my tolerance for bullshit and semantics. I'm in the Navy, remember? It's one of the most cumbersome businesses on planet Earth. I jump through hoops for that. I will jump through hoops for you. Now, will you promise me the same courtesy? You'll stick around when I'm angry, moody, or otherwise mean because you know it comes from a good place?"

"Brody, I saw through that charade right up front. You know that."

Our drinks come, and he drinks his light beer, and I have a mouthful of my water. After a long sip, he pulls the mug from his face, leaving a white foam mustache.

"Do you want to come with me to my brother's lake

house in Montauk this weekend? Nolan and his girl-friend, Catherine, will be there. There are jet skis and a boat."

Brody looks out the window again.

"It's a big house, so your security detail will have space if that is a condition for you leaving your house." He pauses, taking a sip of beer. "Probably not as big as the houses you're used to, but I think it's nice. I don't get out there nearly enough. I'm on a mission to change that."

The way in which he's immediately enmeshing me into his realm and life feels wonderful. I don't have to hide in his world. He must hide in mine. It gives me the best idea.

"Yes. I'm sure it's beautiful, and I don't care at all how big or nice it is. I love that you want to include me already. Thank you."

Tears threaten, but they're happy.

"I can't wait to meet them. I don't know if I'll have to bring security if you're there. Maybe one guy, maybe two. I'll talk to my parents as soon as we get back." I clear my throat. "My parents have a house there too. My sister Bronwyn and her husband will be staying there this weekend."

*Are we doing this?*

"Maybe they can come, swing by? You'll love my sister," I explain, using my hands to talk. Thinking about a meeting between them causes a riot of emotions. Good ones.

"Is she like your mom?" Brody asks.

I pull a face. "Nothing like my mother. But she's also not like my dad either. Bronwyn and her husband are into the art scene, but mostly it's all her charities that keep her busy. You and she have similar charm. The sarcastic wit layered with a pugnacious undertone."

"Fabulous. I can't wait." He smirks, and I believe him. He is excited to meet her. "Are you okay after everything that happened? I'm not good at talking about feelings, but I wanted to ask because you killed two men and endured being caged. That's something I can get over, but I was wondering if you're okay."

"It's kind of sweet when you force yourself to be this thoughtful," I say.

He brushes off his shoulders.

"I had a video call with my mom's psychiatrist the day after I got to Lisbon. I feel relatively okay about the whole thing. The doctor called it psychological robustness. Catchy right? Probably inherited it from Bianca." I snort-laugh. "Thanks, Mom."

Our food arrives, and thankfully, the waitress looks calmer as she asks if we need anything else.

"All joking aside, I might have the mental toughness of a Navy SEAL. What do you think about that?"

"I'd say I met my match, then. Because if you're going to be with me, you're going to need mental toughness."

Brody eats his pasta at hyper speed. He pauses when he asks for another beer.

Soft music bounces off the old stone walls, giving the illusion of a real date, where doors don't have to be locked.

"I talked to my friend, Mark, this morning, and he said Collin and Turner are on their way back to the US. They'll beat us back. No one knows they were rescued because your last name overshadows everything else, but it's a good thing. They'll have peace while they pick up the pieces of their life."

At the mention of the brothers, my heart rate picks up immediately. Maybe I'm not as healed as I thought. They remind me of the guards, and the guards remind me that Ravelo was never found.

"Did they find Rav yet?" I whisper.

Brody looks at me, stoic, handsome, and uneasy.

"They have not, but I'm not going to be able to talk to you about this stuff for much longer. You shouldn't worry about him for another second. He has a flag on his passport. He can't travel without being found, nor will he have connections back home. We're not going to stop looking for him."

"I read on the news that the main ringleaders were captured, along with all the other guards. Do you think another kidnap ring will just pop up on the same base?"

The waitress drops off his beer and another water. I take the beer from the table and drink half while Brody looks on, grinning.

"They can't. We took over the base. No one will have to go through what you did there again." Brody clears his throat. "I don't think we talked about this. Do you like beer?"

"Love it. Won a drinking contest sophomore year in college. I can open my throat and let it slip down. I was sick for the next forty-eight hours, so I won't do it again, but it was worth the pain to be able to see Bianca's face when I showed her the winning certificate. I don't drink often, but this feels like an occasion." I raise the stein, and he clinks with my water glass. "To surviving and thriving."

We spend a couple of hours chatting in Café do Acaso. *Chance Café*. We talk about everything and nothing. Forever, and right now. It's effortless banter, filled with full-chested promises that I believe.

It's not like before, like with Archie, when he would talk about his future without mentioning me at all. Brody includes *we* and *us* speak when he mentions anything, and

I can tell it comes naturally. He's not even trying to impress me or allude in any way. He asks me about work and my projects because that's something we didn't talk about much in captivity. He knows so much about my work that he's interested in the details that would bore most.

He kisses me passionately, fully making me wet in public, in front of the large bay window. Then we have security unlock the door and walk back to the hotel.

This will go down as the most perfect date of all time. Nothing bad happened, even though we were on alert.

No enemy was lying in wait.

Being next to Brody feels like it's where I was always meant to be. It feels too good to be true. When I land back in the States, I'm terrified this will all be a dream bubble popped with the pinpoint needle of cruel reality.

"Do you have brothers, Brody?" Mom asks.

We're sitting at a dining table in the hotel restaurant. I told Brody not to agree to dinner when Bianca asked, but he did. He said nothing blows his skirt up like a challenge. Now he's privy, with a front row view, to Bianca Wyndham's shit show.

Brody smiles at her question, knowing where my mom is going. *Do you have any single siblings because you're attractive?*

"I have a twin brother, ma'am. Older by thirty-seven minutes. His name is Nolan."

I haven't told them much about his family life yet.

Mom sips from the water glass, puckers her lips, then

announces, "Is this water from the tap? I can taste the public infrastructure."

She hails a waiter and asks for Pellegrino.

Then, to Brody, she says, "Nolan is a lucky man to share genes with you. Tell us more about your home life. We know what you do for work. Save reckless women and protect our sovereign country. What about your free time?"

Brody can't help but smile at her antics, even though I'm dying inside.

My former boyfriends have all been like her. In the company of Bianca's friends and family, this is normal behavior. In front of Brody? This? This right here is true zoo animal behavior, I think.

"She wasn't reckless," he defends me. "I know reckless when I see it."

His smile is coy and dimpled.

"Those pirates just needed to be put in line, so what happened to Saylor never happens to anyone else." Brody clears his throat.

He's uncomfortable speaking about himself.

"My family is close, so I spend a lot of time with them, but the truth is I work a lot, so my hobbies are slim. I have a dog, and I volunteer at my local dog shelter here and there. I like to blend tea in my free time."

I nearly choke on my Aperol Spritz.

"Blend tea?" I ask, eyes wide.

"Caffeine messes with cortisol, Saylor. Don't you know that?" Brody claps back, pressing his lips together. "I'm going to stop in the tea shop a few blocks over before I fly home. They have a chamomile that's supposed to be unlike any of the other ones I've tried."

"I...I...You keep surprising me," I drawl, a smile on my

face. "I like tea. Wouldn't know the first thing about blending it, though."

I didn't know blending tea was a hobby. Does anyone know that blending tea is a hobby?

"Oh, I look forward to an afternoon tea daily," Mom says. "That's such an interesting hobby. You will have to make me a blend. Something to unwind and relax. The stress of life really gets to me some days."

My dad rubs my mother's back, trying to comfort her at the word *stress*, but we all know there is nothing resembling actual stress in her life.

The lines creasing my dad's forehead worry me. He seems to have a lot on his mind that he's not talking about. He carries the burden for the family, so perhaps it's still just the mess I got myself in, and the impending circus when we touch down on US soil.

"I'd be happy to do so, ma'am. I'll get to it right when we get home. I'm taking some time off when I return," Brody replies. "The act itself is relaxing. What about you? What do you like to do to unwind?"

"I love reading. I would read a million books a day if it were humanly possible. Roger bought me a book on vacation when we were in our early twenties to pass the time at the beach, and it hooked me forever."

Mom looks at Dad and smiles fondly. The only true gestures from my mom are the ones that involve my dad.

To my dad, she says, "Remember that book, darling? The black and gold cover with the grenade on it?"

My father grins in response.

"I'd have a book at the table right now if it were socially acceptable. No offense to you, of course."

Mom does her best not to make him feel bad, but her best isn't much.

Brody shakes his head, laying a hand on my thigh. "None taken."

We order as soon as I can flag our waiter. I want to get dinner over with and spend the rest of the night with Brody. I plan to eat fast and ditch my parents as soon as we can, but the second I close my menu, the earsplitting sound of shattering glass echoes the expansive room.

The next popping sound confirms what I initially thought. Bullets.

The hotel is an old European structure. It seems to be a castle, with stone walls and stained-glass windows throughout. The restaurant is in the front, where the main street lies, so it's easy to see the dining patrons from the window.

More bullets come whizzing so near that the air pattern changes next to my face. Brody is in action the next moment, tipping our rectangular table over, sending Mom's twenty-euro bottle of sparkling water crashing to the marble floor. Other guests run from the room through a side door.

The scent of delicious food hangs in the air as I watch my dad and Brody eye each other in a knowing way, crouched behind the table. It's hard to grasp what's happening as everything around us seems to move in slow motion. Our security guards flank the walls, guns drawn and gaze trained where the threat looms.

"This table isn't doing anything," I hiss at my mom, who is having a full-on panic attack, mouth open, heavy breathing like some sort of dragon on acid.

Brody grabs my arm and pulls me over to him on the right side of the table.

"We're moving to that stone wall," he says, jutting his chin toward where one of the guards is firing a small pistol.

"That door," he adds, speaking louder because my mother is screaming like an angry goat, while my dad tries to calm her. We're the only ones left in here.

"Why didn't we run instead of hiding behind a wooden table?" I scream, covering my ears when more shots ring out. "I understand," I add, because I don't want to be cumbersome. "Tell me when."

*Bianca is cumbersome,* and there's no stopping her.

"This is why I said they should have flown us to Capri!" Mom screeches. "No one ever gets killed in Capri. They just get divorced quietly!"

Her breathing sounds like a labored peacock.

"This wine was aggressively local. I knew we should have gone to a different restaurant."

My dad has abandoned checking on our surroundings or communicating with Brody because he's worried about my mother. She is in an agitated state.

"We're going to have to make a run for it, darling," Dad explains as I watch on, praying she gets her shit together before whoever is shooting into this room like a funnel reloads their weapons.

"Over there," he says, slowly, pointing with a finger like he's trying to show a toddler something magical. "Then we'll move along the wall until we're in the kitchen. There's a door leading to the outside in the kitchen."

How does he know that? Why did he have this place mapped out? Was he expecting this ambush?

"We have to run, though."

"Run?" Bianca yowls. "I can't run anywhere. I'm wearing Zanotti python skin heels and Wyndham self-respect, for god's sake, Roger. Who do you think I am?"

Dad looks at me, furrows his brow in frustration, then grabs Mom under the arm and hoists her over his shoulder. I grab Brody's hand, and we run, in my sensible shoes, across the glass-littered marble toward the guards who are covering us as we run.

My mom is hysterical by the time my dad allows her to stand on her own two feet in the kitchen. The chef is terrified, and the wait staff is huddled in a corner, sobbing.

"Is everyone okay?" Brody asks, eyeing me like he's an x-ray machine.

"I'm fine," I assure him. "Fine in a way one can be after being shot at while fine dining."

Mom is staring at the waitstaff, targeting her mire and hysteria on to someone else other than Dad.

"Just breathe. Just breathe through it," she chides, trying to calm them down. "That's what I did when I had my second rhinoplasty."

"Darling, I don't think that's the same thing," Dad says, waving at the waiters in apology.

One is on the phone with the police, and Dad directs them on what to say. Then to us, he says, "We need to get somewhere safe. We're sitting ducks in a hotel room. The police are on the way now. This will all be taken care of soon."

"The guards are in the dining room and outside the kitchen door," Brody chimes in. "They are covering. We're safe here."

Brody scans the expanse of the industrial kitchen.

"Saylor, stay with your parents. I'm going to do a sweep."

"Brody," my father says, placing a palm on the center of his chest, then lowering it a moment later, on better thought. "Guys," he addresses us, peeking around the wall that is my man. "This is my fault."

Mom cries. "What do you mean?" she replies, in between sniffles and shock.

It took her a while to lose her humor and understand the gravity of the situation we are in, but she arrived eventually.

"What is going on, Roger?" She wipes her nose.

I don't speak. Brody doesn't speak. You can hear a pin drop.

My dad looks down at the floor, then crouches, putting his hands on his head.

"Jennings Vansickle has hired someone to kill me," he says.

I hear him clearly, even though his words are muffled. Jennings is an attorney at the firm my dad has a close relationship with. While he's not my dad's attorney outright, he's always wanted in on Wyndham's business deals, but my dad hasn't allowed it, seeing through him as corrupt and money-hungry. He has been after Dad for as long as I can remember. Friendly competition turned sour sometime in the last two decades, but kill? That's crazy talk.

Shaking my head, I say, "No, Dad. Jennings isn't capable of that. Why would you say that?"

"The laws are different in other countries. He's hired someone local to Portugal who is going to disappear when the deed is done—if the deed gets done—and there's no trace tying this back to him, but security figured it out quickly. This has been going on since you left, Saylor. This has nothing to do with you or Brody. There was a deal that I cut him out of. I changed law firms while you were being held hostage because we couldn't agree on how your release and ransom money should be dealt with as a last straw. Jennings was irate at the termination meeting. He took the situation personally. The threats began rolling in after that, each one more menacing than the last. They should have known to cross me when it had to do with family." He looks at me. "When it had to do with *my* baby."

Mom cries louder.

"The deed will not get done! Vansickle? Vansickle? Not even God's PR team would touch that mess," she cries. "Maura Vansickle is an ungrateful shrew. Wyndham is why she has anything at all! Her idea of refinement is putting truffle oil on everything!"

*There she is.* Bianca is back from her hysterical terror and ready to rip a new-money woman to shreds.

"Her husband made millions indirectly from your patent deals, Roger, and she still can't figure out how to RSVP properly. The Vansickles throw money at things, hoping it'll turn into class, but even the money is appalled. It just bounces off!"

I stare at my parents while they speak. Mostly it's my father trying to calm my mom down, but he is also giving more details about the deal with Vansickle and the law firm, so I hone in. Brody is talking to the police, and for not the first time this week, I'm left trying to sort out the absolute shit show of the current state of my life.

I zone out, watching the chaos play out around me like a movie, blankly staring at a pot on the stove that has red sauce bubbling over. I walk over, dodging police and a waiter, and turn the knob to turn off the stove.

I spin on my heel just in time to see Brody enter the kitchen. He seeks me out and frowns. I slide down the stove and wrap my arms around my knees. This. This is the breaking point.

"I want to go home."

MY BROTHER HANDS me a bottle of beer, and Grimace lunges to nip his hand from his place on my lap. I smile and pat his head. I missed the little devil more than is reasonable.

"I just can't believe this story," Catherine says, taking the fresh beer Nolan extends to her.

He goes back into the house through the open French doors that lead to the lake house kitchen.

"The whole thing sounds crazy. Insanely wealthy family. A kidnapping for ransom. A freaking hit put out on the head of the family after you think everything has resolved." She shakes her head. "And you go and fall in love with Saylor. That's the best part," she says.

A grin tugs at my lips. "I said nothing about love," I reply.

I miss Saylor. It's been a few days since I last saw her. Checking my watch, I calculate the minutes until she arrives here. She couldn't come yesterday because there was a huge investigation happening at her parents' house, and she had to stay to give her account of the shoot-out at the hotel.

Catherine shakes me off. "No, of course you didn't say it, but it was implied, and I think we all know it's true."

I get along with Nolan's girlfriend in a way that I would have called unfathomable before. Nolan chose someone who may be more sarcastic and straightforward than I am. Nolan sits next to her on the outdoor sofa.

"And no one got hurt during captivity or the shoot-out?" She raises one brow, and Nolan cackles a little. He's entertained by how entertained we both are.

I shake my head and take a long swig of my beer.

A light breeze skates across the lake and reaches us, tousling my hair. I still haven't shaved since I got back to the States. This may be the first vacation I remember since my childhood, and damn it, Nolan was right. This lake house, nestled in the tall trees, with walking trails in the forests surrounding us, is absolutely mind-clearing. I never gave it a chance.

"No one got hurt," I say, meeting Nolan's eyes.

Collin did, but I won't create any ire for my brother right now. Plus, he made a full recovery.

"The last thing my brother wants to hear about is me getting hurt."

Nolan furrows his brows. "But did you? Other than shrinking a bit, you look healthy." His gaze trails over my body like he has superhuman vision. "You are healthy."

Licking the foam off my lips, I grin. "I am healthy, McLan. Cool your anxiety."

"He cares about you," Catherine quips, rubbing the back of Nolan's head. "It's not anxiety!" Her brown eyes slide over to meet mine and hold. "He is the least anxious person I know, and I work in healthcare, so I know many."

"Fine, fine," I say, giving up.

I stroke Grimace, and he sighs, long and contentedly. I missed him so much.

Not that I have anxiety, but this moment is filled with peace. Saylor is on her way here, and she's spending the night with me. I do have nerves about her meeting Nolan and Catherine. Now that I see firsthand how perfect they are for each other, I want that for myself.

"I think you guys are going to like Saylor. She's nothing like you'd expect, trust me. I read about her on paper and expected some heiress with a conflated ego and no survival skills."

Nolan shakes his head. "I need to meet the woman who did this to my brother as soon as possible. Not that you aren't allowed to change, but she changed you. I've been trying to soften you up since the day you began stealing my toys, and she waltzes in and kidnaps your heart without any pain at all." He drinks his beer and looks at Catherine, then back at me. "It's almost offensive."

Catherine turns at the sound of the car pulling up the gravel drive.

"That's her. It's not offensive, it just means he found his person. I hated all men before I met you, remember?"

*Exactly like me,* I think. *Just with women.*

"I always keep an open mind. You should know that about me. I never prejudge anyone."

Nolan squeezes her to his side and says to me, "Go get your girl, McBrode. We'll make ourselves scarce until you're ready for us to meet her." He kisses Catherine on her head. "No, she doesn't prejudge, to confirm. She just judges after."

"Hey, that's not fair. Your buddies were doing keg stands on top of a railing, Nolan. That was begging to be labeled negatively, all right? I can't wait to meet her. I'm a little starstruck after hearing Brody talk about Saylor Wyndham. She's smart and beautiful. That's a lethal combination."

Little does she know the combination is my literal kryptonite.

I set Grimace down on the wooden deck, and he jumps into Catherine's lap. She grins, talking to him like a little baby. He won her over, and the fatherly pride makes me swoon.

Rushing from the balcony, I head down the stairs and into the four-car garage where they've cleared a space for her security's vehicle. They're pulling a black sedan in as I exit, wearing flip-flops and swim trunks. Saylor exits the back seat quickly. Her big blue eyes locked on mine, then they dip down to my abs.

"My god, this is the only sight I've wanted to see since Portugal."

Saylor runs to me, folding into my arms against my chest like a puzzle piece. This is contentment. Full, true, and pure.

Exhaling loudly, it's as if I've been holding my breath while we've been apart. We've talked on the phone and do video calls before we go to sleep at night, but it's not a true replacement for this.

Dropping a kiss on the top of her head, I inhale the scent of her shampoo and settle into tranquility.

"That's your black truck, isn't it?" Saylor asks, her face turned toward the garage that is indeed housing my truck. Nolan's is on the other side, and there's an empty bay that holds a work area with benches, tools, and anything one would possibly need to repair anything in a house.

"How did you know? Do I give off big black truck energy?" I ask.

She shrugs, still captured in my arms. She bites back a grin. "A little."

"There you go again, without missing a beat. I'm not sure if I should be flattered or offended."

Saylor releases the hug and walks over to my truck.

"A little of both. It's exactly how you described it."

A security guard hands me her duffle bag and tells me they'll be covering the outside from all access points. I ask a few pertinent questions while Saylor rounds the vehicle and looks at the tools on the other side of the garage space. I also tell them that the guest house on the side of this property is unlocked and has four bedrooms that they can use as a base. Saylor wants them to stay out of the way as much as possible, and putting them in the guest house seemed like the only option. She runs her hand over a drill, then spins once she hears that our conversation is over.

"Now that the business of my wellbeing is out of the way, I don't want to even think about anything dangerous. I want to languor by the lake with a drink in my hand and not a thought in my mind. I want to meet your brother and his girlfriend and hear baby stories about you. I want to eat BBQ chicken and have sex with you all night long."

Saylor pauses her list of very doable demands, then her smile falls.

"Dad hasn't let me go into the office, so I've been working on a new project from home, not talking to anyone except Angie, our chef, my mom, and her best friend, Bitsy, short for Beatrice, who is breeding prize winning orchids in our greenhouse at the moment." She spins and licks her lips. "I almost forgot. She also curates a personal collection of rare teas. I talked about your strange hobby all day today."

I burst out laughing. "You don't say. Sounds like I need to meet her. I bet she has some good options to blend."

Saylor shakes her head vehemently. "God, no. She's a cougar. The definition of cougar has her photo next to it. She'd have you pinned and under her middle-aged control in less than a day. Heck, maybe half a day."

My eyebrows shoot up. "You must not have any faith in me if you think I can be swayed by a tea-loving bitty."

Saylor's gaze looks apologetic. "You haven't met Bitsy. If she wanted me, she'd find a way to turn me into a lesbian, Brody. I don't know why she didn't go into law as a hobby. No one is better at convincing people of things."

Saylor crosses over.

"Show me to our room?" she says, and the twinkle in her gaze makes my cock hard.

I press my lips together to stifle a grin.

"This way," I say. "Did you learn anything about tea? I can put a pot on if you'd like."

Saylor makes a noise, grabbing my free hand as I lead her into the house.

"I should be happy that you have a random hobby that will endear you to my mother's harem of harlots, but it's still weird. Tea later. Where is Grimace?"

"Let's put your stuff down, and we'll go outside after. Grimace is with them on the second-story deck."

We take another staircase that leads up to the top floor. Nolan had this house gutted and expanded when he purchased it. The seclusion makes it perfect for Saylor and me now.

My first day back from Portugal, I ran onto base to grab some things I left there, and that's when my buddy told me how bad the media frenzy would be surrounding the Wyndhams, and by proxy, *me*. Because Bianca went rogue after Saylor was kidnapped, her face was everywhere. The details about her life are breakfast talk for the average American family. If someone didn't know what Wyndham Technology was before the kidnapping, they do now.

The company's stocks soared during the period that we were captive and continue to climb due to the spotlight on the family and just how intelligent and beautiful they are. It's rare in real life to have a combination of folks who are equally brainy as they are good-looking. They are sensationalized, and Wyndham Tech is capitalizing on it. Some would say at the expense of the family's privacy. That was the disagreement Roger had with his former law firm—they couldn't agree on how this kind of fame should be handled. Even though Roger won in the end, trying to shield his family from the press, the damage was done, and Jennings's holdings in WT were stripped for breach of contract.

I was able to trace Jennings's communications ordering the hit with a little help from friends, and the police arrested him two days ago. While he's locked up, I'm still leery about the whole firm and the actions they may take to punish what they view as bad business dealings. Even though I'm on leave, I'm on high alert, which is just as well, because I don't know one Navy SEAL who knows how to do vacation in a normal fashion. Give us a problem to solve, big or small, and watch us thrive.

Saylor sits on the bench in front of the bay window overlooking the lake.

"This is so beautiful. It's a shame my sister and her husband can't come, but because of the shitshow that is our lives right now, their art gallery is thriving. Everyone wants to visit to get a look at them." She pauses and spins to face me. "Like zoo animals."

It's not an inside joke anymore, though. This is fucking maddening.

"Which is fine because it's good for the charity but also sucks to lose all sense of the people we used to be."

"No more flying under the radar," I amend. "The good thing about the media is they'll forget about you as soon as something else sensational happens. You aren't that important."

I try to joke, but I can tell by the tilt of her eyes she's not having it.

"Saylor," I say.

She raises her chin to look at me. I say, "This will pass, and things will go back to normal."

"At least I have an excuse as to why I can't go get my MBA at Columbia now. It would be near impossible to focus when all anyone cares about is my time on that base."

I sit next to her and have to fight back the urge to take her right here and now.

"I get why you're afraid of your mother. She's terrifying in a way I didn't know was possible, but you don't need an excuse not to go to school. Don't go. Do whatever you want. Your brain is full, anyway. What were you working on yesterday?"

Saylor exhales a pent-up breath. "A no-fail GPS that will stay online at all costs. It uses a hybrid of quantum satellite triangulation and AI-stabilized inertial nav to pinpoint a boat's location within three centimeters, even in GPS-denied environments like urban coastlines. It will have zero latency and a phantom cloak mode, which masks the vessel's digital footprint, or it can make it appear to be somewhere else entirely."

My jaw drops. "That is impressive. When you said tweaking AI GPS when I asked on our video chat, this wasn't exactly what I had in mind."

She continues. "Even masking a vessel from the military. The boat or ship will only be visible on the water to the naked eye, but for that, it won't exist. Sea Tracker failed me," she says, sighing. "I must do better this time. It has to be no-fail."

Her blue gaze meets mine.

"I know I don't need another degree, Brody. But until now, my family was all I had, and making my mother happy was part of my job description. You're right. It's time to do whatever I want. What I'm building now will be life-changing."

Sometimes I forget what resides behind her eyes—how her mind is purely magnificent. She wears her beauty to mask her intelligence instead of the other way around, how many women in today's world function.

"I'll talk to Bitsy, and she'll talk to your mom. We'll make it sound like it was her idea for you to dominate what you're working on now instead of going to college. Sounds like she is the key to getting your mom to believe anything in the world."

Saylor laughs, her smile pulling up in the corner. "It's just one more thing in the absolute circus of my life. I will admit that plan has chops, though. Start with tea talk and then move into the GPS project, though. You have to warm Bitsy up."

She slides her hand over and intertwines her fingers with mine.

"Thank you for sticking by me. This is a lot, and it's going to continue to be a lot. Bronwyn asked me if you were going to deal with the pressure from all the outside sources well, and I said, of course, but then I realized maybe you would get sick of it." She pauses, breathing. "Because anyone would get sick of it."

Bringing my hands up to her face, I pull her to me, kissing her, tasting her, giving her the only answer she'll ever need. What we have together is not something that can be replaced. Nothing that has to do with her would ever be anything that would detract from my feelings for her.

Every nerve snaps to attention when her hand slides over my dick covered by my thin swimsuit.

I curse under my breath. "We have to go downstairs. They're waiting to meet you." The words are spoken against her mouth, our teeth touching.

Her mouth closes into mine, moving soft and slow, making my blood turn to fire. "What about a quickie?"

The need to have her outweighs my plans to take my time and savor her all night long. I can do both.

Her kiss, after being apart, drags something primal out of me, and I don't want to cage it. Never will I cage anything when it comes to Saylor Wyndham. This woman deserves the best of everything the world has to offer.

Standing from the bay window seat, I hold out my hand to help her up. She sees the answer in my eyes, in the telling smirk. Saylor kicks off her slides and lifts the dress over her head.

"You planned this. This was always going to be an all-out assault, regardless of what I said."

The Cheshire Cat smile she's flashing is the only thing she's wearing.

Tilting her head to the side, she flashes a crooked smile. "Learn to plan or plan to learn," she says, leaning up on her tiptoes to kiss me slowly, without urgency.

Her body against my bare chest causes a riot of sensations. Her cool skin against my warmth. She hooks her fingers into the waistband of my shorts and pulls them off in one fell swoop. Stepping out of them, I walk her back to the bed, trying to form all semblance of control when I feel anything but.

The need courses through my body unchecked and unmatched by anything before it.

Saylor sits on the edge of the king bed, then lies down, letting her knees fall open.

"Oh, I have a plan. And then another plan, and several after that, if you'll allow it," I growl as I eye her wet cunt beckoning me.

My jaw works as I swallow down the rest of my self-control. Then, Grimace scratches at the door. I wait a couple of seconds to see if he's going to keep at it, or if he'll leave. He scratches again, and Saylor finds my dilemma entertaining, a twinkle in her eye, and her bottom lip caught between her teeth.

"A quickie," she repeats, opening and closing her knees to tease.

"Yes. Yep. You're right," I rasp, leaning down to lick her cunt, because tasting her before I fuck her is mandatory.

She tastes hot and delicious, and a little moan escapes at the same time I close my mouth over her clit and suck a bit to fill my mouth with her essence.

"Fuck," I say against her pussy. "You drive me mad."

"Good," she says breathily. "You drive me mad too. Now, fuck me."

*Heaven help me.*

Crawling over her body, I let my dick slip inside her as I skim up to kiss her neck. She slams her eyes closed as her tight cunt grips me. I murmur her name like it's the only word I remember, and right now, it is. Nothing exists except her.

Her skin prickles when I kiss her neck. I still myself as she fucks me from the bottom, rocking her hips at a rough pace.

There's nothing timid about her, but Saylor becomes feral when she's with me. She tells me I make her feel safe. Part of me has wondered if it was because I kept her safe in Madagascar.

Was something triggered?

I hate to think this is a trauma bond, but she's clever enough to know the difference. *I think.*

Saylor moans into my mouth, jutting her hips up and circling them. Then her orgasm hits, wrapping my dick and bringing me to closer to my own. She's clutching my biceps, and her body shakes violently before it goes lax underneath me. I thrust my hips into her a few more times, then pull out and come on her stomach in long, hot bursts. Kneeling between her legs with me all over her is a sight to behold.

She smiles sleepily and sighs a contented sigh.

"See? Quickie," she explains, pointing at my mess.

Dragging a finger over her abs, she gets some on her finger, then brings it to her mouth, closing her lips around it.

"Delicious," she moans, flashing white teeth. "Do you want to go down now so I can meet them?"

There's a flicker of nerves behind her simplistic question.

I grab a wad of tissues from the box next to the bed and wipe off her stomach.

"Are you ready to go downstairs to meet them?" I return.

She takes the tissues from me and dabs one inside her belly button.

"I'm leery of everyone these days except you and

whoever you trust, so I'm ready, even if I'd rather lock myself in this room with you until I die." Saylor flashes me a crooked smile.

My chest tightens because I know what it means for her to say that. For her to want me more than anything else. She has a full life, and I'm important to her. I kiss her one more time when she's cleaned me off completely because I can't help myself.

"I'll replace all of that later tonight," I promise. "We can lock ourselves in here. Maybe not forever, though. We have the world to save, you know?" I lean my forehead against hers.

Grimace scratches the door again.

"And a very indigent dog that needs me."

"I love that for you. For us," she says, correcting the term. "I hope he likes me. No, I hope he loves me more than anyone else. More than you."

I find my shorts and pull them on, and Saylor slips her long dress over her head. Knowing she'll be naked under that for the rest of the day might be torture. *Fuck, her body is perfect.*

I open the door and Grimace hobbles in like a grouchy old man pissed I made him wait. He turns up his wiry snout and sniffs the air once, then again, like an oxygen connoisseur on a mission. He waddles over to where Saylor is standing, and we both hold our breath. It's immediate—Grimace's love or hate isn't a gradual occurrence. She knows this because we talked about how hilarious and discriminating it is.

She stoops down, holding out her hands, palms up. And maybe it's because she smells like me, or maybe it's because he senses the peace she brings, he licks her hands, then nuzzles into her pet.

Saylor's eyes widen, and she immediately looks up at me.

"He licked me," she whispers. "I'm going to get cocky and try to pet his head." Grimace nuzzles into her hands more, even when she strokes the fur between his eyes. "He loves me. Oh my gosh, I could cry."

Hands on my hips, I survey as my crotchety old dog falls in love with my woman. She scoops him up, and she follows me downstairs.

"Grimace, you are getting soft in your senile years, aren't you, boy?" I reach over and run my fingers over his back as we descend the stairs side by side.

Saylor makes a pit stop in the bathroom off the kitchen, and I head out to the deck where Catherine and Nolan are bird watching with binoculars.

"I can't believe Nolan sucked you into his old man hobby," I remark.

"I can't believe you disappeared for that long," Catherine claps back. "Are you done hogging her attention?"

Catherine spins, holding out the binoculars to me.

"Look at the double-crested cormorant. It's stunning. I'm going to fix us a cheese board and make some tea."

Laughing, I take them from her and look where Nolan's are pointed.

"It's on the third try. It's going to get a fish on this one. I have a good feeling for him on his next dive."

I grunt. "I think I'm going to marry her, McLan. Nothing has ever felt like forever like this."

Nolan turns slowly, his binoculars the last thing to lower to his side.

"Who are you and what have you done to my brother?" He swallows. "I've known you my whole life, and this is the most shocking thing you've ever dropped on me."

He smirks. "Does she know the real you? Like you've shown her Bitchy Brody?"

"How could she have not met Bitchy Brody? We were sweating in a cage together for a month. She knows him personally. When she looks at me, she sees through the rough shit. I told her about my...past. I'd marry her yesterday if I could."

Nolan is slack-jawed.

"But if you tell anyone about this or that I was mushy, I will kill you with a wedgie. That's a promise."

He stutters, then stumbles over his next words, loud and clumsy. "What-what-what about her family?"

"Hello," Saylor says, announcing her presence.

Nolan and I both jump at the same time.

"Oh god. Hello, I'm Nolan." My brother is embarrassed. We don't know how long she was there. I should, but I was preoccupied.

Saylor has two beers in her hand, and she extends them to us and pulls a third out of her dress.

"It has pockets," she announces with a smile, sipping her beer. "Saylor," she says without any tells.

*Did she hear our conversation?* Am I that out of sorts that I didn't sense her?

"It's so good to finally meet you. Catherine and I were chit-chatting in the kitchen, and she shared all the gory details."

Looking between us for a beat or two is normal. We are identical, but she seems to be puzzling over something.

Catherine comes out, setting the cheese board on the outdoor coffee table in between the sofas.

"Isn't Saylor beautiful? I can't get over it," Catherine squeals. "Cheese and crackers are here. A pot of tea too. A peppermint and lavender blend. We should drink it in between alcohol. Unconventional, yes, but fun none-theless."

"Thank you," Nolan and I say in unison.

Saylor just blushes furiously, the rose color creeping to her chest and neck.

Saylor grins at the unison, as most people do. The in-sync thing is hard to get used to.

"Now that everyone is here," Nolan says. "Catherine and I have some news."

A bead of sweat rolls down my brother's forehead.

"We are getting married!" Catherine squeals, pulling her ring out of her jeans pocket and sliding it onto her finger. "We wanted everyone important to be together before we announced it."

My heart jumps and my stomach sinks at the same time. This is incredible and foreign.

Nolan kisses Catherine, and Saylor claps her hands with joy.

"We didn't want to spring marriage news on you," Nolan says, gaze lingering on mine.

He's still processing what I told him. He clears his throat.

"Happy news all around for everyone," he adds, gaze darting between Saylor and me.

"This is a celebration," Saylor wails, both arms in the air. Her joy is contagious, and I can't help but smile at her. "We need champagne. Lots of it."

Catherine pulls a bottle from behind a sofa cushion. "It's probably a little warm, but we're ready!"

"I'll go get glasses and some ice," Saylor replies, rushing to hug Catherine and then Nolan.

Nolan watches me watching her and shakes his head —that sly grin on his face. We have to do everything at the same time. That in-sync twin shit.

## *saylor*

CATHERINE LOOKS up from bandaging a cut on Brody's leg to meet my gaze. Her lips are in a firm, annoyed line, but her eyes are mirthful.

"But, like, maybe the tenth beer before the jet ski ride wasn't the best idea," she says, trying to get Brody to admit his fault. "Right?"

*Good luck,* I think.

Brody's eyes are hooded and bloodshot. We've been having fun all afternoon, and now we're sitting around the fire pit with rose hip tea and a man waxing poetic about where the leaves came from.

"Beer is never a mistake, Cat. You cannot make me say otherwise."

I grin, tipsy myself, but at ease. I take a sip of the tea, letting it burn my lips, tongue, and throat.

"Do you like the tea?" he asks Catherine.

"I haven't been able to enjoy it, Brody. I just finished sewing up Nolan's finger before attending to this gory shin wound of yours. I still can't make sense of what happened. Nolan threw you off the jet ski, then cut his finger on a rock that sliced your leg as he dragged you back up?"

Brody shrugs.

"I'm shocked neither one of your parents is in the medical field. I feel like they were probably constantly at the doctor's with you two growing up."

"We are grown up and still needing care," Brody slurs.

Nolan messes with the electric switch to lower the fire.

"I'm really glad he's marrying you, you know that?"

Catherine laughs. "Why? Because I'm a nurse?"

"No, because you see him," Brody replies.

Everyone silences at the statement because Brody doesn't say stuff like this sober. It's almost scary.

What else might he say? That he thinks I'm a mistake because of my family? His mind is secretive. I can tell he guards the contents, and the words he chooses to say are presented with care. My fear is he'll say something so truthful that there will be no coming back from it.

"Why don't we get you to bed?" Nolan says, helping Brody stand and wrapping an arm around his waist. "You really let loose today, McBrode, and you need some sleep. We can continue the debauchery tomorrow if you're not hugging the porcelain toilet."

Catherine and I confirm the fire is all the way off, and she grabs the tray with snacks and teacups.

"I mean it, Nolan," Brody continues. "I'm just happy for you."

Nolan side-eyes Brody. "Happy is never a word you use, so forgive me for ordering you to bed."

There's a lull in conversation as we reach the bottom of the stairs that lead up to the second-story deck.

"Don't take me down. Catherine is out of sutures in her medical kit, and she might leave me if we injure ourselves again," Nolan warns his twin.

I notice how Nolan dodges the emotion with his brother, knowing Brody would be horrified if he knew what he was saying in front of other people. Even if it is me.

"Brody," I chime in, walking close behind the twins, keeping my hand on the metal pole handrail.

Never do I believe men deserve the dignity of their thoughts staying hidden, but somehow and some way, Brody does. I've never seen him drunk, but our exposure to normal, civilized settings has been limited.

"Are you always brutally honest when you've been drinking?"

"Yes," Brody and Nolan say at the same time.

"It's how I know when to cut him off," Nolan says alone.

"I only drink like this when I'm with my brother," Brody slurs. "When I'm with the people I trust."

Nolan slaps his back as we get into the house. "I'm flattered. Now go to sleep."

Brody listens, heading up the staircase to our room, where Grimace has been asleep in his bed for hours.

The thought pops up that I should check in with security, but I look at my phone on the counter, and there aren't any messages from them.

There is a group text from my mom and Bronwyn about a small get-together she's hosting next week. My sister is trying to get out of it without luck, and my mom is crying about wanting some normalcy after what she's been through. I roll my eyes, and even though I'd love to skip her party, I won't. I'll respond tomorrow, though.

Nolan locks the French doors leading outside while Catherine goes downstairs to check the door to the garage and the front door.

"You mean a lot to him," Nolan says. "More than I've seen anyone other than his damn dog mean to him."

I nod, knowing exactly where this is going.

"It's serious. We are serious," I tell Nolan.

When they aren't side by side, the resemblance between them is uncanny. The strong nose and glowing eyes, the jaw that's square and strong.

Nolan doesn't look at me as warmly as Brody does, though. As he looks at me, his gaze is sharp, without any trace of softness. He paces a step, rocking back on his heel, and proceeds to continue this cadence.

He picks up a stray half-full bottle of beer on the counter and takes a sip.

"He's been through hell. You know that, I'm sure." He pauses on a rock back on his heel. "But you don't know all of it."

I'm frozen to my spot, one hand steadying myself on the back of a kitchen table chair.

He goes on. "He's seen things. The things he's done? None of it goes away. Here you are, all shiny and sweet, hailing from a world that eats people like him alive."

I narrow my eyes. "If you're trying to scare me off, it won't work. I know who he is, and he knows who I am. I may be from a different place, but I will always protect him. That's what you do when you love someone."

Nolan shakes his head and sets the bottle back on the granite. It makes a loud noise.

"I'm not trying to scare you. I just want to make sure you get it. He's not some project. Brody isn't a man you clean up and bring to brunch."

My hand trembles a little, so I bring it up next to my other.

"There's nothing to fix." I blink slowly a couple of

times, stunned to see this side of his twin, but also thankful he has someone who loves him so fiercely.

Nolan exhales loudly. "Thank God. He doesn't need fixing. He needs someone who stays through the good and the bad. He needs someone who doesn't change him into something he's not."

Finally, he looks up from the floor and meets my eyes. A softness comes.

"He told me he wants to marry you."

There's a pregnant silence as I take it in. Butterflies invade my stomach at the same time my heart rate picks up, throbbing against my neck.

"He did?" I ask.

"He didn't say it like some romantic, idealistic bull-shit, because that's not him." He runs a hand through his hair. "He said it like a tortured man who's never wanted something he thought he didn't deserve."

I watch as he swallows hard, trying to control his emotions.

"So if you aren't all in, or if this is just some phase, walk away now. I'll take care of the aftermath. Again."

"I know who Brody is. I know about the scars you can see and the ones he hides at all costs. I know about the car accident that changed him and the teammates he's lost throughout the years. I know he flinches if you touch him when he's not expecting it, and that he's so inside his head that he acts like a grouch to try to push people away. I know his heart," I say, breathing heavily, a tear rolling down my cheek. "And I will always care for it."

Nolan stares at me, looking for doubt or cracks, but he doesn't find any because they don't exist. He goes to walk away, but turns to look at me before he disappears into the hallway.

"If you hurt him..." He starts, voice shaking.

I cut him off. "I would never hurt him."

"You'll answer to me," he finishes.

"If I ever hurt him, I'll deserve to answer to more than you, Nolan," I reply. "I won't."

He nods, then walks away, leaving me alone.

I turn off the light with shaky hands, grab my phone, and head upstairs. The bedroom door is open, and I can see—no, I can hear—Brody sleeping on top of the bed. He's on his stomach, face turned to the window, so the moonlight illuminates his face.

*He said he wants to marry me.*

Grimace lifts his head from his oversized bed near the bathroom entrance, then puts it back down when he sees it's me.

So this is what it feels like to get the guy fully. In the real love kind of way, not the convenience kind of way that so many of my friends and family thrive on. My heart is still pounding with the knowledge that I'm loved for who I am.

Standing in the bright moonlight, I look out the bay window at the shining lake, and a peace washes over me.

The weight of what I've been through was heavy until I compared it to what Brody has endured throughout his life. It's almost as if by loving someone who has been through so much, I'm able to distance myself from my own trauma.

I use the bathroom, wash my face, brush my teeth, and give Grimace a pet before crawling into bed next to Brody. He pulls me close, and his touch when I'm tired is like a sedative. I fall asleep briskly, and for the first time since I got home, the nightmares don't come.

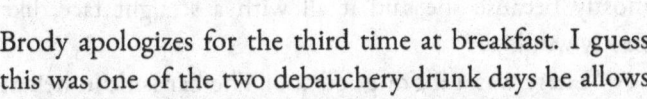

Brody apologizes for the third time at breakfast. I guess this was one of the two debauchery drunk days he allows himself per year, and he wasn't planning on it being one.

"Your security is here, so I guess that's why I felt it was a good time to let my guard down. It's been so long since I've done that."

"Stop apologizing for having fun. You didn't do or say anything that crazy."

I let my gaze drop to his shin. It bled all over the bed last night, stopping just short of soaking the mattress. I've already washed and dried the bedding, and he helped me put it back on.

"That's crazy," I say once again.

I push him a glass of orange juice and headache medicine. He takes it, swallowing the juice so quickly it dribbles down his chin. I finish my bagel and coffee and take our dishes to the sink, where Catherine is.

She's hovering over the sink with a piece of buttered toast.

"I am not twenty-one anymore," she says, voice raspy. "How are you feeling? This was either the absolute best way to meet us or the worst. Be honest and tell me which one." Her eyes are rimmed in yesterday's eye makeup.

"Best. Definitely best. Meeting you guys has been the highlight of my year."

Catherine's smile drops. "You were kidnapped off your boat and taken to a deserted base where they held you captive in a cage for a month with Brody McCoy. They stole your boat, and now there's a media frenzy around your mere existence." She shakes her head. "I'm not sure being the highlight is a compliment. The standard bar is in hell, Saylor."

The laughter that comes next is uncontrollable, mostly because she said it all with a straight face, like Brody would.

"There was a lot of good too. The bar isn't in hell at all. I think I'm able to compartmentalize the whole thing in Madagascar because being with Brody made it bearable. He said it best when he said he's comfortable being uncomfortable, and I guess that rubbed off on me."

I wash my dishes and put them on a dish towel to dry.

"Thanks for embracing me like this. I know Nolan might take some time to come around and warm up to me, but I appreciate you for just taking me at face value."

"You're welcome," Catherine says. "He will come around. You know that, right? He's a softie. He takes that older by thirty-seven minutes seriously."

I nudge her with my elbow. "How could I forget? He has that big brother energy."

"What kind of energy?" Nolan asks, kissing Catherine on the cheek before refilling his coffee cup. "The hungover kind of energy? The taking the dog out early because you slept in kind of energy?"

"Thanks for taking Grimace out," Brody moans from the kitchen table.

"I popped into the guest house to make sure your, ah, friends knew that the kitchen was stocked for them."

"Thank you for that," I reply. His heart is just as big as Brody's. I think it's just on his sleeve. "I know they appreciate it more than you know. This property is beautiful. I can see why you guys love it here."

"Brody rarely comes out here," Nolan says. "Maybe he will now."

"Why?" I ask, aiming my question at the hungover man in question.

He looks up but keeps his head in his hands. "No real reason. I just worked a lot, and I don't know how to be friends with some of our old friends. It sounds like a lie, but I promise it's the truth. My life is just different, and I can't talk about a day in the office or coworker gossip. I don't have kids yet, or have much in common with most folks. Making friends is nearly impossible for people like us. I'll try again with Liddy and Sam if you want to plan something, McLan."

He lays his head on the table and exhales noisily.

"We need to have *less* fun today. I'm going to make us some ginger and lemon balm tea and then I need to hit the damn gym." He moans. "Who the hell let me drink that much?"

"You aren't a baby. We let you self-govern! I have some work to do as well if I don't want to be buried with emails on Monday," Catherine says, walking into the open living room off the kitchen.

I look at him, biting back a laugh.

Brody says, "If you're going to nurse me back to health, at least do it without the smug face."

I lose the battle and cackle. "I'm sorry, I'm sorry, you crank. I'll work out with you if you want."

He nods, like a child embarrassed to admit he was wrong.

"Grumpiness at full tilt today," Nolan declares. "Everyone beware!"

Brody grunts and grabs a gallon of water from the bottom of the pantry floor and begins chugging it.

I go to talk to my security guards in the guest house to confirm that everything was fine last night, only to find out that someone tried to scale the twenty-foot-tall stone walls to break into my parents' home. He was taken down by the elite security guards my dad hired the second we got home from Lisbon. The ones with me are part of that team, but it's disheartening to know that even though Jennings is locked up, the attempts on my father's life continue.

One of the guards flips a laptop around to show me the footage of the suspect. He isn't wearing a mask, and I get a good look at his face.

"I don't recognize him," I say, frowning. "That is the weakest side of the property for break-ins. Whoever is orchestrating this knows things. Things that are personal."

It's probably Jennings running things from jail. Or his wife. If it's the wife, Mom will strangle her with a Chanel scarf. More proof we have to be careful with whom we become close with.

I tell them my plans for the day, and they seem to be in good spirits, probably because they are comfortable in a house as beautiful as the main lake house.

The head guard walks me back to the main house and doesn't leave me until I'm in the door with it locked behind me. Brody meets me at the top of the stairs, face ashen.

"Did you throw up?" I say, trying to hold in the smugness so he doesn't get moody again.

He's changed into a pair of black workout shorts.

"I have to talk to you."

"Talk," I reply.

"How soon will your new AI GPS be ready? Let me rephrase. How quickly can your AI GPS be ready to sell? The Navy needs it. Rephrase again because I'm fucking flustered. The Navy SEALs need it. We need it."

I swallow hard and sweat beads on my head. I've never worked well under a deadline.

"Why would the US military need my system?" I reply.

"Because it's the best. You're the best. I'm confident of that. Your mind works like an evil genius. We can get this put together and delivered soon. I know you can. I'll help you." He looks flustered, nervous. "Just like we're in Madagascar again, except we won't be designing and installing watering systems or fixing tech on the motorbikes. It will be something you love. Something you're good at, and I'm a smart man, but I'm smart enough to know this is your territory, and it's going to fall on your shoulders."

"I'm smart as well, Brody. What is going on? Why do you look like that? All sweaty and unlike your normal cool self?"

"Probably because I have Coors Light leaking from my pores, Saylor."

I shake my head. "Seriously. Be honest with me."

He looks up, his blue eyes avoiding mine. "I can't tell you everything."

"That's fine. I'm not asking for everything."

"There's a threat in the waters off the north east coast. Our home. We need to get into the water and be undetectable."

I widen my eyes. "Let me grab a laptop from security. They don't have a firewall, so I can access my files from work."

My dad told me that if I got this project complete, and it ends up being viable, it would be mine because no one else helped me. There wasn't input from any of the other Wyndham teams—I didn't have to attach it to Wyndham Tech. I could sell the product as a sole proprietor.

I open the door to the garage, and a guard is there. I ask him for a laptop, and he brings me one.

I set up in the living room and open my files.

"You're telling me the Navy is going to buy this from me?"

"If it works," Brody chirps. "I told them what you had, and the capabilities, and I can be your liaison to sell it. I want this to get the recognition it deserves, and selfishly, I don't want to die. We need this."

"Oh, no pressure, then." Another bead of sweat rolls down my face. "Crank the AC, would you?"

Nolan and Catherine are out on the water. I could hear them starting the boat when I walked through the kitchen. Brody must have told him we needed the house alone. Little did they know it wasn't for anything fun.

Brody doesn't reply. He does as I ask, and I bury my whole brain into this dilemma. I know what I need to do to get it working. It's just a matter of time and a lot of testing. Instead of being a little side project to distract me, this will have to be more important.

He sets a glass of water down on the coffee table in front of me. "Unless you'd rather have beer. Or tea."

I shake my head. "Brody," I say, looking up, meeting his gaze. "I know the Navy already has tech like this. What exactly do you need me to tweak?"

He pauses, searching for words.

"Under the radar," he says. "We need to be all the way under."

*I know what I'll call, it at the very least.*

# CHAPTER SIXTEEN

## *brody*

THE ATLANTIC IS a graveyard at night. Cold. Dark. Quiet. Especially because the waters surrounding the SEAL base are protected by guards to keep civilians out of our water and off our training beach.

Our Zodiac boats skim just inches above its surface, slicing through the chop like a whisper. The only light comes from the soft, purple—yes, purple—glow of the navigation system blinking at my knee. Four SEALs. Two Zodiacs. No plan B. No screw-ups. We have one chance to do this our way before the big Navy cascades in and fucks this up, bringing more attention to Saylor and me.

This is personal in many different ways for me.

*ALL THE WAY UNDER IS ACTIVE.*

I have stared at these words more times than I could count.

The system is almost completely Saylor's brainchild—quantum satellite triangulation fused with inertial AI nav that can hold position in a hurricane and fool every eye in the sky. It doesn't just tell us where we are, it tells us where *they think* we are. Phantom cloak mode makes our boat appear as a wandering fishing trawler two miles northeast of our actual location.

I love this system so much that I helped Saylor as much as I could with testing, trials, and backend engineering. I was the main person spearheading the deal to sell ATWU to Naval Special Warfare. They wanted it straight away, of course, because nothing like it exists in the world.

Saylor made her own millions on the deal, so it was easy to tell her mother to beat sand with regard to returning to college. Saylor made this possible, and my name as a co-creator probably wasn't earned, but I still have pride in the part I played in making this a reality together. I hate that she is on land, pacing around a smelly operations van, waiting for a voice in her earpiece that tells her I'm not dead. And that her firstborn works as it is supposed to.

Mark sits beside me, chewing on a piece of gum like it owes him fucking money. "You hear that?"

I narrow my eyes to hear better. I hate that it's my thing.

"Nothing," I reply, speaking over the chop.

"Precisely." He grins, adjusting his rifle. "Not even greedy beak bastards. They know something's about to go sideways. The gulls are always honking."

Mark is second-in-command on this operation for a reason. Smart in more than one way. Steady in all the ways. He's also funny when I forget how to be, which is often. He's like a Nolan while I'm at work. If something bad happens, Mark will be the guy dragging my ass out.

The other Zodiac, fifty meters off our starboard, holds Reyes and Dalton, two SEALs I trust with my life and no one else's. We are operating tonight as a four-man team for one simple reason: to keep the noise down. Fewer people die if this mission goes bad.

We are hunting pirates. Ravelo and the new crew he put together when we decimated the others—his first crew, his family.

I explained to my team that these are not the rum-swigging, AK-waving kind of pirates. These guys are smarter. Former contractors, warlords, opportunists, or so my research showed.

Ravelo and his crew hijacked two US Coast Guard interceptors and stole enough military-grade weapons to arm a small country. Just to show he could, and as a threat to the Wyndhams, he kidnapped a billionaire tech exec and his bodyguard. No ransom has been paid yet. We did get, addressed to me, a livestreamed proof-of-life video from what looks like a lobster trawler turned fortress. This is why it's personal. Motherfucker.

We are here to end this charade before there's a third act.

"Range?" I ask, squinting into the darkness.

Mark casts a glance at the nav screen. "Six hundred meters. They're drifting off Deadman's Elbow, just west of the inlet. Looks like three boats—main command vessel, center mass, two flankers. Same location as thirty minutes ago. Either they're getting sloppy, or they think we're too dumb to find them."

I adjust my grip on the throttle and can't help a sideways grin. "They have no idea what they're up against. Let's show them how dumb we are."

"Team," I whisper into my mic on my chest. "Split and surround. Phantom cloak active. No shots until I call it."

"Copy that," Reyes comes back.

"Roger," says Dalton.

We cut our engines and let the tide carry us, hidden behind a perfect veil of salt spray and quantum deception.

On the pirates' systems, we don't exist. Or worse, we exist in the wrong place entirely.

The nav shows the enemy fleet in eerie detail, every hull marked, every movement tracked. *All the Way Under* doesn't just show us the battlefield, it writes it in real time. Our actual position is marked in white, the cloaked projection hovering five hundred meters in the opposite direction in red. If anyone pings us, they're looking at an apparition.

I think of Saylor, hunched in that van on shore, watching the same feed we are because I went to bat to get her clearance to do so. It wasn't easy, but where there is a will, there is always a way. And when there's not a way, there is money. Plus, if anything went awry, she would be who they need to problem solve. Saylor's system, far surpassing its predecessor Sea Tracker, is the reason this op will work. And if it doesn't, I won't be the one to tell her.

We breach the perimeter in under two minutes. We are close enough to see the outlines of the boats—stolen US interceptors, modified and stripped of Coast Guard insignia. They are teeming with American-made guns. I think that's the worst insult of all of this.

Mark points forward. "Visual on command boat. That's our brain."

Aboard, we count six hostiles visible with night vision, and more inside. There's one man on the roof, scanning with his own pair of night vision goggles. Fucker.

"He's about to get a surprise," I mutter, tone low and cold.

"Want me to say hi?" Mark growls, eager.

"Yes, but use your manners," I reply.

Mark steadies his rifle, then squeezes the trigger once. The spotter with the night vision crumples without a sound. The rest of us surge forward.

We are over the rails, hooked on the side, and on deck in less than ten seconds. I lead the breach. First door off hinges, flashbang through the smoke. The cabin fills with light and screaming.

I move left. Mark moves right. We are muscle memory precision together. Three are down embarrassingly quickly. One tries to toss a grenade, but we double-tap him through the chest before he has a chance to pull the pin.

The boat goes eerily still, wrapped in the silence of death.

Mark kicks aside a chair, and I shove a table off two feet to confirm no one is hiding beneath. "Command boat's clear," he says, barely breaking a sweat.

I check the nav hanging on a tablet near my chest. *Jammer offline. Phantom broadcast expanded.* We are now spoofing our position to every known frequency. Hell, we could've made it look like we were in Portugal if we wanted. The nerd thrill shoots up my spine. This is going to change so much for our Teams. This system is going to protect my brothers more than anything else.

I confirm the trawler we're aboard is fully anchored, and we move out.

"Hostage boat is northwest," says Reyes over comms. "Moving in."

We leap back into the Zodiac, Mark already spinning the engine back to life. I key into Saylor's custom interface and lock our nav pin on the hostage ship. The boat shimmers on-screen, marked in red—eight combatants, two civilians, and one .50 cal on deck, unmanned.

We move fast and low to the water, no spotlight, barely a sound, and definitely no warning. They never see us coming.

Reyes breaches from the starboard side. Mark and I

take port. Explosives blow the hatch just as we hit the deck.

*Chaos. Gunfire. Cries.*

I shoot one through the wall. Mark lobs a flashbang into the galley.

Dalton's voice crackles in my ear. "Hostages alive and present. Mild resistance."

Two more hostiles come charging up the stairs. Ravelo. *You asshole*. I drop him with two shots—light work.

The memories from my time in Madagascar flash through my mind, but I don't have time to dwell on emotions right now. Ravelo made his choice, and we all pay for the wrong ones. That's the way the world works.

Mark tackles the other, stabbing his blade deep into the bastard's collarbone. He falls to the ground, unconscious, and after one last gurgle, he stops moving.

"Clear," I say.

Ravelo had to die, I remind myself. Even if he allowed me to live, he had to die tonight. It was the only way to cement this ring into the ground for good. I hate that guilt bubbles up, but I need it to remind myself I do have feelings. I am a human, not a machine. I have a good heart.

"Clear," comes back from the Team chorus.

They find the hostages zip-tied, blindfolded, and shaking. One of them is bleeding from the shoulder, but alive. We pull them up and haul ass back to the Zodiacs, engines roaring now. The ghost projection shifts as we move, the AI cloaking system adapting to our path, throwing up new false echoes in our wake. I can't help a small smile.

"They'll never find us," Mark mutters as he steers us toward the open ocean.

I glance at the console. Purple. Steady. The cloak holding like steel armor.

Back on shore, an emergency extraction team is rolling in from the operations van. Saylor mobilized them the second our green light pinged on her screen. I didn't even have to tell her. She knows what every light means.

We land fast. Reyes and Dalton escort the hostages to the med team. I step out last, boots crunching on gravel, body aching like hell from banging against the waves in a low-profile seacraft. They're tactically perfect and incomprehensibly uncomfortable.

The van door opens.

Saylor stands there, arms crossed across her Navy SEAL sweatshirt, face ashen.

"You're late," she says, bottom lip trembling.

I bite back a smile. "Your clock is wrong," I reply.

"You told me no hero stuff."

Shaking my head, I say, "I didn't do anything heroic."

"You guys killed them all."

I look away, feeling awkward that the woman I love knows the nitty-gritty about my job. This isn't a part of myself I readily share with anyone. Not even Nolan. It's already over, so there's no sense dwelling now.

"They had it coming," I reply

Will she think differently of me now that she's seen *this* up close?

Saylor crosses the distance and punches me in the shoulder. Hard. Then she hugs me like I'm made of glass, and she's forgotten how to breathe. I allow it, in full gear, covered in sweat, smelling of flashbang smoke, diesel fuel, and death. I let her hold on as long as she needs. I inhale her hair, and it calms me like a salve. This is why I do what I do now. Everything is for her.

Mark jogs past us, coming from one of our vans,

holding two lobster rolls. "Hey! They had warm butter tonight!"

"Give me one," I say, my chin resting on Saylor's head.

"Already ate it," he replies, shaking his head.

"Then give me the one in your hand."

He grins, running to Reyes, who has beers in his hands. "Come and take it, grandpa."

I look down at Saylor, pride beaming. "Your system worked. Like clockwork. On the ride back, all I could think about was how proud I am that this is your brain-child, and it works better than anything I've ever used."

She tilts her head, eyes wet. "I knew it would work. It had to. Your life was on the line. I won't fail with that. I might mess up in every other area, but I'll never mess up with that."

It baffles me that she somehow has low self-confidence.

"Didn't mean I wasn't scared," I say, letting a bit of vulnerability slip. If she can show vulnerability, so can I.

She exhales. "Me too. So damn terrified."

I pull her close again, content to just be. "But we're here."

"All the way under," she whispers.

I shake my head, then growl. "All the way home. That's where I'm taking you right now."

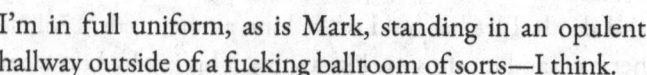

I'm in full uniform, as is Mark, standing in an opulent hallway outside of a fucking ballroom of sorts—I think.

We're inside Roger and Bianca's house. We agreed to attend this party because it's also a fundraiser for Bronwyn's art gala, and well, the Wyndham's PR firm said it might lessen some of the fucking interest around us if we did something public together. Take some photos. Let people see us together.

It also shows whoever is trying to get to Roger that we're a united front, and we aren't scared. Bring. It. On.

This isn't a large party by any means, but enough people are here tonight that it's the biggest risk we've taken since we've been back from Portugal. Security has a guest list at their gate, and only certain folks are allowed in. Metal detectors are being used, and the room is covered with security. I've never seen so many suits in my life.

"I feel like a fucking show pony," Mark says, grabbing at the collar of his uniform. I help him fix it. Perfection is the only option in uniform. "I can't drink. Can't smoke. Can't cuss. This is going to be awful."

Catherine glares at him. "You're upset? I bought a dress at Macy's because that's what high class means to me," she hisses from next to Nolan. "These people are dressed like celebrities, Brody. What were you thinking, bringing us to this?"

"You look beautiful, Cat. You don't need a thousand-dollar dress to look like my dream girl," Nolan replies, clutching her arm to his side. "No one cares what you're wearing. I promise you. Look at those two." He nods his head at us, fussing with our uniforms before we enter. "All eyes are going to be on them." He smiles widely and shakes his head. "We're here because Saylor invited us. She doesn't care what we have on. You know that. We're her friends."

I stand shock still at his admission because it feels nice. Saylor has been accepted, but I can't deny the whiplash we feel from chilling at the lake house, drinking beer, to this *house*, and whatever awaits us behind these gilded golden doors.

"He's right. And I don't say that often," I say to Catherine. To Mark, I say, "Go in and mingle. Saylor just texted. She'll be down in a second. We need to split up tonight. Remember what I told you. Regardless of what they say, they mean well, okay?"

He's met Bianca, so he has some idea what we're up against, but a horde of them together is going to be jarring.

"They're making a donation to our command."

"Do we need donations? We are the highest funded unit in the entire military," Mark says, sweat forming on his forehead.

It's always uncomfortable to be on display like this. Before I met Saylor, I'd eat my arm off before willingly participating in something like this. When she explained it in more detail, it's hard to deny it's not useful.

When I don't reply, he pastes a fake smile on his face, turns on his heel, and enters the room. *What a goddamn hero.*

Nolan and Catherine are speaking to each other in hushed tones.

"He's right, Catherine. You look beautiful," I say, tasting the compliment as it feels foreign.

Nolan smiles in appreciation.

"The food is fucking delicious. Go eat, get some stories, find the tea lady, and talk about your work. You are both accomplished, successful people. Don't let this house fuck with your mind. We all put our damn pants on the same way, one leg at a time."

Catherine exhales loudly. "Thanks," she says, inhaling deeply. "I've never been to something like this." Then she swallows hard, links her arm into Nolan's, and says, "For Saylor. We'll do this for her."

They enter the room next, the door clicking closed behind them. There's a low roar of conversation and light classical music. I was here when they were setting up, but I haven't seen any of the guests, or even Saylor, since I changed into my uniform.

My phone buzzes in my pocket.

> **SAYLOR**
>
> Wardrobe malfunction. Request for assistance. Use the elevator behind the kitchen.

I don't reply. I jog down the hallway, then another, finding the kitchen.

"Elevator?" I ask Angie as she bustles in with a tray of empty champagne flutes. She nods to the corner where there is another hallway.

I see the elevator. It's gilded and wooden, not silver like the ones in basic hotels. I hit the up button and wait. It dings open, and she's there.

I lose my breath, and my brain scrambles. I couldn't tell you the difference between up and down. She's wearing a long cobalt blue gown that's covered in crystals. Her hair is in loose curls hanging over her shoulders.

"Fuck," I say, forgetting to enter. She has to hit the open button again.

"I didn't think I'd have to text you," she says. Her gaze dances down my body, then back up. "This is better than I imagined."

The doors close behind us, and she raises one brow.

"I lied about the malfunction. I wanted you. Like this." Saylor bites her bottom lip.

"Here?"

I must look shocked because she raises one brow.

"What? We can't ruffle the SEAL before a performance?"

"Forgive the shock. I've never been in full uniform while being propositioned by the most gorgeous woman in the world."

I take a step forward, then another. She's pinned against the back of the elevator. I toss my cover on the ground.

Saylor kisses me, and the premeditation is everywhere. I pull away from her mouth.

"You did plan this. You didn't even put on lipstick," I say. "How bad did you want this, then? How long have you been thinking about this?"

Her blue eyes melt into mine as she reaches behind her body to unzip the dress. It falls to the floor in a pool around her feet. Nothing but skin and the body I cherish.

"I've been thinking about it since I last saw you."

I take off my jacket and set it gently on top of my cover. Saylor leans over and presses a button on the panel. It lights up red.

"No one can come in. Or out."

"We'll see about that," I reply, casting a cocky grin.

I collapse to my knees in front of her, eyes wide as I stare up in awe. She slides her legs over my shoulders, and I pull her ass forward to taste her pussy. She's so wet for me as she works herself against my tongue. The way her face remains soft with ecstasy, yet her pace harried with intent, is mesmerizing.

I lose track of time after she comes and slowly steps down, ordering me to stand. One hand holds the elevator door to steady my body as Saylor unzips my pants, then swallows my cock. Watching her work propels me closer to the brink, and she knows, because then she slows her pace, popping off to savor my balls. She licks a trail up and down the underside of my rod until I shiver, then she slides it back down her throat. The pace picks up when she uses her hand to guide her mouth up and down.

When I don't think I can hold back any longer, she looks up at me, all whale-eyed, fucking perfection, and says, "Fuck me," around my cock.

I lick my lips, nodding furiously. "Get up and turn around."

Saylor knows exactly where I'm going because she splays her hands on the closed door and spreads her legs. The invitation couldn't be warmer and inviting. I plunge into her, grabbing both of her hips to steady the fuck. Her blonde hair bounces with each thrust, and one side of the elevator has a mirror, so I watch, and even though I know it's my reflection, I still feel jealous of the lucky bastard.

Who gets to fuck a woman like this? Who gets to call a woman like this theirs? Couldn't be me.

The mere sight of my cock pounding into her firm tan ass in my hands is enough. She's in nothing but gold high heels, and fuck if they're high.

"Where do you want me to come?"

She grinds back against me and circles her hips when I'm already teetering on the edge.

"Inside me. I want you with me all night."

Saylor turns to the side to meet my gaze. Her body was made for me, and those ocean eyes tell me her heart was too.

My grip tightens on her hipbones at the same time she readjusts her palms on the door. I thrust into her a few more times, and I spill inside her with a groan that echoes in the small space.

"Keep going, I'm..." she says, breathy. "Almost there."

Wincing against the desire to stop, I slam into her

once and then again, and I feel her orgasm hit, the muscles in her body tightening.

"I love you. I love you. I love you," she says, gasping the words.

I look down as I pull out and immediately regret the hot load I just put in her.

"This is going to leak down your legs all night."

"Maybe that was the point," Saylor says.

I wrinkle my nose. "We haven't had sex in a couple of days, so there was...a lot," I explain, trying to be tactful.

She looks at me with big eyes, wet lips, and absolute reverence.

"I'm trying to say those beautiful gold shoes are going to be slippery when wet."

Saylor reaches between her lips and slips two slim fingers inside. My whole body tenses. The sight makes me frenzied. A shark circling blood. I bite back the desperation because I know we're on a timeline. She pulls her fingers out, and some of my cum is dripping down her fingers onto her palm. She licks it up, then licks her lips, without tearing her gaze from mine.

"You're really just torturing me now."

She shakes her head. "No, I'm just trying to solve the problem you pointed out."

My heart pounds against my ribcage. "I love you too," I say. "In case I forgot to respond while I was distracted."

Saylor slips her dress on and picks up her purse that was on the floor, and I dress quickly.

When we exit, Angie has a knowing look on her face as she loads another silver tray with flutes. This tray has Aperol Spritzes as well as champagne. The people in the other room are going to be loaded, and I'm fearful about keeping myself in check if someone says something inappropriate.

Saylor stops in the powder room to freshen up and put on lipstick. I adjust my bars and make sure my trident pin on my lapel is straight in the mirror when she's finished. I'm vaguely aware that both of our phones are buzzing, but there's no time to check them.

I hold the door open for Saylor. She straightens her shoulders, and I watch, curiously, as her face changes, a mask covering who she really is. The smile is not quite right, the stance a little prouder, eyes completely blank of any emotion.

She enters the room, and unfortunately, this is a moment the room has been waiting for. There are about seventy-five people in here, and conversation is buzzing along with the music. Even if there's not a spotlight, it feels like there is. I crook my arm, walking up next to her, and she links her arm with mine. We don't speak as we begin walking through the crowd.

I hear our names as the crowd parts to allow us through. I spot Mark right away. I also spot the other exit point because it's flanked by guards. My brain doesn't allow me to process this situation. I'm on alert. It's the only way I can keep my heart rate down. Treat this like work.

We run into Bitsy first. She hands Saylor a spritz.

"Nice to see you again. Especially looking like that," Bitsy says, nodding her head to me.

"Thank you, ma'am," I reply. "Thank you for the tea leaves," I say.

After she realized our shared hobby, she had some sent over from her house. I spoke with her earlier today as they were setting up for the party at depth about many things. Saylor said to be careful, but she just seems like a horny old lady who likes tea—and men half her age.

"Oh, you're welcome," she says.

Her red lipstick is smeared on her front teeth.

"Saylor, darling, there's a surprise for you in a little bit," she adds.

Her tone changes completely when she speaks to Saylor.

Bitsy grins, takes a drink off a silver tray, and heads into the crowd to bid on the auction pieces from Bronwyn's gallery.

"I think my dad went rogue and bought me another sailboat. I told him not to," Saylor says, leaning toward me to speak so no one else hears. "I'm not ready for that yet, and I wanted to buy it for myself."

I wrap my arm around her. "He feels bad. Just because you have a boat doesn't mean you have to sail it around the world. You could just trick it out with all your projects and take small sails to test things out."

"You're going to sail with me? Help me with all the projects? Even though you said, what did you call it, a *fucking dreadful pastime*?" Saylor raises one brow. "Did I get that right?"

I exhale, stifling a laugh. "We are giving each other grace for the things we said while in a cage. That's what we decided."

"Fine, fine, but you were definitely meaner."

"Because I didn't know you yet. It takes me some time," I chide.

Mark is in conversation with Bitsy now. Catherine and Nolan are at the buffet table, people watching. I can tell they're entertained, so I don't worry about them for long. Saylor is staring at someone by the bar. He's laughing, loud, meant to be noticed.

She visibly pales.

"I might have left one, tiny detail about Bitsy out," she says, voice shaking.

I narrow my eyes at the man. He sees Saylor and brushes down the front of his tailored suit, not even sparing a glance at me.

"Go on," I say, intuition telling me before she says it.

"My awful ex, Archie. Well, Bitsy is his mother. She convinced me to date him in the first place."

Saylor takes a sip of her drink. Then another, looking anywhere but at him or me.

"He's by the bar, staring at me like I owe him money."

"Ah," I say. "He knows we're a thing," I say, motioning between our bodies.

Her blue gaze flicks with an emotion I hate. Sadness.

"You don't get it, Brody. It doesn't matter." Shaking her head, she whispers, "My family is tactful for the most part. Some of these people just take what they want. They're relentless. I was going to marry him because they were so convincing, and I'm honestly almost positive he hated me."

She holds up a hand when I go to argue.

"It's messed up, I know. I had no idea he was going to be here. He's predictable, though. He'll drink too many Negronis, then move on to expensive tequila, and he'll black out outside in a pool chair. He's harmless."

Anger rises, and I eye Mark. He seems to be enjoying himself with Bitsy. Jesus effing Christ. Of course he is. But he's looking around, and I can tell he's looking for someone.

"It's fine."

"Don't say it's fine when I know it's not." Saylor finishes her drink, puts it on a tray, and engages in small talk with a woman who approaches her.

I don't even comprehend what they're talking about because all I see is red. Archie is staring at Saylor like she belongs to him. There's no respect for the man on her arm.

I can overlook a lot of things, but disrespect and a low moral compass when it comes to basic human decency? Fuck that. I have to remind myself not to cause a scene. It would accomplish the opposite of what we need.

"Excuse me for a minute, Saylor," I say. "I need to ask Mark something."

She glances at me warily, but nods, returning to her conversation.

I'm almost to Mark and Bitsy when something tells me to check on Saylor. I look over my shoulder to see Archie crossing the ballroom, people separating to make way. Her smile drops, and the corners of her eyes turn down when he stops in front of her. She doesn't breathe. She tips her chin up, and it trembles.

"Hi," she says.

Archie takes a microphone from a man next to the woman Saylor is talking to.

"Here is the woman of the night. Saylor Wyndham, everyone." His voice is even worse when he speaks instead of laughing. "I'm proud to be one of her most trusted friends, Archie."

He is rattling on about memories when Bronwyn runs up to me.

"We tried calling her, and I had Nolan and Mark try calling you, trying to tell you this was about to happen. Where were you two?" Bronwyn says, tone whispered but words rough.

No sense in lying now. "The elevator," I say. "Tell me what?"

"Good god," Bronwyn hisses. "There's no service in that damn elevator. Archie and Bitsy had this insane plan all along, and we found out about it by happenstance when Archie was talking to one of his friends. No one could find you two."

"Saylor Wyndham, will you marry me?" Archie's voice booms through the room, loud and pompous.

Bronwyn holds out her hands, extending them to Archie on his knee, presenting Saylor with a box.

"This. We were trying to tell you this was about to happen."

"What the fuck?"

My heart sinks, slips, slides, and I think it stops for a beat or two. Saylor looks around the room, but I'm in the back. I can see Bitsy, and she's glaring at me, a half smirk playing on her lips.

"We're here together," I stammer. "Bitsy talked to me all afternoon."

"It doesn't matter," Bronwyn says, echoing what Saylor tried to tell me.

It doesn't matter. I don't matter. I'll always be a lowly military employee. A man not sufficient for a Wyndham.

Nolan and Catherine slide up to where Bronwyn is explaining the semantics of this fucked-up world. But all I hear is how I'll never truly be able to fit in here. How I'll never be good enough for Saylor.

Love doesn't mean anything here.

Saylor grabs Archie's wrist and drags him out the side door without responding to his proposal.

"I have to get the fuck out of here right now," I say, and I don't recognize my voice.

Mark is there in a flash, covering for us as we leave. The hallways are colder than they were mere hours before. Bronwyn tries to get me to stay, but I can't. Not right now. The betrayal wasn't by Saylor, but it might as well have been. The chandeliers burn low in the hallway as we exit the mansion of lies and cheats.

When I'm in my truck, and Mark is next to me, I scream.

I scream so loud that the guards jump from outside the closed windows.

Nolan and Catherine get into the back seat.

"It's not fine. It's not okay. But this needed to happen," Nolan says, voice low.

I meet his eyes in the rearview, and it's a small salve in this moment.

"I know," I say, voice breaking.

## CHAPTER SEVENTEEN

*saylor*

"I HATE EVERYONE," I wail, covering my eyes with my forearm when Bronwyn presses the button to open my bedroom drapes.

I'm staying at my parents' house until the new wave of publicity dies down. While I also have a home nearby, I like to stay with them, and now, it's just safer.

"I don't understand why I can't call him and tell him why I'm not calling him."

My face is red and puffy from crying.

She sits next to me in the bed, rubbing my back.

"Keeping him in the dark is the only way this works, Saylor. Why don't you go work on the boat Dad got you? Get your mind off him?"

"The boat? The boat reminds me of him now. Everything reminds me of Brody."

I cry again, a little less jagged this time, because I'm fresh out of tears. I said fuck no to Archie, but after Brody left the party in a rage, our PR said we need to run with this new story. It would be beneficial to Brody and his family and friends if the world thinks I said yes to Archie Beaumont.

"I miss him. I miss his voice. I miss his angry little tirades when I get snippy. I miss everything. How much longer do I have to pretend, Bronwyn?"

"One outing with Archie. Today. We've hired paps to take some photos so they can run with it, and then you can go to Brody and explain everything."

Her voice is tired. She's been dealing with me because I'm angry with everyone else at the moment. There's no way Bianca wasn't in on the proposal. I bet she and Bitsy schemed for a week straight about how it would play out. Those crazy bitches actually thought I'd say yes to Archie with Brody, a real man, my man, standing right next to me.

"The way it happened gives me nightmares. I still can't believe he had the gall to ask me."

"I heard he had a change of heart about breaking it off with you when he realized that not only did you have Wyndham money, but you were also independently wealthy and made your own fortune with ATWU," Bronwyn explains. "It makes it worse. These guys are the pariahs of society, I swear. I bet he went to his girlfriend's house the second he left here."

I scoff and wipe my nose on my sleeve.

"You know Bitsy had a hand in this. She probably told him about ATWU and how I was branching off on my own. There's no way he's smart enough to read the news," I hiss. "He got through college on the Beaumont last name, manipulation, and cocaine. For the first time in my life, I have a real man to compare him to, and there's no comparison, Bronwyn. Like, none at all. Brody is patient and real. So real it aches because I know I hurt him."

"No, Archie did. The people we're surrounded by

hurt him." Bronwyn exhales. "I know what you mean. When I first met Edmund, and he didn't try to manipulate or gaslight me, it confused me because we're so used to that callous behavior that it's normal. I know what you mean when you say real. I promise you."

"I know you know. That's why I hate you," I say, laugh-snorting. "You got out of here, and you got love."

"Okay," Bronwyn says. "Answer this question right, and I'll go talk to Brody."

I sit up in bed and get lightheaded. "Ask it."

"If I tell him you said no to Archie and you are madly in love with him, will he be able to lie to the press sufficiently? Like, if they ask him, how do you feel about Saylor's engagement to Archie, will he be convincing enough? I know he's a SEAL, and they're supposed to be experts in handling stuff like this, but I'm here to tell you he was anything but cool, calm, and collected when I was talking to him during the proposal."

She pauses. I wait on bated breath to hear more.

"He was crushed, Saylor. I don't think he has any sort of self-preservation when it comes to you."

I'm already nodding. "He can lie. He can be mean. He won't answer the questions. I'll go on the date and smile for the damn photos, if that's what they want, as long as you go talk to him and tell him I miss him and this had to happen."

My sister shakes her head sadly.

"Why are you sad?"

"I feel bad for you. I know how hard you're going to have it. Mom and Dad followed their hearts, but it almost feels like that right wasn't granted to us. You remember the hard time I got for marrying Edmund, even though he was wealthy? He wasn't Mom's first choice. You choosing Brody is going to complicate things. Especially for him."

Her brown eyes meet mine.

"Are you saying we should break up?" I ask, mouth ajar, unable to process.

"No, because I know you're too deep for that, but know he's the one who will make the sacrifices, Saylor."

My stomach sinks. "I don't want him to make any sacrifices for me."

She blinks once, then again.

"Therein lies the reason we're guided to the multiple-choice options in our world. It's easy for both parties when it makes sense. Mom isn't as callous as you think. I'm not defending what she did, only giving you the reason she might have allowed it to happen in the first place. Sometimes it's not as simple as it should be when money gets involved."

I shake my head. "I don't want easy. I want him. He's the right person for me in all of the ways. He sees me, Bronwyn. The person who I really am, not what I present to people to hide. I'm sick of pretending I'm someone I'm not. I'm myself with Brody, his brother, and Catherine. It was freeing to just be able to be myself without any false pretenses. If you have that with Edmund, you must want that for me too."

"I do. That's why I'll go against Mom and their PR firm for trying to fix the mess you got us in in the first place."

"Hey, this isn't just my mess. The Wyndham attorney situation heightened it."

She nods. "That's true."

Bronwyn throws my covers back, exposing my bare legs. I'm wearing one of Brody's T-shirts and panties.

"I'll go tell Brody if you want me to, but Saylor, have you truly thought of the consequences he'll face for being with you? I love you more than anything and want you to be happy, but I need to know you've thought this through before we complicate things more. You're an educated woman. I trust your judgment implicitly, but sometimes love has a funny way of blinding us to things we should see." She clears her throat. "You see, right?"

I stay silent. I turn from my sister and look at the ocean view from the tall, expansive window. Standing from the bed, I run my hands through my tangled, long hair. It's a mess.

*Everything is a mess.*

My new sailboat, even more ostentatious than the last, bobs in our harbor. It is a taunting of sorts. I slam my eyes closed.

"I could walk away from this. I have my own money now. I could move away with him."

"His life is here, Saylor. His base. His family. It's here. You wouldn't take him away from that."

I hear her stand from my bed and walk to stand next to me.

"Plus, you can't leave your family. You're loved."

"So...marry Archie and be miserable? Try to forget true love exists? That's the easy, safe option?"

Bianca is the one who responds. "No. That's not an option. Archie Beaumont is an evil nitwit. I prohibit you from entertaining that proposal in the least," she says, clomping on my hardwood with her high-heeled mules. "Saylor," she deadpans.

I spin, my discontent evident in every fiber of my being.

"Bianca," I reply.

She looks out the window, then back at me, the resolution finalized.

"I want to apologize for the part I played in what happened at the party with Archie. I stayed away this long because Bronwyn said it would be best to give you space, but I heard this whole conversation because I'm nosy, and you need to go get that man. I don't care what's easy, or what everyone thinks, or what the PR team says. This has gone on long enough. If it's meant to be, it will be, no matter how hard it is."

"You mean that?" I ask, unable to hide my shock.

She presses her lips together. "Do I lie, Saylor?"

"Yes," Bronwyn and I charge at the same time.

She rolls her eyes. "Oh god, white lies don't count. Those are required to keep feelings and save face."

I have to hand it to her. She's acting civil and normal, so I believe her.

"If I listened to all the people in my ear about your dad, you wouldn't be here right now, so I mean it. This suffering has gone on long enough." Mom looks at me up and down. "And I'm not sure how much longer you'll last looking like that."

*There she is.*

"I love you, and I know I don't always show it, but I mean that too."

"I love you too, Mom," I reply.

She approaches slowly, steps tentatively, then she wraps me in a hug that lasts longer than any I remember in recent memory.

"You do need a shower. And a toothbrush," she adds. "Some Givenchy perfume and a nice sundress, and you'll feel like a billion dollars."

I step out of her embrace.

"I shouldn't worry about how this will affect Brody?"

"Let him worry about that. We're Wyndham women. Men make a way or make room. Trust in your heart."

"Wow, Mom. This may be the best advice you've ever

given," Bronwyn says, letting a giggle slip. "It's almost an out-of-body experience hearing it."

"Yes, well, someone had to tell her the truth, and you were doing a poor job of it. Oh, we sold all of the paintings, in case no one told you."

"Thanks, Mom," Bronwyn replies. "Thanks for the party too. Edmund is over the moon. He had a feeling the paintings sold would provide enough capital for another studio."

Bianca Wyndham returns, smiling at Bronwyn. "I aim to please. There was also a very sizable donation sent to the Special Warfare command too. In Brody's honor, for his part in saving you."

I sit on my bed and scrub my hands down my face. I do need a shower.

"It feels like so long ago. A dream almost."

I haven't spoken to them about my time in Madagascar in depth. I'm afraid of how they'll react.

"Not a nightmare?" Mom asks, nose wrinkled in disgust.

"How can it be?" I throw up my hands and let them fall on my bed. "I met him."

"I get that," Bronwyn says. "You really are okay after enduring...that?"

"I promise I am."

"You're just like your father," Mom says, and I think this may be the nicest thing she's said yet. "You do what you need to do and keep on moving. Did I tell you we eliminated the threat? Well, your father did, himself. The man who kept trying to break in to get my sweet Roger...it was Jennings's twenty-year-old son from his mistress! The scandal runs deep. His name was Ryan Smith, and he got a stipend every month from Jennings's account as hush money. Jennings got locked up, and the payments stopped. Ryan said there was a price on your father's head, and he needed it to survive once the payments stopped."

"Eliminated?" Bronwyn asks, voice cracking. "Like Dad killed him?"

Mom groans. "Don't be so crass, darling. Your father took care of the problem before the problem took care of him."

She's an ace at attorney speak.

"So did you get rid of the security team?" I ask, hopeful.

She shakes her head. "Not until the world is less interested in you."

"I'll meet Archie for dinner. I'll go. I'll smile. I'll tell the bastard I never want to see him again. We'll let the paparazzi take the photos. They'll post them. The world will know Brody and I are finished. Then I'll go see Brody and try to talk to him. I want to help fix what I can, and this will make them less interested in me. I'll do it for the family. If I'm marrying Archie, someone everyone expects me to be with, then that can be the end of the interest."

"Only if you want to," Mom says. "The photos will disperse quickly."

My legs are shaky from rotting in bed, but I walk into my bathroom and crank on the hot water.

"I got this," I toss over my shoulder.

Bronwyn comes in to talk to me when I'm in the shower. The glass is fogged, and she tells me the plan. She tells me how to look and what to say, so the pictures look authentic. When she tells me I have to kiss him, I tell her there's not a snowball's chance in hell I'll agree to that.

I wear the sundress. I put on the Givenchy perfume. I strap on red-bottom sandals and the Van Cleef bracelet stack. I play dress up one last time before I can be myself. Before none of this matters.

I'm shaking when I step out of my car, still reeling from sitting with Archie.

I saw the camera flashes from the corner of my eye. Archie didn't because he's not observant, and he's stupid. He actually thought I'd changed my mind and wanted to accept his great, great, grandma's fourteen-carat diamond and live a life of misery next to him.

I told him I wanted to see him for closure, and that's all it was. For him. I'd closed that book the second I realized Brody existed.

I rub the hood of my car and feel relieved. It's the first time I've been allowed to drive anywhere. Sure, I was followed, but I also have security. They're parked along the street, watching me like a hawk.

It doesn't look like Brody is home. The lights are off, and Grimace isn't standing on the back of the couch, barking his head off.

*Where are you?*

Every time I call him, it goes to voicemail. Every time I text, it bounces back as undeliverable. I sit on the front step and decide to wait.

I call him a few more times before I give up. If I lose him like this after what we've been through, it will not only be embarrassing, but it will also haunt me.

My stupid life that I don't identify with anymore ruins my chances for happiness. That's the headline, I decide.

I fold my arms over my knees and put my head down. The thoughts run so quickly they blur together. The first time I saw him. Our first conversation. The waterfall. The projects we collaborated on so effortlessly. The escape. The elevator. The lake house. It's a dream that's interrupted by the roar of a loud engine. I stand. His black truck pulls into the driveway.

He steps out, Grimace in his hands.

"What are you doing here?" he says, cold, emotionless.

"I wanted to see you," I say.

My body buzzes from seeing him and hearing one sentence from his perfect lips. He's in his cami uniform. The normal one, not the formal one he wore to the charity event.

"Brody, please, I need to talk to you. I'm sorry. I'm so sorry."

He looks behind him to where three black cars line the street in front of his house. He turns his tired gaze back to me.

"Just go, Saylor. Go home, back to the palace with your guards and the people who know you best."

He doesn't make a move to come closer.

"Hey, don't you say that. Don't you stand there and lie to me. You know that you know me best. You know my heart."

Brody shakes his head, looking down at the sleeping dog hanging limp over his arm. "I have to get him to bed."

He brushes past me and unlocks his door.

"That's it?" I say, tears forming in the corner of my eyes.

He puts Grimace down on the couch, but doesn't invite me in. He leans against the doorframe, tall and looming.

"What we had was nice, but we can't pretend this had staying power. I was blinded by obsession. I didn't see all the glaring signs telling me that this was never long term. We went through something traumatic together. You bonded with me, and I think it clouded your judgment too. I took this time away to really think about what a life together would look like, and it's not something sustainable, Saylor. You're a Wyndham. I need anonymity. Fuck, not just need, it's required from me *to do my job*."

My worst fear is coming true. Bronwyn is right.

"You're brilliant and beautiful. It doesn't take a rocket scientist to know you'll do okay without me."

"You're breaking up with me?" I say the words like a string of curse words.

"Your ex and that whole fucking display of fuck knows what did give me clarity. You may want to get married for love and live a happily ever after, but that's not what you need. We both know that. You need someone who blends in."

Tears fall over the rims of my eyes, hot traitors slipping down my cheeks. Brody looks at my jewelry and dress and shakes his head.

"I'm just a dirty ole SEAL. I'm not good enough to be next to you, anyway."

I hold up my arm and peel off the bracelets, tossing them to the ground.

"This shit doesn't mean anything to me. I want you. I want you to want me enough to figure it out. My mom was the one who sent me here. She said it didn't matter. That if you wanted me, you'd figure out a way to make it work."

That shocks him, but I can tell his mind is made up. His eyes tell me all I need to know. They're lifeless. Nothing is there. Like when I first met him.

"I can't figure this out. I can't. I've tried. Do you know how maddening it is to admit there's a problem I can't fix, and this is the cost?" He holds an arm out to me.

"Then keep it. Keep me. I'm yours."

He smiles sadly. "You were never mine to keep, Saylor."

"You're mistaken. I was always yours to keep. You toss me away so easily? That might hurt more than being cheated on. At least I know what I'm getting with a man like Archie. It's not love. It's not even loyalty. It's an agreement. You can't make up your own mind to save your life."

He grins. It doesn't meet his eyes. "Now you're getting it."

"Don't patronize me, Brody McCoy. Don't do that." I swallow down a lump. "Say you don't love me and don't hold back. Tell me you didn't love me at the waterfall. Or the lake house. Say you didn't love me at all, at any time we've been together, because I won't believe you ever did, because love doesn't just stop."

"It does."

"What, like a switch?" I retort. "If that's true, then maybe who you were when we met truly is who you are. Mean, corrosive, and condescending. Maybe I was wrong about you all along. This is who you are. Someone who can toss a person aside so easily because of circumstances out of her control."

"Saylor," he says, and it's condescending. "My profession dictates things. It dictates I can't be in the press. It tells me who I can date and who I can't. I was so numb to the reality of it because I wanted you more than I cared about everything else. The rest of my life cannot look like this." He points to the street with the guards. "My neighbors don't even know what I do, for Christ's sake. You are too much."

The last sentence causes physical pain.

"I'm too much for you, is what you mean to say. Rephrase it, Brody. Tell me the truth."

I sniffle. Brody looks away, like seeing me in pain is too much for him.

"Tell me you don't care."

He leans into the doorway, further away from me.

"Then you'll leave? If I tell you I don't care?"

My stomach turns to lead. He's serious.

"Better make me believe it, McCoy," I sling back, jamming a finger into the name patch on his chest.

He hangs his head. "Don't make this harder than it has to be. I've had a long day. I've had several long days."

"I didn't hear you say you didn't care."

"*I don't care,*" he says. "Sort your life. Get back into sailing. Invent. Discover. Make the world better, Saylor. You don't need a man to do the things you love. You changed the world with *All The Way Under*. The military forced you to create it. We blocked the signal of the original system you were using. It was us. We are the reason you got kidnapped in the first place."

"I can't believe this," I say.

He won't meet my gaze. They blocked my signal. I knew it didn't fail, and this is confirmation. I try to suppress my anger at this information so I can have a conversation with the man I love.

Brody presses his lips together. "It wasn't personal. It could have been anyone. We just needed a reason to go to the island. If we knew the brothers were already there, they would have been enough." He lets out another sigh. "You don't realize it now, but I am doing the right thing. Not just for myself, but for you too."

Another longing look that ends too quickly.

"I did learn something important, though. Sometimes love isn't enough."

"What if it's always enough?" I retort. "That's just your opinion. My opinion is that it is enough."

"Nah, it's been proven a couple of times now. I won't test the theory again, that you can be sure of."

"So you and Grimace are just going to live in this house by yourself, and you're going to do the same job forever? Lonely and mean?"

"He won't live forever," he replies sadly. "But yeah. That's the plan."

"That's sad," I say.

"Not as sad as it could be, though."

I remain silent. Studying his face. He does the same. It breaks my heart.

"Goodbye, Saylor. Fair winds and following seas."

He closes the door. Then locks it.

I sit on his cement steps for longer than I care to admit, processing everything that just happened.

My GPS signal was jammed by the United States military, and he knew it. All this time, he knew it.

Brody couldn't handle the very thing I warned him about in my life—people do what they want, and they manipulate to better position themselves. I offered to give it all up for him, and he rejected me.

I pick my bracelets up off of the ground and drop them into the mailbox attached to the side of his house. I meant it when I said I would give everything up for him.

My GPS was jammed, he knew it, and waited until now to tell me.

# CHAPTER EIGHTEEN
## *brody*

## ONE YEAR LATER

**THE FRENCH DOORS OPEN,** and the bridesmaids flow through, their purple dresses floating down the aisle one by one. I swallow hard, doing my best to maintain all composure in a situation that makes me feel...feelings.

Grimace is by my feet on a camo leash, wearing a black bow tie. I glance down to make sure he's watching. His second favorite person is about to walk down the aisle. I tighten my grip on his leash. Catherine walks out, and I peek around Nolan's shoulder to see his eyes watering. That little baby. I lock it in the memory bank to make him pay for it later and pat him on the shoulder.

"She looks so |beautiful," Nolan says, wiping at his eyes.

I hand him a hanky, and he dabs the tears away.

"I can't believe this is real."

Her slow walk gives everyone in the audience time to appreciate her, and I can't hide the happiness I have for my brother. Our parents are sitting in the front row, beaming at Nolan and Catherine. She finally gets to the pastor and Nolan after her father hands her off, and it's like I'm looking at a celebrity. She looks like herself, but better. Nolan is enamored, but that bastard never stood a chance. Catherine is perfect for him in every single way.

"We're doing this," Catherine says, handing her bouquet to her sister, the Matron of Honor, before grabbing Nolan's hands. "This day is finally here." Her voice is low, but the excitement in her words is visceral.

There was a time when I thought I deserved this, what my brother and Catherine have, but life truly showed me a different path. One that means I live my life to serve my country. I will die for my country too. I can't be certain of that, of course, but at the deployment schedule I've been going at, it would make the most sense.

I've thrown myself into my job. I got the promotion. I'm only a part-time grouch now that I realize this was always how my life was supposed to turn out. I'm a good man with a good heart. I wasn't missing anything in my life except self-validation. I never needed someone to complete me or turn my life around.

They wrote their own vows. I listened to Nolan practice his in front of the mirror at least a thousand times over the past months. Like he thought if he got them wrong, she might say no at the altar. Their love is made of something I've only witnessed once before between my own parents. It's how I knew their relationship would stand the test of time. Together they are one, but separately they also kick ass.

Nolan trips over a few words as he's reading the vows, but surprise, surprise, she says yes when the pastor asks if she'll take him as her husband 'til death do them part.

The rest is a blur of pure happiness. Nolan let me

wear a tux instead of my uniform. I didn't want to draw any attention on my twin's day. The reception is being held at a nice restaurant on the water. There are buses taking guests from the church to the venue, and I'm squeezed in between my parents in a row as we ride.

"Son, you know we have to keep everything even, so we make it to heaven," Dad says. "We're proud of you."

I chuckle. "You don't have to be proud of me on Nolan's wedding day. I don't think this counts as keeping everything even by saying that."

My smile falls. It will never be even in the same way. Nolan will forever have Catherine now. I'm still his brother in every way, yet my role has shifted. I'm not the most important person to him anymore, and that's the way it should be.

"I'm happy for them. Catherine is perfect for Nolan."

"She reminds me a lot of you," Mom says, smoothing a wrinkle on my pants. "Is that weird to say? Your brother's wife reminds me of his twin?"

"No, it makes sense. We make a great team, and we are very unlike each other. They'll make a great team because opposites attract. She is the me to his glee." I'm proud of my analogy. "You and Dad gave him a good example of what it's supposed to look like."

"We only gave *him* a good example?" Mom asks, cheeks falling.

Her blue eyes have wrinkles next to them, and I hate that I can see pain in her question.

I clear my throat. "Of course you set a great example for both of us. It obviously just resonated more with Nolan." I smile, but they don't.

"You act like it's a foregone conclusion you won't find someone, son. Why is that? You've given up completely?"

"I have to, Dad. I have to. No one will ever stack up,

and there's no sense looking back on something that was never going to work out. Before you ask, of course, I'm over her. It's been a year. It's not worth the effort of dating."

Mom sighs. "You really haven't gone on one date in a year?"

The bus hits a bump, and I hold on to the seat in front of me.

"How is that possible? You're a handsome, strapping man. You're not even as grouchy as you used to be!"

Dad cackles. "You're a straight catch, is what Mom is saying. Weddings have a way of making people talk about relationships, and we've been wanting to talk to you about this for a while now. You deserve some company."

I shake my head. "I'm never home. It wouldn't be fair."

"You could be home. You could accept the shore duty they've been trying to give you for months and settle down. You could have children and be home at night. It's not the running and gunning you've been doing, but it could be something special," Dad says.

He only knows this because I told Nolan. Have to love the game of family telephone, don't I? At least Nolan gave the details correctly.

I don't shoot him down straight away. I'll give them hope before I snatch it away.

"What if I get bored?"

"There is never a dull moment with children, son. I promise you that. Boredom won't be in your lexicon."

"Grimace would hate kids," I say. "I hope Mark does what I told him and gives him a treat before he leaves."

Mark was running Grimace back to my place before coming to the reception. He offered, and he never offers to do anything with Grimace.

Mom groans. "Grimace would not. That dog is as soft as you on the inside. You love to play the mean dog card, but that dog doesn't have a mean bone in his body. He's a reflection of you."

"Oh, I indeed have a *mean bone* in my body," I say, elbowing Dad gently.

A wheezy laugh escapes his wrinkled lips. Signs of aging on my parents make my chest tighten. The signal that time is passing, and there's nothing we can do to stop it.

"You are foul," Mom claps back. "But I do love you and want you to have a fulfilled life."

"I am fulfilled. I promise you."

Dad puts his arm around my shoulders. "We accept this promise under one condition."

I look at him. "I'm afraid to ask. I'm not going on any dates Mom sets me up on."

They've tried that before. Mom has ladies at the doctor's office she works at who have daughters they've been trying to set me up with all my life.

"No, no, we've given up on that," Mom says.

"We won't bring up dating or women again if you promise that the next time something scares you—and we know that doesn't happen often—but if it scares you, lean in. Stop treating your heart like a grave. It's a garden, son. A beautiful garden with lots to offer the right woman."

The right woman. The right woman.

The thing with talking about her, which I don't do often, is that now I'll dream about her. Saylor will be visceral in my dreams, and when I wake in sheer excitement, she vanishes—a figment of a lost promise.

"I promise when something scares me, I'll lean in. Then I'll probably shoot it, but hell, I'll lean in first."

"Stop making jokes," Mom says, slapping my shoulder. "We're serious. We think that Say...*she* scared you. What could have been scared you. How close you were to having...something terrified you. Having something to lose," she adds. "Be scared. Embrace it. Everyone in the world is scared at some point or another in a relationship. If you're scared in a good way, you're blessed."

I hang my head. They're right.

"Okay, okay. I got it. I'll let myself be terrified, like a little pussy."

Another slap. "Get off the bus. We're here. Don't embarrass us when you give your speech. Do you hear? Nothing wild. The girls from bridge are here. So are all of the ladies from work. The daughters too."

"Moooom," I groan.

She shakes one finger at my face while holding back a laugh. "Don't embarrass us with your raucous childhood stories. I was a good mom."

"You did everything you could, honey. They're just unruly kids," Dad says, wearing his devil-may-care smirk.

We walk off the bus, grinning. It's sunset on the water, and it is fucking beautiful. I love looking at the water from land, knowing I'm not going to be *in it* when blackness takes over.

"Where did Catherine find this place? I've never been here before."

We live in one of those small, big towns. Big enough for people and places you've never heard of, but small enough that people tend to know, in a roundabout way, everyone.

Mom says something under her breath, and Dad claps me on the back once before heading in the opposite direction with the other guests.

I was given orders to enter through the side, where the

deck wraps around. There's a room where the bridal party is supposed to wait so we can enter together.

I stop at the deck to admire the sunset. I'm here early, so there's no sense going in yet. A waitress with a tray filled with drinks spots me from inside and comes out to offer me a drink. I take a foamy glass of beer and thank her.

My parents' conversation and their worry have me feeling melancholy, so I drink my beer and watch the horizon until dark settles. I set my glass down on a tray in the corner and head inside. I pull down my tux and read-just my shirt before turning a corner.

"Boo!" A flash of purple and blonde pounces in front of me.

I actually startle, my heart tripping.

Saylor. She's standing in front of me. Like a dream vision of perfection.

"I'm sorry," she says, but her smile deepens, crinkling her eyes. "Your dad said he'd pay me ten bucks to jump out and scare you."

*My damn dad. I should have known.*

Her big blue eyes hold me to my spot. I don't move. I can't. She enters my bloodstream like a hit of a drug after I've been sober. My heart beats a familiar rhythm again after a year of heartbreak.

I'm alive. That's what this feels like. Her scent fills my lungs. Her presence brings me back to life.

"Saylor," I say, her name trembling on my lips.

I forbade myself from saying it after the breakup. Thinking of her was unbearable. It was easier to wash myself of her existence entirely. Which is easier said than done.

"What are you doing here?"

She's eyeing me up and down.

"Cat sent me an invite, but obviously I sent back a no RSVP straight away because I didn't want to intrude. Then a guest needed a last-minute plus one, and he convinced me it would be a good idea if I came."

I push the jealousy aside because she isn't mine. Was never mine, honestly, but who could she possibly be here with?

"I can leave if you'd rather me not be here. It's why I wanted to talk to you first. Should I leave?"

I don't trust my voice. I shake my head to reply.

Her gaze darts away.

"I didn't keep up with anything to do with you. I couldn't. When I got the invite, it was still fresh pain, you know? It was too hard to think about you."

Saylor turns her face, and our oceans lock.

"I set the world record, though. I didn't report it to the record book. That attention didn't seem like something I wanted." She smiles, then it drops. "I just needed to prove to myself that I could do it. It was never going to be safer than it was right after the SEALs squashed the terrorist group, so I took advantage. I spent a few months being upset, loaded my new sailboat, and went."

She shakes her fists next to her shoulders in an exaggerated way.

"Didn't get captured this time! I used ATWU the whole journey, and somehow my signal didn't get jammed," she smirks. "It took a long time and a lot of therapy to work through that, but I know it wasn't you."

"You took my advice," I say.

"I dated a few guys when I got back too."

"I did not give you that advice."

Saylor tilts her head and smiles. "You gave up rights to stop me."

Fair.

"I didn't keep up with you either, for what it's worth, so I didn't know about the sail. Congrats. That's a huge accomplishment." I pause. "The new update on ATWU is pretty crack too, by the way. Used it a few weeks ago and thought of you."

I regret the last sentence the second it leaves my mouth.

She blushes. "Oh, good. I thought that update might change things for the better. I have an open-ended contract with the military now. They want first dibs on anything I come up with." Saylor crosses her legs at the ankles.

"There you are," Mark says, coming up from behind me. "Ready to go in? Nolan and Cat just got here."

Saylor nods. "Yeah, sure. Was just saying hi to Brody really quick."

Ah, that's all I needed to find my voice.

"Wait, you are here with Mark?" I ask, looking between my best friend and the woman who haunts me.

My woman.

He wouldn't.

"I'll see you both in there," Saylor says, turning to walk away, looking just as perfect leaving as she does coming.

As soon as the door closes, I grab my friend by his collar.

"Unhand me. It's not what you think," Mark deadpans, rolling his eyes.

I release my grasp. "Talk."

"Nolan told me I should ask her so she would be here to talk to *you*." He huffs. "She's here as my platonic, nothing at all, friend. Jesus, Brody. Who do you think I am? I'm your best fucking friend."

"I trusted motherfuckers before, and that's what got

me here. I'm sorry. Seeing her has me on edge. I don't know how to act. I haven't spoken about Saylor in months. Why would Nolan think I wanted to talk *to* her?"

He raises one brow. "You're joking, right? Just because you haven't spoken about her doesn't mean everyone doesn't see the romantic fool you are about her and the past you had with her. Your parents were part of this. It might be Nolan's wedding, but it's your fucking intervention."

"Intervention for what? I'm happy. I'm fine. I'm over her."

"So we're not going to talk about the ten minutes that happened before I walked in? That looked like anything except you being over her. She was willing to be here. Saylor moved on with her life, and now it's time to start over with her in a new space." He coughs into his hand. "If you can convince her."

"If you think I'm fuck-all stupid, and I'd put myself through *that* again, you're crazier than I realized."

"It's not the same. No more security. Did you notice that? The circus around the Wyndhams died down. You avoiding their name isn't the only reason you didn't hear about them. They began a huge campaign to disappear into obscurity after you broke up with Saylor. They're still filthy fucking rich. They just don't use their name and lay a little lower." He looks away. "And don't act like that rich fake shit is the only reason you pushed her away. You know you freaked and were being pusillanimous. You know you didn't think you deserved it. We all know you do."

"You're a pussy," I fire back.

"I used the refined word. Stop being so crude. It's a blessed day," Mark says, flashing a half smirk. "A joyous wedding!" he exclaims.

Nolan and Catherine rush down the hallway, big smiles on their faces, looking at each other, speaking low. Nolan turns and sees me, and the smile drops.

"You can't kill a man on his wedding day! Let's go in!" he calls to me.

"I'm going to kill you all tomorrow, then. It's settled."

We go into the room where guests are cheering. The bride and groom do some dumb, rehearsed dance, and we follow after, but I can't stop myself from searching for her in a crowd. It's automatic and infuriating.

When I see her, she's watching me, a smile on her lips.

I bite back any emotion and take my seat at her table, right next to her, because the entirety of the humans who care about me put my name card next to hers. Hers just says S.W.

"All this fuss just to tell people you're going to be together for the rest of your lives. Seems excessive," I say, folding my arms, leaning back in my chair.

I can feel her stare at the side of my face.

"Well, not all weddings have to be the same. This is very beautiful, and they both look happy."

Happiness is a gateway to pain. That's what I know to be true. You allow it in because it poses as something light, and then it sucks you all the way under and anchors you to the depths of despair.

"It does give off a bit of the zoo animal vibe, though," she says, voice quiet.

Biting my lip, I stave off a grin. It's impossible to shoot down the feelings the memory forces. Even though it's been a year, my body reacts like I was fucking her in an elevator yesterday. I think it's what a true connection must feel like. We pick right back up where we left off. It's not just a twin thing. It has to be a *real* thing.

I do my best to make conversation with the others at

our table, trying not to talk to Mark too much or stare at Saylor too long, until after dinner.

The toasts begin.

I wrote one on the note app in my phone before I went to bed, but with the turn of events, and my fourth beer tasting like I-should-wing-it, I go up to the small two-person table Nolan and Catherine are sitting at. I see my mom glaring at me, so I get out my phone. I'll just ad-lib a bit.

The spotlight hides all the tables and faces from me, which is a good thing. Public speaking is not my strong suit. Sweat rolls down my face, and I can't wipe it away quick enough. My free hand is in a fist by my side. I can keep a steady pulse rate when I'm clearing a room or exterminating villains, but being in front of these people, knowing Saylor is out there, makes me tremble.

Nolan stands up, grabs the microphone from me, and puts his arm around my shoulder. "We're twins. I know exactly what he was going to say anyway," Nolan says.

The shadowy figures boom with laughter in front of us. It doesn't quiet my nerves, though.

I look at my brother, and I remember to breathe because he is. Nolan turns back to the spotlight.

"He was going to make a joke about how he's younger by thirty-seven minutes and somehow that time alone made him darker, wiser, broodier, and obviously more intimidating."

Nolan looks at me. It's wistful.

"And then he was going to tell you that I'm the sunshine twin. The optimistic one. The one who believes every situation can be fixed with a good cheeseburger and a big smile."

Nolan beams at me.

"But he'd get through the jokes, and he would've,

eventually, he would say something real. Under that whole emotionally allergic exterior, Brody is the most loyal, deeply feeling person I know. He's been my other half and best friend since the womb. He's my mirror. The only one who knows when I'm lying, even to myself, and calls me out for it."

Nolan turns to the crowd, and I hear the words come slower because he has to push through the emotion.

"And even though he couldn't say it, I know what he meant to say. You would tell them that you've never seen me more myself, and at ease than I am when I'm with Catherine. You would tell them you're not sure how, but she's made me better than I was before. You know that she gets me in a way that no one else has. And Catherine," he says, turning to look at his bride. "Brody was going to tell you that he likes you because you terrify him. In only good ways, though."

The audience laughs.

"That your twin flame sarcasm is a love language, and you share a mutual understanding that eye-rolling is a valid form of communication. He would say that you're already family, and we're better for it. On behalf of my twin brother and my favorite grump, let me say," Nolan says, picking up a glass of champagne and handing me one. "Here is to finding someone who makes your stubborn heart feel safe and to the people who love us even when we freeze at the mic. To Catherine and me, and to Brody, thanks for standing up with me today. Cheers."

We clink glasses and take a sip. I can't help the traitorous tears forming in my eyes. Nolan is the only person who has been saving me my whole life. I hug him, but then I take the mic.

"That was exactly what I was going to say. More or less. Thanks, brother."

I pause, the crowd shifts, but I forge through the nerves because my brother paved the way for me.

"But I think I've got a few words left in me after all. Catherine, I expect you to keep him in line, and Nolan, good luck."

The guests laugh.

"Nolan talked about love and people getting each other, but he didn't talk about timing. Timing is something that you can't fake. It's either right or it's abysmal. If you can't fake it, maybe you can fix it or try again. It's been a hard, life-altering year, but it had to happen."

I shrug to control my shaking.

"I'm not here asking for anything crazy, like I'm sure my parents and Nolan want from me. This isn't a grand gesture. I am asking, S.W., if maybe we can start over. As friends. Two people who once meant everything to each other, and who might again. One step at a time. That's it."

I raise my shaking glass.

"To fate. To timing. And to second chances, if we're brave enough to ask for them. I love you, Nolan." I say it out loud for everyone to hear.

The spotlight dims, and I can see my parents smiling. I set the mic down on the table, and I leave the room. Returning to my seat isn't an option when I'll have to face her. I grab another beer—a mistake—and head back to the deck and walk down it as far as I can. Past where the lights from the restaurant cascade out. Hidden in the silence. The way I'm intended to be. The ocean hums softly.

I don't turn when I hear the click of her heels.

Her voice is soft. "So...you want to be my friend, huh?"

I swallow the last of my beer and set the glass on the rail.

"It was either that or pretend that seeing you didn't wreck my entire emotional stability. I couldn't even give a damn speech."

She lets out a laugh. The kind she does when she's trying not to cry. I don't dare turn to look at her or risk losing all control.

"You surprised me in there. That wasn't the Brody from a year ago."

"The Brody from a year ago let you walk away without a fight." I pause. "The new improved Brody taught himself how to fight something other than bad guys, and also how to sail."

She blows a breath from her nose.

"You learned how to sail? Like not pretending to sail so you could get captured and make it look real? Like, sail, sail?"

"I mean, I knew the basics when I got captured, but I still crashed into docks. I figured if I ever met another woman who was obsessed with sailing, I should probably brush up." Another long pause. "You know?"

She reads through my bullshit jokes easily.

"You didn't need to change for me. You know that, though. It was me who was required to change because of the family I was born into."

Now I'm certain she's crying, and I can't ignore that. I turn, and her face is illuminated by twinkling fairy lights that someone inside turned on. My family truly did orchestrate an intervention and knew every move I'd take. Got to love them and hate myself for being so predictable, I suppose.

"You never needed to change. I wasn't brave enough. It's really that simple. I was always going to worry you only loved me because I saved you. Our time in the jungle wasn't normal or reality. It fast-tracked our feelings, or that's what I told myself, anyway."

God, I missed looking at her face. Her lips. Eyes that scream adoration. Forever.

"I changed because not having you wrecked me in ways I didn't know were possible. Sailing helped me figure out who I am when I'm not running from what I feel."

Silence stretches on, and I'm a fool for thinking I could be her friend. I want to kiss her right now and never stop.

Saylor tucks her blonde hair behind her ears. An invitation?

"Here's me being brave enough to ask for a second chance when I botched the first." I grab her hand, and I feel it throughout my whole body. "Saylor, will you go on a date with me? A real one. No timelines. Or media. Or guards. Or looking over our shoulders. My boat isn't as nice as yours, but she's fucking fast." I grin. "A sailboat date. No pirates." I shake my head. "Just us."

Saylor studies me, really stares. I know she's looking for a tell, and I know she'd see it if I were trying to hide something. She smiles real and slow.

"Only if you let me captain the boat. You have to be my first mate."

"Deal," I say, too eagerly. "But I'm bringing the snacks. Fancy ones. Friendship-level snacks, at least, because that's what we are."

"Yeah, sure. That's what we are," Saylor says, raising a brow.

She squeezes my hand, and it electrifies me, making my heart knock against my chest and my mind race.

"Good. Good. Nice talk," I say.

"It's a date, Brody."

"I have to know. Did my dad actually pay you ten dollars?" I ask.

Saylor tilts her head and looks up through her lashes, smiling.

"I didn't take money from your dad, but I did promise to make you jump."

"I am going to kill them all," I blurt, noticing them all standing in a large window overlooking the dock, staring at us.

I give them a thumbs up. Mission complete.

Those fuckers have the audacity to cheer.

# CHAPTER NINETEEN

## *saylor*

"WHY AM I SO NERVOUS? My hands are actually clammy. I didn't know that was a real thing. It's absolutely disgusting," I say, checking my outfit in a full-length mirror.

I'm at my parents' house, in my childhood bedroom, because my date with Brody is tonight, and I wanted everyone around me for moral support.

My mother sips her drink from a chaise nearby.

"Because you've been waiting for this night for a year," she says. "I think the other dress was too *look at me*. This one is understated. You are beautiful in both, though. Which bikini did you put underneath?"

I lift the dress. "Baby pink crochet, not full coverage, not a thong, a cheeky bottom. Does it scream desperate?"

She shakes her head. "No, red is desperate. This is perfect. Oh, that reminds me. Let me fetch the box. The chauffeur went and picked it up from the jeweler."

I got Brody a gift. Like, a proper love gift that I hope doesn't freak him out. Mom comes back ten minutes later and hands it to me.

"I love you, Saylor. I don't say it enough because something about saying those words itches my windpipes, but I love you, and I'm proud of you."

I hug her. Bless this crazy woman. She would lay down her life for me, but maybe not if she was wearing couture.

"I love you too, Mom."

This year changed all of us. Our perspectives shifted in a way that brought us closer. We understand each other more.

Brody was right. I needed this time. I needed him to set me free. I hated it, but the reality check saved us all.

"I say a lot of stuff about stuff, but follow your heart," she whispers. "He's not a dumb man. Don't be nervous."

I face myself in the mirror as she leaves, and I worry. I put on makeup and a pair of deck shoes, even though they don't go with my dress, because they make more sense than wedges.

The drive to the marina is quick, and I park next to his truck. I toss the jewelry box into my tote bag with my laptop and transfer cords, because I'll never go on the water without my programming again. I see the boat from the parking lot. Brody is on a step stool hanging lights as I walk up.

"Those friend lights look pretty romantic," I say, letting my voice carry on the slight breeze.

He hooks the strand and steps down, turning with his hands on his hips.

He has on a white linen shirt and khaki shorts. His hair is longer than it was the last time I saw him, and there's a five o'clock shadow around his jaw. He's had time off.

*He's had time off, and he hasn't called you*, my subconscious hisses.

"You're early," he says. "And that dress doesn't look very friend-like either," he says, licking his lips.

Damn. I'm in trouble. Exactly where I want to be.

"Let me help you up."

He extends his hand, and the view of him, at sunset, is something out of a fairy tale.

"I've been working on this all week long," he says, pride evident. "I wanted it to be perfect for our date."

Tears well.

"It is so perfect, Brody."

The details. The flowers. The soft lights. The high-tech equipment that looks like he stole from work.

"You do know the way to my heart."

That slipped and wasn't very friend-like, but at least he knows how I'm feeling.

"I can't believe you did all this for me."

He lifts and lowers one shoulder. "There's a whole picnic down below. It was no big deal."

He reaches out an arm, and I think he's going to wrap me in his arms, but instead says, "Here, let me take your bag."

My stomach sinks. Is this really a friend date? I'll die of embarrassment, and then I'll perish altogether if it is.

He takes it, and I follow him down to the berth where there are electric candles, more flowers, and all my favorite snacks. I take off my shoes.

"You stay here and have some snacks. I need to finish up, and I don't want your help."

"I was supposed to be captain," I say.

"If this isn't perfect, I'll never forgive myself, so just do what I say."

"So grouchy," I say. "Fine. Aye, aye, captain."

His eyes light up. "God, having you here doesn't feel real."

I pop a grape in my mouth. "Oh, I'm here all right, and I'm ready to date."

His smile turns into something feral. *Yes*. I recognize that. My stomach leaps.

"Be right back," he says.

Another grape. A piece of cheese. A gummy bear. I can't eat much. I'm stuck in a feedback loop, operating in a place I'm not familiar with these days.

The hull groans and adjusts, and the creak of dock lines releasing tells me we're off. The water laps in a calming slap, slap pattern. There's a thump as the mooring line is pulled in. More calmness and peace fill me. There's a palm-sized velvet bag on the board of food and the temptation is too strong. I peek inside to see my bracelets. The ones I left in his mailbox when I never thought I'd see them...or him, again.

The picnic is set up on the bed, and there's a small bathroom down here. It smells like new construction has taken place. As I look at my bracelets, I wonder how long it took for him to know that he'd give them back. How long until he knew I'd be on this boat with him.

I call up, pulling my sweater out of my bag. "Can I come up yet?"

"Yes!" he calls back, faint with the wind and the water rushing around us.

He has music playing as I come up, something soft and classical. The sunset is magical. Although it always is, this one feels special.

"We won't go out too far. There's a perfect cove to anchor that I checked out yesterday."

"Foxglass Cove?" I return, standing next to him so my shoulder brushes his.

He seems intent on the water and the navigation, so I keep talking.

"While we weren't together," I say, clearing my throat. "I saw a fundraiser for Conner and Turner. They both lost their jobs while they were captured. I donated and made sure they'd be set up for a long time. I just...the guilt was too heavy. We didn't worry about that kind of stuff, you know? It was anonymous, so they don't know it was me. I didn't want recognition, but I hope they figured it out."

He smiles down at me warmly.

"That was really nice of you, Saylor. There's no guilt to be had with that, though. They may not have escaped at all if you and I hadn't shown up. They got their lives back. I'm sure they're thankful for that," he replies. "Yes, Foxglass Cove. That's the spot. I should have known you would know."

We stay silent, appreciating the view as we near the cove, thinking about the rescue and the brothers. I help with the lines as we approach, and he lets the anchor down when we've reached the correct depth. The land blocks the wind, and the water is glass still here, hence the name.

"I've never been on a sailing date before, believe it or not. This has always been a dream of mine."

"I kind of hoped that was the case," he says.

When we're finished with the tasks the boat requires of us, he stops on the deck, hands on his hips, nothing else to distract him from me. Us. This chemistry crackles between us.

"I should have done this before. A year ago."

"You would have crashed us into a house if you did this a year ago," I tease. "Turn around and look at me."

He's staring off at the horizon.

"I used to think the world was flat when I was a kid because I couldn't see what was beyond there, you know?" He points. "I'd watch the sun set and think it just vanished below dirt because I couldn't see where it went."

"You didn't have a lot of faith as a kid," I reply. "A flat-earther, I never would have guessed!"

He shakes his head. "It's hard to put faith in something and end up being wrong. I eventually got to science class, and it was proven to be round. When you and I broke up a year ago, I thought that was it for us, and then you showed up at Nolan's wedding. There you were—a burden of proof. That no matter how hard I tried to distance myself from my feelings, your mere existence proved me a fucking liar."

He turns, and his blue eyes sink into my soul.

"Because when I look at you, I feel forever, Saylor. When I touch you, it brings me to life."

He takes a step closer. I can smell his cologne and taste his breath now.

"When I left you, I lost part of my heart."

I put a finger up to his lips.

"It's okay. I'm here now. We're together."

I replace my finger with my lips. His hands slide up to the sides of my face, and his lips taste like home. The kiss is short and sweet.

"You know that I came back because we were meant to be together, and you were right. *You truly were*. I needed to sort through my life and fix aspects, and *you were right*." He holds my face close to his as I speak. "You were wrong about one thing."

"What?"

"Love is enough. That's what this is. I could have met you on the street, and it would have felt like this. I went to therapy because Bronwyn was going to disown me if I didn't, and the therapist said I was right. The things I said about you and how I feel aren't because of some trauma bond. It's what true love is supposed to be. Textbook."

He lets go of my face and steps away so he can see me fully.

"You were busy this year," he replies.

I wave my arm. "Back at you. Mark told me that you were also deploying more than usual as well."

"It was fast and furious. But if I were going, then that meant someone could stay back who wanted or needed to stay back home. It just worked out, I guess. And I did this in between. Even me trying to forget you led me to pick up your favorite pastime. Should have known we were textbook," Brody says. "I'm not going to be deploying much now, though."

"Why? Isn't that what you do? What you live for?"

"I put my name in the hat for shore duty," he says, clearing his throat. "I have so many good years and ops under my belt, it was no question. My commander granted my request instantly. That means I'll be working on base here, supporting my Team from home."

I can see in his eyes that he's still getting used to this idea.

"Brody," I say. "When we were at the lake house, you said you never wanted shore duty. You called it the *Broken Flipper Club*. That real SEALs never ask to stay back."

His neck works as he swallows. "I think I said SEALs never ask to stay back unless they have a reason."

"What's your reason?"

He looks away.

"I'm tired, Saylor." He meets my gaze, and he smiles, but it doesn't reach his eyes. "And Nolan found Catherine. I want that. I want what they have. I'm not a jealous person by nature, but I'm jealous of him because now he's never lonely. Seeing him reach a milestone has never affected me the way it did when he found his person. It made the jagged hole in my heart and my life glaring."

He strokes my cheekbone with the back of his knuckles.

"I'll never assume anything about you again, but I want you to be my reason."

I cup his hand and hold it against my face. The sun sets completely, and now the only light is from the fairy lights and the lights embedded into the deck.

"I thought you wanted me to be your friend," I say. "This doesn't sound like friendship territory."

"I do want you to be my friend. What's that saying? Marry your best friend, and there will be laughter every day?"

"Whoa, whoa, whoa. That sounded suspiciously like a marriage proposal, Brody McCoy."

"If it was?" he asks, a line forming between his brows. "If it was, what would you say?"

His blue gaze dances over my face.

"I'd probably ask if you were feeling okay," I say, honestly. "Because you didn't ask in a cantankerous way, but then I'd say yes." I lick my lips. "That is, if you had actually asked," I amend.

Brody bends down on one knee, taking a box out of his shorts. He opens the ring box, exposing the most stunning sapphire ring I've seen in my entire life. It's a color I've never seen before. Then it hits me where it's from.

"You got that stone in Madagascar. It's native there."

He nods. "I found it while we were installing that sprinkler system and knew I had to keep it for right now."

"Brody," I say.

He waves me off and looks like he's going to pass out. He exhales noisily.

"I've been shot at, dropped out of planes, nearly

drowned, dragged teammates out of hell, and none of that scared me like this does. Like you do. Marry me, Saylor Wyndham. Marry me and do life with me. I'm probably going to mess up, and God knows I'll be an asshole every once in a while, but I will be loyal to you. I will love you like no one else can. All in. Every damn second. I can't live without you."

"Are you done? Are you going to put that ring on my finger or make me wait another year?"

He slides the ring on. A perfect fit. It's so beautiful and perfect that I cry.

"Next time you propose to me, maybe lead with the part where you can't live without me instead of war."

"I did live without you, and it was unbearable. I don't want to relive that." He stands, pulling me to him. "Was that a yes?"

I'm still looking at my left hand, holding it out, watching the cobalt stone sparkle in the moonlight.

"A thousand times, yes. A million times, yes. I can't believe this is real. I was so nervous for tonight that I played out scenarios all day, and this one wasn't even on the list."

"Can I kiss my fiancée?" he asks, tone lowering. "Please."

I reach my hand around his neck, and he leans down to kiss me. His hands rove over my ass, and he pulls me against his hard-on sharply. I can't help the quiet moan that escapes my mouth.

This is the connection that's been missing. Most of the pieces of the puzzle of my life were in place, and even though I knew this was what I was missing, Brody needed to be ready.

I taste him this time, and it makes my head swim and

my stomach dance. His big hands are warm as he runs his hands up my sides, and then he holds my neck in place.

The hollow ache is finally dulled.

Brody pulls back. "You like the ring?"

"I love the ring."

"When we got back to the States, I took it to my dad's friend, who is a jeweler. It looked like just a dark blue rock when I found it. He turned it into that. I don't know fuck-all about jewelry, but I designed the setting and stole one of your rings for twenty-four hours so I could get your size. It was a mission in and of itself."

"I'm so impressed. It's the color of your eyes. It's perfect." I shiver.

He pulls two notecards out of his back pocket and holds one in each hand.

"I planned a few things, but I wanted to make it fun. Pick one."

"Right," I say, grabbing the one on my right and reading it. "It says, Brody McCoy is certifiably insane." I flip it toward him. "Night swim? Are you crazy?"

"There are no sharks here. It's too shallow. Just a quick swim so we can say we did it," he says.

"I don't even know who you are anymore," I say, folding my arms. "What's the other card say? I pick that one instead. Black water swimming is terrifying, Brody."

"It's sailboat sex," he says coyly. "Which we can do after we swim."

I take off my dress to expose my bikini and toss it down into the berth.

"Take off your clothes," I order. "The sooner we dunk ourselves in that ocean, the sooner we can move on to more entertaining, safer options. Plus, I have a gift for you too."

He's undresses, except he doesn't have a bathing suit underneath.

"Oh, this is just not fair," I say, licking my lips. "I've waited a year for this, and you're going to parade it around, yet make me wait?"

His smile is white against the dark sky, and his dick, like it always is around me, is hard.

"You could make it fair if you wanted to."

"Skinny-dipping? Here?"

He nods firmly. "Break some rules, Wyndham. We're living a little tonight, McCoy style."

And I do. First, I make him check the sonar system to make sure nothing big is swimming near or under us, then he holds my hand, standing starboard, and we jump off the gunwale.

The water is electric cold, but Brody pulls me into his body—his warmth—and I stop shivering. He treads water so easily. I just lean my head against his wide chest and savor the closeness and this connection. The embrace is gentle, but his arms are strong.

"I feel like nothing can touch us here," I whisper.

"Nothing can ever touch us. I will always protect you," Brody replies, bringing my ring up to kiss it. "Look. The bioluminescence."

The tiny blue lights float and sway in the distance like stars trapped in the ocean. That's always what I think about when I'm sailing at night, and I see the living light the marine plankton emit. It's alive, just like the stars, swirling and warping with the waves, never breaking, always flexing. Always bright and stunning.

Brody pulls me down and kisses me underwater, just for a few moments, running his hands over my breasts and down my sides. The warmth from his hands sends a thrill through my body, my stomach flipping with excitement.

We surface, bodies entangled as he swims us toward the ladder and lets me climb back on board first.

There are two big towels folded nearby. I grab one and drape it over my shoulders. I hand a towel to Brody, and he does the man thing, dries his hair, then a half-assed towel off for his body, then wraps it around his hips.

I head to the berth where it's always warmer and climb onto the edge of the king-sized bed. The tray of food is in the center, so Brody gets on the other side.

"From the moment I began working on this fucking time suck, I thought about you. I wanted to show you stuff as I went. It almost made it bittersweet because I couldn't."

"Or it makes it sweeter now because I can see how well it came out. You did a fantastic job, Brody." I pause. "I got you a little gift too. Let me give it to you," I say, reaching into my tote bag and handing him the box.

"When I sailed around the world, I did stop in Madagascar. Not because I'm crazy, and only for a brief stint to get some of the sand." I pause as he opens the box, eyeing what's inside. "The cage wasn't there anymore, but of course I knew exactly where it was. They did convert it to a base like you said, but I talked them into letting me do this."

I look away, hoping this brings back the same sweet memories as it does for me.

"Sand is mostly silica or quartz. You can heat it, and silica can crystallize into a gemstone." I nod at the leather bracelet he's tightening on his wrist. "I was going to have Cat give it to you if the wedding run-in didn't go the way I wanted. I thought you should always have a piece of that time. To remind you of how sweet life can be in the middle of madness and desperation." I swallow down the emotion. "I still think about our time there, and the good outweighs the bad."

"Saylor, I don't know what to say," Brody says, voice breaking on the last word. "I love it."

I blow out a breath. "Good. I'm glad. You don't wear jewelry, so this could go one of two ways. I made the stone myself, but I did have to send it to our family jeweler to get it mounted and put on the leather so it would last forever. You can get it wet and everything."

He fingers the stone, tilting it so the dim cabin light catches the nuances.

"I can't believe you went back on that base," he says, finally. "Alone."

"Sometimes we have to do things alone," I say, shrugging. "If I had it my way, you would have been with me, remember?"

His face drops. "I'm sorry. Torturing myself is one thing. I'm used to it. I thrive in hostile environments. Torturing you is quite another thing entirely."

"If you love someone, you have to set them free. If they come back, they're yours. If they don't return, they never were yours. It's a proverb I told myself when I began to feel sad or when I missed you. You can't keep someone with fear. You were right to let me go." I meet his big blue eyes. "Because we're together now. Forever."

"What's truly yours will seek the sea. And sail back home through storm or blue, to rest again inside of you," Brody says, eyes turning down in the corner. "If they return on winds so true, then fate has stitched their path to you." He nods. "I told myself the same thing a million different ways when I realized my mistake. When Nolan was writing his vows, I sat with him in solidarity and wrote my version of that same proverb. The sailing one I wrote was my favorite. It suits us."

"You wrote that?"

"I had to. It was the only way to make sense of my assholery at the time. You said yes, so you forgive me."

I nod, smirking, then I let the towel drop. "What are we doing first? Eating or card option number two?"

His gaze darkens as it wanders down my naked body and back up. He picks up the large wooden tray holding the snacks and moves it to the deck, out of the way. He drops his towel and turns, looming, to stare at me.

"There's a part of me that never thought I'd see this sight."

Kneeling on the bed, I move toward him, reaching out my left hand. His eyes catch on the ring, then move to my face.

"This was always going to be the sight, Brody. I knew. Woman's intuition."

He takes my hand and lies down between my legs on top of me. He interlaces his fingers with mine and slides them so they're over my head.

"This is my favorite place in the world."

"On a sailboat?"

"No, with you," Brody says, sliding into me.

I'm already wet and ready. His moan is low and deep as he thrusts once and then again. I lock my legs around his waist and bring my lips to his neck. My touch drives him wild, feral, my lips edging him closer as he fucks me.

"I'm going to come," he says. I stop kissing his neck and hold his face to kiss his mouth.

"Look at me when you come inside me," I order, lips on his mouth.

His thick lashes open, blue eyes meet mine.

His smile, against my teeth, turns feral, calculating the challenge. With effort, he keeps his eyes open, barely, as he empties inside me with a groan.

RACHEL ROBINSON

"God, that was way too fast," Brody says, eyes apologetic. "Let me finish this for you," he adds, sliding out of me and settling his face between my legs.

He licks my clit at a precision pace while I hold on to his hair. His tongue is hot and skilled, and I come, riding his face, screaming his name. He slides his fingers inside me.

"I want to feel you come," he says as my waves of pleasure squeeze his fingers.

I'm flushed and panting, the scent of sex lingering in the air. He covers my pussy with his mouth and sucks long and hard one more time. Dragging his mouth up my body, he kisses me. I taste him. I taste myself. They intertwine, creating the most intoxicating combination of us. I lick his teeth as his tongue dances with mine. The frenzied erotic kiss slows and ends with me sitting on top of Brody, his half flaccid, half hard dick inside me.

"Better than my dreams," Brody remarks, exhaling. "Way fucking better."

He takes my left hand in his and kisses my ring. "I get to have this for the rest of my life."

"Well, in my dreams, you lasted more than one round," I counter, granting him a half-smirked challenge.

I circle my hips, riding him slowly until his cock stiffens more and more.

"Careful what you wish for, baby. I'm good for the next month. I'm on leave."

"You took a month off?" I say, sliding up and down, trying to focus on the conversation as he slides against my G-spot. "What if I said no to the proposal?"

"If you said no, I was going to have to take two months to nurse the heartbreak," he says, voice strained.

We're both distracted, but I won't be the one to give in.

"You're telling me we get to do this for the next month," I say, closing my eyes. The orgasm is building. I don't even have to focus.

Brody pops one of my nipples into his mouth.

"Shit," I hiss. "That feels so good."

"We can do this everywhere. Your house, my house, this boat, your boat. Anywhere you want it, I'll give it to you."

The last sentence sends me. I come apart around his dick. He keeps pumping his hips as I fold over him, riding the high sensations of coming with him inside me.

"I love coming on you," I say.

"I love coming in you," he replies, rapid fire fucking me from the bottom. Then he comes again, like he promised he would.

We're both sweaty and panting when we finish. I cup my hand between my legs to push his come out and wipe it on my stomach.

"We're going to need another ocean dip to clean you up," Brody says, smirking. "This could go on all night."

"I'm going to take you up on that," I say, catching my breath, rubbing my swollen clit, tracing his come onto my body. "I'm filled with you," I say, breathy. "It feels so good."

He moves my hand out of the way and fingers me, making sure to hit my G-spot when he enters.

"Close your eyes."

I do as I'm told.

"I'm going to finger paint on your stomach. Tell me what I'm drawing."

He drags more of his come onto my stomach, and the first shape is easy.

"Heart," I say, teasing my legs open so he'll go back.

He fingers me a little longer the second time, then

slips his hand back to my stomach. My pussy is cold and bereft.

"That's a raindrop," I say, slamming my eyes closed further to delight in all my senses.

Brody gives a low, throaty growl before he eats me out, making me arch my back and come apart another time. He doesn't stop, though. He doesn't stop eating me until I'm a sweaty pool of limbs and bones, every orgasm slaked from my body viciously, and I'm begging him for a rest.

He's not tired. He doesn't ever get tired when it comes to me and my body. We do this dance all night. Eating and fucking. Carnal and feral sometimes, and sweet and slow the next round. His perfect body is my playground, and mine is his.

We don't sleep until the sun is rising, my head on his chest and his arms protecting me like the safest cage in the entire world.

# epilogue

## BRODY

## SEVEN YEARS LATER

THE SUN'S coming up over the sound, and there's something about mornings like this—warm breeze, hint of salt in the air, toddler laughter rolling through the screen door—that makes me pause. Savor. Reflect.

I didn't know I had it in me to build a quiet life. Not back then. Not when I was all calloused edges and bite. But here I am, watching my daughter amble across the deck in her little sailor-print dress, dragging her stuffed narwhal like it's an anchor she refuses to cut loose from.

Saylor swears she gets her grip from me. I say it's all her. She held on to me when anyone else would have cut their losses.

She giggles when she sees me, and I crouch low, catching her just as she careens forward on chubby legs.

"I got you, squirt," I murmur against her fine, honey-blonde curls. She smells like lavender lotion and jelly toast. "Where's your brother?"

As if on cue, a blur of sandy curls sprints past us, our

five-year-old son, Caspian, shirtless and barefoot, wielding a wooden sword like he's storming a pirate ship.

"Mom said I could be captain today!" he announces, breathless. "You're the deckhand!"

I glance over my shoulder at the woman leaning on the doorway, mug in hand, hair messy and pulled into a knot that somehow still makes her look like a goddess.

My goddess. My forever.

"You gave him rank?" I ask Saylor, smirking.

"He bribed me with a strawberry he didn't eat," she says, shrugging like she's not proud of her weakness. "Besides, you were a Navy SEAL. You're used to taking orders."

I snort. "That's mutiny."

"Consider it training," she says, stepping forward to ruffle Caspian's hair and steal a kiss from my cheek before her lips slide to mine, slow, sweet, like morning sun on cold skin. She brings me to life.

This life...I never could've imagined it. Not seven years ago, when everything felt like it might slip through my fingers if I breathed too hard. The way it came together feels something like a fairy tale.

There are always villains in fairy tales, but the only ones in my life come in the form of Bianca's friends who love me in their own weird way. I learned how to deal with them and shut them down quickly, though.

After I left the Teams, it took time, years, for the restlessness to settle. The only thing that kept me grounded was Saylor and the mission we created together. MacSay Technologies started as a whisper of an idea on a boat deck in Madagascar, back when we were more scars than hope. It's turned into something real now. Something big and far-reaching.

We design satellite-integrated navigation systems for

civilian sailing vessels and long-range maritime security networks. Our goal? Make the seas safer. Give adventurers like Saylor better tools. And maybe, if I'm being honest, it's also my way of ensuring no one ever goes through what she did. The fear, the isolation, the fight for survival. No one should have to do that alone. Sure, I endured the same, but I was trained for misery. No one deserves that without warning. We're fixing it.

I'm the COO, but Saylor's the heart. She's the visionary, the dreamer who knows when to take the helm and when to let me calculate the tides. She's still wild at her core, still Saylor Wyndham, daughter of a dynasty and breaker of rules. But now, she's also a mom, a founder, and the woman I get to call my wife every damn day. Reality turned out better than fiction.

I never imagined love could stretch like this. That it could hold us through boardroom battles and three a.m. diaper changes, through funding rounds and sleepless nights nursing fevers, through fights about school schedules and decisions over where to dock the boat for the summer. But here we are. Building. Choosing each other again and again.

It wasn't all easy. I remember the day I officially turned in my trident and stepped into civilian life fulltime. Saylor met me outside the command with our son on her hip and tears in her eyes. There was something final about it, like I was shedding a skin I'd worn for too long. I was proud. But I was terrified too. What comes next? Who am I if I'm not the SEAL? It turns out I didn't need to worry. The world has a way of giving you exactly what you need.

We celebrated quietly that night. No party. Just the three of us on the deck of our first family house, wine in hand, and our baby asleep between us in a portable crib.

She looked over and said, "So what now, sailor?"

I laughed, and the words came out before I could stop them.

"Whatever you want, baby. Wherever you lead, I'll follow."

Saylor took those words seriously. First, a trip to Madagascar. Six months later, we were knee-deep in the formation of MacSay Technologies. The name still makes her laugh. A mash-up of our names, born from a joke Nolan made over beers at the lake house. I wanted to call it Neptune Navigation. She vetoed it.

That first year was rough. Investors weren't sure what to make of a military guy and a former society yacht racer with a reputation for vanishing off the grid. I was adamant we do things the traditional way and not use family money or connections through Wyndham Technology. We did pony up some of our cash, but the big investors came because Saylor had ATWU as her proof of success. We worked out of the sunroom with a few employees. Took meetings while passing the baby back and forth. But then came our first contract—a private expedition company outfitting their fleet for Arctic routes. And everything changed.

Now we have offices in three states and a research team in Norway. Just last month, we launched our first satellite. Caspian watched the live feed with wide eyes, holding his sister's hand.

He turned to me and said, "That's ours, Daddy? In space?"

"Ours," I said. "Yours too."

Nolan calls every day. Sometimes twice. His voice always fills the space like an old song. He's the godfather to our daughter, Marina, and he takes that job more seriously than anything he's ever done before.

Catherine's pregnant with their third, and she still somehow manages to run half the pediatric wing at the hospital and keep Nolan in line with her whip-rich sarcasm. She is my acerbic rival and cynicism nemesis. She just learned when and where to rein it in. We get along so well, it's as if she were born to take my place next to my twin.

They visit often. Their boys are rougher and rowdier, but treat Caspian like a little prince. Sunday dinners with them and our parents are sacred. Barbecue on the back porch, kids tearing through the yard like pirates on shore leave, my mom screaming at my dad to put down the water gun before he accidentally squirts her.

There is laughter that rises with the smoke. I traded gunshots and flashbangs for giggles and scraped knees. Life is wild and wonderful.

One night, after the kids were down, Nolan and I sat out by the fire pit, passing a bottle of bourbon between us, stars above, the sea whispering nearby. It felt like the old times, just him and me. Black and white. Good and bad. Except the lines aren't the same anymore. We're similar in ways I never dreamed of. I got to be a little bit like Nolan, and that makes me choke up.

"You ever think we'd make it here?" he asked. "Us doing life like this together?"

"No," I said honestly. "But I wanted to be here. Even back then. Even when it felt impossible."

He nodded slowly. "It still scares me sometimes. The quiet. The stillness inside of you."

"Same. But I earned it, brother. I survived the fire," I said, winking. "Now we both learn how to live in the warmth."

The moment was poignant. It was a full-circle

moment. I finally got to be the person I always idolized. Myself, but better, so him.

Saylor travels now and then to give keynote talks. Just last spring, she stood onstage at the International Women in Navigation Conference, radiating grace and authority. I sat in the back, Marina asleep in my arms, and watched every man and woman in that room hang on her every word.

She spoke of resilience. Of knowing fear but choosing courage. Of refusing to be defined by what almost broke you.

When she said, "Sometimes, the best way to find your way home is to first let yourself get lost," I had to blink fast and hard.

After the talk, she found me in the lobby, dropped her award on the floor, and wrapped her arms around me.

"You make me brave," she whispered.

I didn't say it then, but she's the reason I breathe easy. The reason I'm alive and well.

Leaving the military, while it was an easy decision, needed to happen. She made the transition effortless. No nightmares. No regrets. No thoughts of my past at all unless I feel like dwelling. The right life and the right support system can sometimes be enough to combat a past filled with fight.

Support doesn't always mean solving the problem. Sometimes it means sitting with you in the struggle, reminding you that you're strong enough to keep going.

We took the kids to Greece last year, rented a catamaran, and lived on the water for a month. Caspian learned how to cast a net. Marina danced on the bow in her floaties, arms wide like she could fly. We made love beneath the stars, the old wood creaking with the rhythm of the tide. It was the freest I'd ever felt.

Then there was the vow renewal. Five years. On the beach near our home. Barefoot. Friends and family in a half-circle, Caspian as the ring bearer, Marina scattering petals like a giggling storm.

Bianca orchestrated the whole thing with the precision of a CEO and the flair of a Paris runway. She flew in custom florals from Holland, and there was a string quartet that played our favorite songs, note for note. There were fairy lights in the trees, champagne in seashell flutes, and a cake so tall it required internal engineering. It was perfect.

It was hers, and that was fine, because all I cared about was that she was still mine. Just like the first wedding.

Saylor wore a simple ivory dress, her hair down, curls catching the breeze. I wore linen and a smile I couldn't hide despite my best efforts.

When I repeated the words, I added something new. "I promise to follow you, always. Even if it's all the way under." Or across the ocean. Into enemy territory. To heaven. Or to hell. I'd follow her everywhere and anywhere in between.

She cried. I did too. Much to Nolan's delight, might I add.

Now, tonight, I sit on the deck with Marina in my lap, Caspian curled up on a pillow beside me, the sea murmuring its sweet, sweet lullaby. Saylor hums in the kitchen, barefoot, pouring wine and brewing my cup of tea.

The moon is full. The house is quiet. The tide rolls in steadily and surely, like it always has. Like it always will.

This is our forever.

I'd go all the way under to keep it.

# *author's note*

This story has been fully formed, living in my brain for the past two years. I didn't write it sooner because I never gave myself full permission to make my SEALs do things that they wouldn't do in *real life*. Let's face it, this mission was never going to play out this way in the real world, but I think that's why I loved writing it so much. Brody and the operation to save Saylor (I mean, she saved him) had to happen the way it did. I took creative liberties with my SEALs and gave Brody permission to stray from a normal tactical operation. I'm sorry, but I'm not sorry. You read the story. It was exactly as it needed to be.

*All The Way Under* flowed out of me like *the* waterfall in Madagascar. Yes, it was that rapid and torrential. The humor was the glue sticking the parts of the story together, and also the antibiotic, curing the ailments that the darker moments created. I loved writing flawed, sometimes insane—I'm looking at you, Bianca—characters, showcasing a blending of personalities and worlds. To me, *All The Way Under* had a *Romeo and Juliet* feel without the tragic ending. Different worlds. A love that transcends

EVERYTHING. Brody and Saylor were always meant to find each other. In my head, I have a whole different story where they DID meet on the street and the story transpires in an entirely different way, but ends the same. This story could have been double the length, maybe triple, because I wanted to stay with these characters as long as I could. I love them dearly, and I hope you did too. The cast of side characters are some of my favorites I've ever created, and they leave me with a smile whenever I think of them.

# a look at: the forgotten seal

## THE REAL SEAL BOOK ONE

**Two shattered souls. One unexpected chance at healing.**

Carina Painter has it all—on paper. A bestselling author with a carefully curated life, she hides the truth behind her smile: a childhood of chaos and an engagement that left emotional wounds she can't outrun. When a chance meeting offers her an escape, she grabs it—desperate for something real.

Smith Eppington, a Navy SEAL scarred by war and a tragic accident, is a man haunted by memories he can't fully recall. With most of his body burned and his best friend lost, he's given up on finding peace—until Carina enters his world, pen in hand and curiosity burning.

What starts as an interview quickly turns into something deeper: a connection born from pain, resilience, and the possibility of something more. But as Carina helps Smith unearth the truth about his past, the answers they find may cost them the fragile hope they've built.

Can love rewrite the story of their lives—or will the truth end their final chapter before it begins?

***AVAILABLE NOW***

# *acknowledgments*

Thank you, as always, to my family. My husband, for pushing me to finish on a timeline and answering all my crazy questions about SEALs (even when I go rogue and make my own rules). To my daughter, who told me what trauma I needed to grant Brody to explain away his positively EVIL grumpy personality. To my son, for asking me every single day how many words I wrote and if I was done yet.

I love you guys.

All the way under and back.

Rachel grew up in a small, quiet town full of loud talkers. Her words were always only loud on paper. She has been writing stories and creating characters for as long as she can remember. CRAZY GOOD and SET IN STONE, and TIME AND SPACE, three of her Navy SEAL novels are INTERNATIONAL BESTSELLERS. After living in San Diego, Virginia Beach, and then Fairfax, VA, she now resides in colorful Colorado with her badass husband, two children, her Sphynx cat, & her dog, Polly.

www.racheljrobinson.com
Rachel Robinson's Racy Readers

www.ingramcontent.com/pod-product-compliance
Lightning Source LLC
Chambersburg PA
CBHW011758010726
47497CB00013B/3256